BOOKS BY L

HOLLOW WITCH

SECONDHAND MAGIC #2

LORI DRAKE

Published by Clockwork Cactus Press

PO Box 1874

Leander, TX 78646 USA

HOLLOW WITCH (SECONDHAND MAGIC #2)

ISBN-13: 978-1-955545-00-6

Cover by Christian Bentulan

Edited by Rebecca Hodgkins

Line Edits by AE McKenna

For Pauline.

Thanks for your support and inspiration.

...and tolerance.

CHAPTER 1

Detective Mike Escobar screeched to a halt next to the curb and killed the siren. "Wait here," he said, letting a burst of cold air into the warm cabin of the nondescript sedan as he climbed out.

"Are you kidding?" I unbuckled my seatbelt, poised to open the door.

Leaning into his open door, he fixed me with a no-nonsense look. "Damn right I'm serious. You're not a cop, Davenport." He slammed his door and jogged around the front of the car to take off down the alley after our perp.

I growled and flung open my door, scrambling out onto the sidewalk. He only called me by my last name when he was trying to boss me around. "I'm your partner!"

"Still not a cop!" His voice echoed off the alley walls in his wake.

I slammed the door shut. Kicked it for good measure. He was right. I wasn't a cop. But I was still his partner, even if my laminated badge read "Consultant," and I didn't like him running in on his own. He should've waited for backup. We'd been working this case for a week, investigating a rash of petty theft centered in the downtown area. The perp was a witch and had been using magic to evade the police. They'd kicked it over to Magic Crimes—aka me and Mike— as soon as they'd put two and two together. So far, no one had gotten seriously hurt, but the witch was getting bolder, and I didn't like Mike's odds going up against a practitioner with nothing but a service pistol and a can-do attitude.

Also, I was itchy to field test my new toy.

"Not the boss of me," I muttered to myself as I spun away from the car and took off down the alley in hot pursuit.

"Stop, police!" Mike's voice echoed through the alley again, but this time he wasn't talking to me. No, his words would've been much more colorful if he'd known I was legging my way down the alley behind him.

I knew this area well. We weren't far from the Tin Whistle, my favorite cafe. There'd been road construction in this area for months, and I'd learned all the shortcuts to bypass the worst of it. This particular alley continued for about six more blocks, crossing several busy streets in the process. Unless the punk had a death wish, he was going to have to turn one way or another. Since he was on foot, odds were good he wouldn't head for the highway. I took a left, darting through an open gate and through someone's backyard. Picking up speed, I leaped over the low chain-link fence out front, spilling out onto the sidewalk of a quiet side street. I turned right and raced down the street, but the moment I reached the next intersection and started to turn and see if I'd gotten ahead of them, someone bowled into me and we both went down.

The cold concrete made for a rough landing, and my hip took the worst of it, but I banged my elbow pretty good too. I caught a whiff of tobacco smoke and a glimpse of magenta-tipped black hair as our target scrambled to his feet. I grabbed for his leg, but my fingers failed to find purchase on his denim pants.

"*Puta!*" he snarled and took off.

Mike was at my side a few seconds later, jaw clenched but concern in his brown eyes as he held out a hand. "What part of 'wait in the car' was unclear?"

I grasped his hand and pulled myself to my feet. "The part where you went running off without calling for backup."

He made an irritated growly noise in the back of his throat. "Come on, he's getting away."

We took off after the witch who, favoring one leg, hobbled along like his knee was suddenly difficult to bend. We were gaining steady ground when he looked behind him, eyes widening in panic as he saw how close we were. A magical glow sprang to life around him, and he flung a spell over his shoulder at us. It was a knockback spell, simple but effective. Also, invisible to the mundane eye. I grabbed Mike and spun, putting my back to the spell. I felt nothing as it impacted against my back, the wards lacing my trench coat causing the spell's threads to dissipate on contact.

A thrill of victory rushed through me. Getting the coat warded had cost me nearly two months' rent, but it was already paying off. I wasn't sure what I'd do when the weather warmed up, but that was a Future Emily problem.

Mike froze, unable to see or sense anything, but trusting me. There weren't many reasons why I'd put myself between him and a witch like that.

The witch was only digging himself in deeper. Using magic against a police officer was a considered aggravated assault—a third-degree felony that could put a witch in jail for up to three years.

When I looked back, the witch was still casting, but this

time I couldn't tell what he was doing. The spell wasn't directed at us, at least. He changed course suddenly and leaped at a nearby building, climbed its wall like Spider-Man, and vanished over the roofline. The last thing we saw of him was his middle finger over the edge of the roof.

Mike pushed past me and ran to the wall the witch had disappeared over.

"Uh, Mike . . ."

My partner jumped, but the witch hadn't cast the spell on the wall—he'd cast it on himself. Gravity pulled Mike back down. At least he landed on his feet.

"Dammit!" He smacked his hand against the wall, staring up at the roofline.

"Over here!" I ran around the corner of the building. But by the time we got to the other side, there was no trace of the perp.

"I told you to wait in the car," Mike said between heaving breaths.

I snorted, lips twitching with the effort not to grin. "Yeah, and after almost two months of working with me, you actually expected me to listen. Not sure which one of us that makes more a fool of."

He growled and clenched his hands into fists, then marched off in the direction of the car. My amusement fled as I hastened to catch up with him. He was actually pissed, and I wasn't sure what to say.

We walked in silence for several blocks. When I couldn't take it anymore, I blurted, "I'm sorry."

"No, you're not."

I sighed. "Okay, I'm not. But you can't just hare off after a witch like that on your own. You didn't even radio dispatch to tell them you were leaving your car in pursuit."

"I may not have a fancy warded coat, but I'm not

completely defenseless." His voice rumbled like he had gravel in his throat.

"Yeah, yeah. You have a badge and a gun." I was getting tired of this argument, and yet I kept engaging in it like the outcome might be different.

He spun, fixing me with a stony glare. "What do you want me to do, Davenport? Call in a few uniforms to back me up? It'll just put more 'defenseless cops' in the line of fire."

I lifted my chin and glared back. "I'm your partner, Mike. You have me."

"You're not a cop. You're a consultant." He inched toward me, chest puffed up like a rooster, as if being closer might intimidate me more.

"You're the one that asked me for help in the first place!"

"Yeah, to help me with investigating things, not chasing down suspects! Christ, Em, you can't even sling a spell."

Of all the things he'd said, that one stung the most. He was the one who'd made me register as a practitioner in the first place. Now he was going to take pot shots at me for not being a "real" witch? Hell to the no. I shoved him out of my personal space. "Well, maybe this isn't working out."

"Maybe not." He shoved his hands in the pockets of his leather jacket and resumed walking.

I watched him go for a moment, then sighed and followed him. I didn't hurry to catch up this time, just trailed along in his wake. Okay, so maybe I was sulking a little bit. I hadn't really meant what I'd said, and I certainly hadn't expected him to agree. He'd come to me for help because he couldn't find another witch, a real witch, to take the job. And I was the sucker who'd thought maybe, just maybe, I was a desirable option rather than the only option.

It was a long, quiet ride back to the station. After pulling into a spot in the parking lot, he glanced at me, expression unreadable.

"You working tonight?" he asked, calmer now, but his tone was chilly.

"Yeah." I studied his face in profile, uncomfortable with the way he stared straight ahead, one hand resting on the wheel even though the car was in park and the engine was off.

He nodded. "I'll take care of the paperwork. You should try to catch a nap or something. I know you've been burning the candle at both ends."

I turned toward him. "Mike . . ."

He opened the door and climbed out of the car. "I'll see you tomorrow."

The door closed before I could answer. He was still mad, but at least I wasn't fired. Yet.

CHAPTER 2

In what sometimes seemed another lifetime, I would've had a prayer of getting that nap Mike suggested. Instead, I got to go home and deal with my brother. Six weeks after moving in with me, the newest black sheep of our family was still broke, unemployed, and spent most of his time sitting on my couch eating junk food, watching television, and—perhaps the most galling offense—not gaining a single pound. I wish I'd gotten that gene.

When I opened the front door, he was—true to form—lounging in his nest of blankets and pillows on the couch with his feet propped up on the coffee table and my cat sprawled across his lap. As always, my eyes drifted to the colorful painting hanging directly opposite the door, above the couch. I should've hung it somewhere it wouldn't make me think about the artist every time I walked in my front door. I hadn't spoken to John Warren in almost two months and was content to let that streak ride for a variety of reasons.

"Hey, sis! Did you have a nice day fighting crime?" Dan

flashed what was probably an attractive smile were I not immune to his charms.

I sloughed my coat and hung it on the rack by the door, thinking briefly about Mike's tense posture and cool dismissal. "I don't want to talk about it."

This, of course, only roused his curiosity. He grabbed the remote and turned down the TV. "Uh oh, that doesn't sound good. What'd you do?"

"Nothing. How did the job search go today?"

He draped an arm along the back of the couch. "I've got a few irons in the fire."

"I'd believe that if you weren't wearing yesterday's shirt and covered in Dorito dust. You know the rules, Danny. If you want to stay here, you have to get a job."

"Well, quit hogging all the good ones. It's not fair that you have two."

Snorting, I headed for the kitchen to snag a glass of water. "You'd never survive nursing school—or any occupation that involves empathy and compassion."

"Hey! I can be compassionate. But I'll leave the emptying bed pans to you if you'll put a good word in for me with Detective Escobar."

The reminder that Mike had picked me over Dan when it came to choosing a consultant momentarily cheered me. I hadn't been his last choice after all. Then again, my brother set a low bar to clear at times.

"You can't have that job either." I unscrewed a bottle of water and carried it over to the dining table to sift through the mail. "You brought in the mail?"

"Uh yeah, if answering the door when Matt came by earlier counts."

I'm terrible about checking my mail. I've been known to go as long as two months between checks. But I missed a jury summons once, and that taught me to at least check every two weeks. Sometimes Matt—my ex and bestie—would grab my mail for me when he dropped by. Even now, years after he moved out, some of his mail still showed up in my box. Among the bills and circulars I sorted through was a small envelope with a Boston postmark and my name and address scrawled across it in my mother's carelessly elegant script.

I grimaced and nearly tossed it in the junk pile. "Did you give Mom my address?"

"What, in our weekly check-ins that we don't have because she disowned me?"

I grunted. That left only one other option that I could think of: Liam. But my older brother had been keeping my whereabouts to himself for a decade. Why would he suddenly turn me over to the Wicked Witch of the East?

Maybe she'd never asked before. But why would she ask now?

Didn't know, didn't care.

I put the letter aside with the bills and promptly forgot about it. "What did Matt want?"

"Snuggle time with Barry."

"I asked you not to call him that." I rubbed my face, suddenly feeling every ounce of fatigue I'd earned from a night shift followed by inadequate sleep and being on the go with Escobar all afternoon.

Dan scooped my cat up under his arms and held him up. "Does this look like a Barrington to you?"

The cat flattened his ears and squirmed until Dan let him go, then leaped onto the back of the couch to lick his mussed fur down. An image immediately flashed into my mind of Barry, the man I'd been seeing for almost two months but couldn't quite call my boyfriend, attempting a similar maneuver. One of those things you can't unsee, you know?

I dropped onto the opposite end of the couch from Dan. "Just . . . Don't call him that."

Dan snickered but relented, slouching back into the corner of the couch. "I had an idea today, about a job."

"Great. Go for it."

He nudged my leg with his foot. "Don't you want to know what it is first?"

"As long as it's legal, I'm fine with it." I leaned my head against the back of the couch and closed my eyes.

"Oh, it's legal. Can't get more legal, in fact."

I cracked an eye open and eyed him. "Okay, I'll bite. What's the job?"

"I'm going to apply to the police department."

"As what, a target for the gun range?"

He rolled his eyes and nudged me again. "As a cop, what else?"

I burst out laughing. The idea of Dan—irresponsible, irreverent Dan—as a law enforcement officer was nothing short of hilarious. I laughed so hard that I ended up clutching my stomach. I couldn't breathe. My face ached. It wasn't until the tears cleared from my eyes that I noticed Dan's crossed arms and sullen expression.

I forced myself to take a calming breath and wiped my eyes. "You're serious."

"Of course I'm serious! I'm more than qualified, and they don't have a witch on staff. They'd be lucky to have me."

"And what, pray tell, are those qualifications?" I massaged my cheeks to encourage the aching muscles to relax again.

"I'm young, healthy, of sound mind . . ."

"That's debatable." I studied him while he floundered

for more. "You didn't even look up the job requirements, did you?"

"I'm a witch! They'll probably take me on that alone."

"Uh-huh." I fished my phone out of my pocket and pulled up a browser, then typed "santa fe police requirements" into the search field. Dan snatched the phone from my hand before I could get far, so I settled down to wait.

"Okay, here we go," he said. "US Citizen. Check. At least twenty-one years old. Check. High school diploma. Check. Valid driver's license . . . well, I've got one for Massachusetts, getting one here is no big deal."

"You're supposed to get an ID within thirty days of moving." It wasn't the first time I'd reminded him.

He ignored me. "No felony convictions or other disqualifying charges. Check." He paused, eyeing the screen, then pushed the lock button and tossed the phone to me. "See? I told you."

Suspicious, I unlocked the phone and scanned the list myself. It wasn't until I got to the very end that I discovered what had given Dan pause and barked out a laugh. "Be of good moral character? You couldn't even say that with a straight face, eh?"

Dan crossed his arms and grumbled quietly. "I knew you'd just give me shit about it. Go on, laugh it up."

I bit my lip to keep the laughter at bay because I wasn't completely heartless. The idea of Dan as a cop was just so, well, laughable. "I know you're on a quest to be a better Dan, but have you really thought this through? It's not like all you have to do is charm an intake officer. There are probably written exams, physical tests—hell probably even drug tests."

"I don't use drugs!"

I held up a hand. "I'm not saying you do, Danny. I'm just

saying it's a process. You'd have to go to the police academy, and who knows if any of the training is paid training . . ."

He slumped in his seat, and not that careless artful slump he usually managed. No, it was like he was shrinking in on himself, and that gave me pause. He—my baby brother, who usually didn't have a serious bone in his body —really was serious about this, and what kind of a sister was I being? Guilt tugged at my heart when I thought about the way I'd laughed at him. I was positive that Dan attempting to join the police force would be nothing short of a shitshow, and I'd undoubtedly be on the hook for whatever application fee was required. But there'd be no living with him if I blew him off. And I did have to live with him. Okay, well, technically I didn't have to live with him, but kicking him to the curb when he was at least trying to fulfill the tenets of our roommate agreement would've been a dick move.

"Hey," I began.

He raked his fingers through his blond hair and stood. "Never mind. You're right, it was a dumb idea. I think I'll go out for a bit, give you some quiet to take a nap or whatever before your shift."

I vaulted from my seat and grabbed his wrist. "Wait. I'm doing this wrong." He gave me the side-eye. I went on before he could spoil the moment with a wisecrack. "If this is something you want, something you're serious about, then do it. I'm behind you one hundred percent. Just make sure it's what you really want because at the end of the day, it's a dangerous job."

Dan tugged his wrist from my grasp and studied me for a long moment. A slow smile crept across his face. "You're worried about me! That's so sweet."

I slumped back on the sofa with a sigh. "Weren't you going away or something?"

"I love you too, sis."

He ruffled my hair in passing, and I swatted his hand. He was out the door in under a minute, and while I had no idea where he was going, at least he hadn't asked me for walking-around money. Peace and quiet wrapped around me in his wake. I scooted down the sofa and closed my eyes rather than take in the empty soda cans and food wrappers on the coffee table.

I tried to imagine Dan in a police uniform, but couldn't quite manage it. Chances were, he'd forget this flight of fancy as soon as the next cute girl walked by. If not, well, maybe he'd be on his way to having a job and getting out of my hair for good. But it raised a troubling question: If and when the police department did get a witch on staff, what would that mean for my consultancy?

I liked working with Mike. It challenged me in ways nursing didn't while allowing me to help an underserved community. The idea of being pushed out didn't sit well with me.

Even if another witch—or, let's face it, any witch—would have been infinitely more qualified.

CHAPTER 3

I peeled my purple nitrile gloves off and chucked them into the waste bin with a scowl. It wasn't enough. I wanted to kick the damn thing, send its contents flying across the scuffed linoleum. My fingers curled into fists, nails biting into my palms. I took a deep breath and did what the hospital counselor always tells us to do: breathe it out and move on to the next chart. Breathe out the frustration, the disappointment, the anger . . . whatever it is that went on behind that curtain, and leave it there so your mind is clear for the next patient.

After seven years as an ER nurse in the only Level III Trauma Center in Northern New Mexico, I'd gotten pretty good at compartmentalizing. It was my job to empathize with patients, to see to their comfort and facilitate their treatment. But you can't get too close, can't make their problems your problems. I glanced behind me at the sheet-draped body of a seventeen-year-old boy who'd been rushed in by paramedics less than ten minutes ago. He hadn't even lasted long enough for his parents to arrive. That would be a fun conversation. I hoped I didn't draw the short straw. My throat started to close.

Breathe in. Breathe out.

A hand landed on my shoulder, and I turned to find Dr. Russell Carson, St. Vincent's least eligible yet most desirable resident, standing there. My eyes skittered away from his, avoiding the knowing look he gave me.

"I'm fine. Just . . . rattled," I said.

"Young ones are the hardest." He squeezed my shoulder before turning his attention back to the tablet in his hand, no doubt updating the kid's chart.

"Yeah." It was easier to agree than tell him what was really on my mind.

Another witch. Another mysterious overdose—and not because overdoses are uncommon in my ER, mind you. The health department distributed a flyer a few years ago with some grim statistics. On average, one New Mexican dies of an overdose every eighteen hours. Two out of three of those deaths involve an opioid. And those are just the ones that result in fatalities. We treat overdoses daily, to the point where there's kind of a rhythm to it.

But these weren't normal opioid overdoses. Not by a long shot.

Sure, they started out with the classic symptoms: slow or erratic heart rate, difficulty remaining conscious, blue lips and fingernails from low oxygen, etc. But things quickly went off the rails once an opioid antagonist was administered. Once their high was reversed, they started hallucinating. Restraints were involved. Sedatives were administered. But whatever cocktail was swimming around in their veins made them infuriatingly resistant to going under. In their panic, they started throwing magic around. That's where I, your friendly neighborhood Conduit, came in.

If it happened on my watch, I could siphon their magic away and ground it safely, buying time for the sedative to kick in. But if I wasn't there, someone got hurt, whether that was an EMT, doctor, or nurse struck by a juiced-up knock-back spell or the witch drawing too much power and burning themselves out—if they didn't code first. Sometimes they coded anyway, and that . . . rarely ends as well in real life as it does on TV. Just ask the high school student cooling on the gurney behind me.

Whatever it was these patients were overdosing on, it was new and it was dangerous. What no one at the hospital but me realized—in part due to my own interventions, granted—was that all of the afflicted patients were witches. Not all of them were registered practitioners, and I couldn't flag the unregistered ones as witches without explaining how I knew. My witch status was still on the down low around the hospital, and I liked it that way even if I wasn't sure how long I'd be able to keep it that way. Regardless, these mysterious overdoses were getting more common. There'd been three this week. This dangerous new drug was killing witches, and it was time I talked to Mike about it.

But first, I had to finish my shift. So I headed down the hall toward the nurses' station with heavy steps and a dull ache in the center of my forehead. I was running on fumes, between the fatigue of another long shift on limited sleep and the adrenaline crash from the ill-fated trauma. I covered a jaw-cracking yawn as I bellied up to the counter.

"Who's my next contestant?" I leaned my elbows on the counter and blinked owlishly at the woman sitting behind the computer on the other side.

Gracie looked up over the top of her monitor and her dark brows drew together. "You look like shit. When's your next break?"

"An hour ago." I fought the urge to yawn again. "I'm off in ninety minutes. Can I have a nice old lady with low blood sugar or something?"

"Ha! You're a funny gal." She clicked her mouse a few times, eyes returning to the screen. "Oh, but this isn't too bad. Next in line is a guy with a suspected broken nose. Curtain six. Hector Gomez."

Cheered somewhat at the prospect of a patient that probably wouldn't die, I nodded and headed off down the hallway. But when I pulled back the curtain and found a familiar witch sitting on the edge of the gurney, I had to bite the inside of my lip to keep from frowning.

Our eyes met as I stood stock still for several seconds, one hand still on the curtain.

"Well?" His voice was nasally on account of the bloody tissues stuffed up both nostrils. Faint bruising smudged his eyes. "Are you going to just stand there or what?"

Hector and I had crossed paths a few times since I'd helped solve the rash of magic burnouts that'd taken out two of the members of his small local coven, but it'd always been at the Tin Whistle—a cafe we both frequented. Our interactions might be best described as cordially tense, and I'd never gotten his last name. He knew I worked with the cops, and he knew I knew most of his coven was unregistered. What he didn't know was if he could trust me. And he definitely didn't trust my brother.

I forced a smile and headed for the blood pressure cuff on the wall so I could start taking his vitals. "Good morning, Mr. Gomez. Nice to see you again." Okay, maybe nice wasn't the right word. "What happened to you?"

He grunted. "I ran into a door."

I tucked my tongue against my cheek as I slipped the cuff onto his arm and fastened the Velcro, but I couldn't quite stop myself from asking, "Tracy got a mean left cross?"

Hector just glared at me, and since antagonizing a patient while taking their blood pressure wasn't a good idea, I kept my comments to myself while the machine inflated the cuff and did its thing. Still, Hector being decked by his pint-sized pixie of a girlfriend was an entertaining thought. It stuck with me while I recorded his vitals, and it must've shown on my face.

"Do you make a habit out of making fun of victims of domestic abuse?" he asked.

That sobered me quickly. I cleared my throat and looked him in the eye. "Of course not. Do you, uh, I mean, did she . . . ?"

He snorted, shaking his head. "It wasn't Tracy. Just making a point."

"Point taken." Chastising myself inwardly, I put on a fresh pair of gloves and approached him, but when I reached for his face, he leaned back.

"What are you doing? Isn't a doctor going to check me out?"

"I need to see if it's still bleeding. Trust me, removing bloody tissues from your nose isn't on my wish list."

He narrowed his eyes but held still while I plucked the tissues free. I'm no doctor, but I've seen more than a few broken noses in my day, and Hector's was definitely broken. It had to hurt, and I wish I could say that was probably the reason for his sunny disposition. But he had been a sour-puss since the day we met. The only time I'd seen him smile was when he was picking on Dan, who hadn't been able to defend himself from magical mischief at the time. But his nose wasn't bleeding anymore, so I tossed the tissues and plucked a few fresh ones from the box on the counter to hand to him.

"In case it starts again," I said. "Try not to fiddle with it. The doctor will be in to see you shortly." I turned to go but paused and turned back. "Since you're here, can I ask you something?"

He eyed me but gave a slight nod, dabbing gingerly at his nose like he didn't believe it wasn't still bleeding.

"You know anything about a new drug on the streets?"

Hector rolled his eyes. "Why do you think I would? Because I'm brown?"

"Uh, no..." I blinked, taken aback. "That's not it at all. I just thought as a co—community leader"—I gave him a significant look—"you might have heard something. Whatever it is, it's having some really strange effects on witches."

"Uh-huh. And why should I tell you?"

I crossed my arms. "Because it's killing people. Your people."

"My people?" He sat a little straighter. "Who?"

"Your people, as in witches. Not your people, specifically." I watched him relax, then added, "Yet."

"*My* people don't do drugs."

I leaned toward him and sniffed, sure I'd caught a skunky odor when I'd been close to him.

He leaned back again. "Jesus, what are you, a K-9 unit?"

"Good thing I'm not." I smiled, then sighed. "Come on, Hector. We're on the same side here. I'm just trying to look after the community. Whatever's causing these overdoses . . . It's nasty shit."

"I don't know anything about it, Davenport."

He looked me square in the eye when he said it, and I didn't get the sense he was being untruthful. Not that truth-sensing is a talent of mine, he just seemed like he was on the level.

"Well, if you hear something, will you let me know? I'd really appreciate it. We have a chance to stop this before it becomes a full-blown crisis."

"Yeah, sure. You'll be the first to know. Now can you get a doctor in here?" He shifted on the gurney, the paper crinkling beneath his butt.

"You're on the list." I nodded toward the computer terminal where I'd marked him ready for the doctor after taking his vitals. "It shouldn't be much longer."

I turned and headed for the curtain to let myself out, pausing on the threshold to look back. "Oh, and Hector?" I waited for him to meet my eyes again. "Thanks."

He nodded. "Sure. And while we're doing favors for each other, there's something you can do for me."

"Oh?"

"Yeah. Tell your shithead baby brother that if he puts a hand on Tracy again, I'll break *his* fucking nose."

CHAPTER 4

I shook Dan's shoulder until he opened his eyes and hissed like a vampire, flinging up both hands to ward off the sunlight streaming in through the open blinds. I also had every light in the living room on, because even hours later I was still pissed.

I grabbed one hand and then the other, utterly unsurprised when I found the knuckles of his right hand bruised and swollen. He yanked his hands away and pulled the blanket up over his head.

I grabbed the blanket and pulled it entirely off him, wadded it up, and threw it on the floor. "What the hell did you do?"

He squinted up at me. "Wha?"

"I had an interesting talk with Hector this morning. In the ER. While treating his broken nose."

Dan put the pillow over his head. I yanked that away too, then smacked him with it.

"Hey!" He covered his head with his arms to ward off further blows while I contemplated switching to soap in a sock. Okay, not seriously. I wanted to beat sense into him, not actually beat him.

"I told you to steer clear of Tracy. But you just didn't listen, did you? I don't know why I'm surprised. The only thing I should be surprised about was that *you* aren't the one with the broken nose."

Dan groaned, lowering his arms when no further blows came and squinting at me again. "Tracy and I are just friends. Hector's an asshole. That's nothing new, and definitely not something worth waking me up to physically and verbally abuse me over."

I hefted the pillow again. "I'll show you abuse . . ."

"Wait!" He flung a hand out, palm facing me. "Just give me a minute. I can explain."

I sat down on the coffee table and placed the pillow across my legs, waiting while he pushed himself up into a sitting position. He rubbed his face with both hands, then ran his fingers through his hair, which just made the way it stood up in different directions worse.

"Waiting," I said.

Dan leaned back with a sigh, flexing his right hand. "Tracy and I hung out last night. We were out late, and she had a few too many tequila shots, so I drove her home. Hector was there, waiting. Which is kind of overbearing and creepy, if you ask me. I mean, he has a key but they don't live together."

"I didn't." Ask him, that is. But I didn't disagree; sitting around your partner's house while they were out late did sound a bit overbearing and creepy. "So, you punched him for being overbearing and creepy?"

"No, I punched him for calling her a slut."

I didn't know Hector well, but that still sounded out of

character. "He called her a slut because you dropped her off at her house?"

Dan rubbed the back of his head. "No, I think that was because she was half-dressed, and I had to carry her in from the car."

"Why was she half-dressed?" And why couldn't he tell a story in a linear fashion?

"Wet T-shirt contest. Her idea, not mine, I swear. She was the runner-up, and she was robbed. You should've seen the—"

"Daniel. Focus."

"Right. So . . . her shirt was all wet, and it was cold. I let her wear my jacket, and after she fell out of the car, tripped over the curb, and nearly face-planted into the sidewalk, I decided to carry her the rest of the way. I had to set her down to unlock the door, and we kind of stumbled into the apartment with her arms around me and—okay, I admit it looked bad. But all I was going to do was get her to bed and grab a rideshare home. But Hector didn't even give me a chance to explain. He lit into her, and she was too drunk to defend herself. She just started crying, and I—well—I didn't like how he was talking to her, and figured it'd be better if his attention was on me."

"So you decked him." My anger and righteous indignation fizzled out. The story was just crazy enough to be true, and while my little brother had plenty of unfavorable attributes, spinning tall tales wasn't one of them. He'd always insisted nothing was going on between him and Tracy, and I believed him. I wouldn't call him a braggart, but he was pretty open about who he was sleeping with.

"Yeah." He looked me in the eye. "And I'd do it again, in a heartbeat."

"You'll be lucky if he doesn't press charges."

He waved a careless hand. "Not his style. He's more the 'get revenge in a dark alley' type."

"He did ask me to tell you that he'd break your nose if you put a hand on Tracy again."

Dan rolled his eyes and flopped back down on the couch, pillowing his head on a folded arm. "I'm not afraid of him. But I feel bad for Tracy. She deserves better than him."

"Someone like you?" Smirking, I held out the pillow as a peace offering.

He took the pillow and tucked it under his head. "Nah. She definitely deserves someone better than me. Can I have my blanket back now?"

I sat there in stunned silence for a moment, turning his words over in my head. *She definitely deserves someone better than me.* For all his protestations about nothing going on between him and Tracy, he obviously felt something for her. I was no stranger to being stuck in the friend zone, so I decided to let sleeping dogs lie.

After tucking Dan back in, I headed down the hall and found Barrington curled up on my pillow. I leaned over and gave his head a little rub, and he cracked his eyes open briefly before squeezing them shut again. I scratched behind his ears since he was in a tolerant mood, then got ready for bed myself but hesitated while reaching for the charging cord draped across my nightstand.

Bringing up my contacts list, I thumbed through it until I found Hector's entry. After editing it to plug in his last name, I started a new message. Whatever was going on between him and Dan—and Tracy—wasn't really my business. Except that it kind of was. He'd made it mine when he'd asked me to relay his threat. I wasn't sure what annoyed me more, the way he'd manipulated me or the way he'd unloaded on Tracy. Typical insecure macho man bullshit, that was. If I'd been there, I would've been tempted to break his nose myself. He just couldn't handle the idea that his girl could have a platonic male friend. Granted, Tracy wasn't doing herself any favors by maintaining a friendship with Dan behind Hector's back. And Dan's reputation as something of a player wasn't helping anything either. I just hoped that Hector's mistreatment of Tracy didn't go beyond angry words.

The thought chilled me. What if it did? I backed out of the message and started one to Tracy instead.

Are you okay? If you need someone to talk to, I'm a good listener.

I felt silly after I sent it, but there was no taking it back. I barely knew Tracy. If she was going to open up to someone, it wouldn't be me. Surely. But I wouldn't have felt right not offering. Battered spouses often felt like they had no one to turn to. Maybe a virtual stranger was better than no one at all.

CHAPTER 5

I had no response from Tracy when I woke seven hours later and rolled out of bed to start a new day, but the read message indicator told me she'd seen it. That'd have to be good enough. I did have a message from Mike, however, telling me we had a complaint to follow up on once I was up. I texted him to pick me up in an hour and threw myself in the shower. Dan was nowhere to be found, which was honestly for the best.

When Mike pulled into the parking lot, I was sitting at the bottom of the stairs, sipping coffee from an insulated mug and finishing up the slice of toast I'd made for breakfast. Not exactly protein-rich, but after the incident the day before, I hadn't wanted to risk making him wait.

I brushed crumbs from my coat and hopped up to join him in the car. The heater was on full blast, and I wanted to take my coat off immediately. But that was hard to do while buckled in, so I settled for hoping it was a short ride.

Spoiler: It wasn't a short ride.

I wasn't sure what to expect from him after yesterday's kerfuffle, so I played it cool. "Where to?"

He pointed at the dash-mounted GPS unit. I leaned over to peer at it. "Um, I thought you said we had a complaint to follow up on. Isn't that a little outside our jurisdiction? It's practically on the Pueblo."

"Not anymore. You're looking at the newest member of the State Police's Magic Crimes task force." He plucked a small brown paper sack from the console and held it out to me, then put the car in reverse and twisted to look over his shoulder.

Inside the sack was a still-warm foil-wrapped breakfast burrito. "Oooh, thanks!" I peeled back the foil and took a bite. Fluffy eggs, gooey cheese, soft potato, and green chile delighted my taste buds. New Mexicans will put green chile on just about anything. It took some getting used to at first, but now it just tastes like home.

Mike finished backing out of the parking place and put the car in drive, but paused before pulling forward. "I'm sorry about yesterday, but—"

"Mmm, just what a girl likes to hear. I'm sorry, but . . ."

His jaw tightened and he shook his head, accelerating toward the exit. Me and my big mouth.

"Sorry, sorry. What were you going to say?" I took a big bite of the burrito to keep myself from butting in.

"Just that I'm sorry. I was frustrated about losing the perp, and I took it out on you."

"I appreciate that."

A few seconds passed in silence, then he glanced over at me. "This is the part where you say you're sorry for not staying in the car."

I sighed and peeled back the foil a bit more, toying with it. "That'd be a lie. And you would've lost the perp either way. If I hadn't stopped that spell, it would've knocked you on your ass."

"Part of being my consultant means doing what I say." His eyes remained on the road this time, hands at ten and two.

"Does it?" I picked up my consultant badge and peered it, front and back. "I don't see that in the fine print. But you did bring me breakfast, so . . . I'll do my best."

He grunted in response as we pulled out in traffic.

"So, what's this task force about?" I asked between bites.

"Pooling resources for better coverage. You know how Deputy Payne is the only witch on the county sheriff's payroll?"

"Yeah."

"Well, Payne is stretched pretty thin. It's a big county, and the population is really spread out. The troopers put together a task force of Magic Crimes officers in the region, so we're all authorized to respond to calls, conduct investigations, write tickets, and make arrests."

I mulled this over a moment, chewing and swallowing. "Does that include tribal police?"

"Not unilaterally. Some opted out. But it's still a step in the right direction. It means that we can respond to this call while Payne's tied up in Los Cerillos this morning."

"Like we didn't have enough to do, serving the most densely populated city in the county?" I mused aloud, more thoughtful than upset. "But I guess it works both ways, and if we need extra hands in Santa Fe, they can send someone?"

"Exactly."

Of course, that meant my position as a Magic Crimes consultant was somewhat less valuable, aside from me being conveniently local. My breakfast suddenly weighed heavy in my stomach, and I glanced down at the remaining half a burrito briefly before wrapping it up and tucking it into the bag.

"Tell me about the complaint we're following up on this morning," I said.

"Ever heard of Nate Alan Reed?"

"The self-styled shaman-slash-life-coach that charges gullible, desperate people thousands of dollars for wellness retreats and holistic healing?" If I sounded caustic, that's because I was. I hated people who preyed on the weaknesses of others the way so-called gurus like Nate Alan Reed did. "Yeah, I've heard of him. What's he complaining about?"

"He received a death threat, and since he's a registered practitioner . . ."

"It's our problem. Great. I have to imagine a con artist like him receives death threats on the regular, though. Is there something different about it this time?"

"He's got a pretty thick file. I looked it over while I was waiting for you to gussy up. Reed is an alias. His real name is Randolph Hirshman. He's been in the area for about five years, and his land butts up against Tesuque Pueblo land. There've been a few altercations over the years. The Pueblo even filed a lawsuit over encroachment at one point and made him move his sweat lodge two feet back so it wasn't over the property line. He's gotten threats before, but nothing ever came of them. The last one was nearly a year ago."

"This should be a fairly easy outing, then."

"Fingers crossed."

I glanced at the GPS again. We had a solid thirty-minute drive ahead of us, give or take. I settled in to sip my coffee and gaze out the window. Mike and I had never had a problem with silence. Neither of us felt a driving need to fill it. But as we passed the high school on our way out of town, the memory of the dead teenager in my ER drifted to the surface, and there seemed like no time like the present to broach the subject.

"I think there's a new drug on the streets that's especially bad for witches."

"Oh? What makes you say that?"

Where did I even start? I hadn't thought that far ahead. "We've been seeing these weird ODs at the hospital. They present like opioid overdoses, which we deal with all the time, but there's something else to it. They don't respond to treatment or sedatives the way they're supposed to. They hallucinate and throw uncontrolled magic around on the way down, then often suffer massive cardiac arrest."

"That sounds bad. All witches, you say?"

"Yeah. I mean, mundies can't sling spells no matter how high they are, but the rest of the symptoms, nothing like it."

"I wonder why this is the first I'm hearing about it. Seems like that would've raised some red flags."

"That's probably my fault." I winced faintly but pressed on. "I've been intervening with the ones I come across, draining their magic so no one gets hurt. And not all of them have been registered, so . . ."

"Ah. Got it." He hummed thoughtfully. "Still, if you're encountering enough to notice on your shift, surely they're happening outside your shift too."

"Yeah, but if they don't know some of them are witches, they might think it's affecting both humans and witches the same way."

He nodded. "I'll reach out to Narcotics, see what they've got. Do you think you can get me some names of the affected witches?"

"Sorry, bud. Little thing called HIPAA standing in the

way." The Health Insurance Portability and Accountability Act put a lot of restrictions in place to protect patient privacy. The only way we were going to get the info was with a court order, and if I tried to go around it, I could—no, *would*—lose my license.

"Right, right. How long has this been going on?"

"I'm not sure. Maybe . . . December?"

His head twitched aside as he glanced at me. "That long?"

Guilt stabbed at my heart. "That's when I saw the first case. I think. I know it was before we started working together, but not by much. It was weeks before I saw another case, but they've gotten more frequent recently. I know I've seen three this week."

"Troubling," he murmured.

I nodded my agreement and went back to watching the landscape slide past as silence settled between us once more. Had I waited too long to say something? Maybe I should've tried harder to ask the witches what the hell they'd been on before they left the hospital, but so far, the ones who hadn't gone out in body bags had been released before my next shift.

"Don't let it eat you up," Mike said a few minutes later, dragging me from my increasingly bleak thoughts.

"I should've said something sooner."

"You could've said nothing at all."

He had a point, but I wasn't sure it'd help me sleep at night.

CHAPTER 6

We headed out of the city, then roughly northwest on a series of progressively narrower roads. This part of Santa Fe County was relatively flat, though dotted with a few hills here and there, unlike the mountainous region on the western side of the county. Brown earth dotted with scrub brush and the odd patch of days-old snow stretched as far as the eye could see between distant, snow-capped mountains to the east and west, too arid to be grassland but not quite dry enough to be desert. Beautiful, though, in its own way.

We passed various communities along the way, but the farther we went, the farther apart and grander the homes became. Mike eventually pulled onto a private drive that terminated in a wide wooden gate between two low adobe walls that were more ornamentation than security. He pressed the button on the callbox, and the gates swung open once he'd identified himself as a police officer. We proceeded down the paved driveway, soon reaching an ornate courtyard with a fountain at the center of a circular drive.

The massive single-story adobe home at the end of the drive sprawled across the landscape, carrying a sort of false humility with its deceptively plain exterior. The home's only decorative touches were architectural, in the form of varying roof height and the ends of logs sticking out in a tidy row along the top. Flat spouts were built into the rooftop here and there for runoff, a built-in gutter system. The grounds around the home were xeriscaped with native plants. Big sagebrush, yucca, common yarrow, and desert marigold were all things I was used to seeing, but there were a few shrubs—like the spiky sage-colored ones in the waist-high glazed pots flanking the front door—that I couldn't identify at a glance. A four-car garage sat off to one side of the house, and a compact sedan sat parked in the gravel alongside it.

Mike parked in front of the garage, and we climbed out to head for the house. I was sweating like a beast under my coat by then, so the chilly air was a welcome change. He nudged me with an elbow on the way to the door.

"Try to play nice," he said.

"Why wouldn't I?"

"You made your opinion of Mr. Reed clear on the way here. Just be cool." He unbuttoned his coat so his badge on the chain around his neck was visible and rang the doorbell.

I pulled my lanyard out from under my coat, a rebuke on the tip of my tongue. I eyed him but only said, "Yes, sir."

He eyed me back, but we were saved from further discourse by the opening door. A short, older Hispanic woman in a traditional maid's conservative black dress with a white apron stood on the threshold, looking us over with critical brown eyes.

"Good morning, ma'am. I'm Detective Escobar, and this is my associate, Emily Davenport. We're here to follow up on a report of a death threat received by Mr. Reed."

The maid nodded and held the door open. "Please come in," she said in heavily accented English. "Señor Reed is expecting you."

I followed Mike into the tiled entryway, assaulted by warm air once more. I shucked my coat, and we wiped our feet under the maid's watchful eye before she led us deeper into the house. The entryway's tile gave way to hardwood covered here and there by a woven rug. The interior walls were the same adobe as the exterior, but unweathered. High ceilings with large, exposed beams created a lodge-like atmosphere reinforced by large pieces of rustic furniture in dark, earthy tones. Native art was everywhere, from paintings to shadowboxes, baskets, blankets, rugs, sculptures, and pottery. I was willing to bet it was all authentic too. There wasn't a tourist trap Kachina in sight.

The maid stopped in front of a closed door and rapped lightly upon it before opening it a crack. The scent of incense wafted out. "Señor, the police are here."

There was a pause, and then a rich baritone rolled out of the room. "You may enter."

The maid pushed the door open and motioned for us to head inside. The scent of incense grew stronger as I followed Mike into the room, squinting because of the abrupt change in light level. Morning sunlight streamed into the east-facing wall of windows, which was a very non-traditional feature for an adobe home. Our host sat cross-legged on a large pillow in the center of the otherwise furniture-less room. A conical incense burner sat on the floor in front of him, wisps of fragrant smoke curling from its tiny chimney.

Nate Alan Reed unfolded his long legs and stood in a graceful movement, generous mouth curving in a warm smile. He was an older man with a full head of gray hair plaited into two braids that hung down over his shoulders. His bronze-hued skin reminded me of spray-tanned contestants on a celebrity dancing show, and he flashed twin rows of perfectly straight, pearly white teeth as he smiled. The man could've been a politician with that picture-perfect smile. Then again, it wasn't a big jump from politician to con man. Regardless, his green eyes were bright as he greeted us.

"Gracias, Alma. Come in, detectives. I was just doing a bit of meditation, but I was expecting you. Grab a pillow." His welcoming baritone filled the small room, wrapping around me like a sonic hug. "Oh, and Alma, bring us some refreshments, if you would."

He just felt . . . genuine somehow. I scanned him for charms but found none. No, the guy was just naturally charismatic. He wasn't using a lick of magic to—wait. There wasn't a lick of magic in him at all. At least, not that I could detect. And I could always tell a witch from a mundie, even if they weren't actively casting magic. I'd only recently found out just how unusual that was. But regardless, I could've sworn Mike had mentioned Reed was a registered practitioner. Hadn't he? He had to be, for us to be here.

Mike cleared his throat. Distracted, I turned to find him holding out a large purple floor pillow. He arched a questioning brow as I took it, but I shook my head and carried the pillow over to set it down across from Reed's.

Mike set his pillow beside mine, but we both lingered on our feet while he introduced us to Reed. Once settled, he took out his notebook and got straight down to business. "I understand you received a death threat, Mr. Reed?"

As I studied Randolph Hirshman—aka Nate Alan Reed —through the haze of incense, an old Stephen King quote came to mind. Something about liars sitting in chairs and friends sitting around campfires. Reed was no Randall Flagg, but he had the same sort of dangerous charisma. His smile dimmed in response to Mike's question, and he nodded.

"Yes, yes. A troublesome business, that." Reed turned his head slightly, but his gaze touched the north wall rather than looking out at the picturesque landscape beyond the glass wall. "I have trouble with the neighbors from time to time, and then there's the anti-witch crowd, those so-called Sons of Humanity . . ." He shrugged his shoulders like there was nothing to be done about it.

"You picked an interesting spot to settle if you didn't want trouble with the Pueblo," I said. I usually let Mike take the lead in these sorts of situations, given that the extent of my law enforcement training consisted of a three-hour, pre-recorded orientation seminar for civilian consultants. But I was too curious to remain silent.

Reed smiled again, however briefly, and gestured out the window. "Have you seen this view? I regret nothing." The corners of his eyes crinkled with mirth, but it faded in the face of his unamused audience. "This is a deeply spiritual location, Miss Davenport. It resonated within my soul the moment I arrived, and I'll not be driven off by troublemak-ers. This is my home, a peaceful sanctuary. I am far from a disruptive neighbor. I pay my taxes, maintain the property, and mostly keep to myself. Host the occasional quiet retreat for bruised souls seeking tranquility and enlightenment. Those who take offense to my presence here—or my mere existence—ought to look inside themselves for the wicked-ness they wish to expunge."

I had a few thoughts about his tranquility and enlighten-ment, but I kept them to myself.

"May I see the letter you received, Mr. Reed?" Mike asked, steering us back on track.

Reed blinked owlishly. "Letter? There must be some misunderstanding. I mean, it was written but . . . perhaps it's best if you see for yourself." He stood once more and we followed suit, then he led us back out of the meditation room and down the hall, past an expansive dining room and through a humungous kitchen Matt would've found drool-worthy. Alma barely gave us a second glance as she arranged earthenware mugs on a tea tray.

I put my coat on when Reed opened the back door, which opened onto an expansive patio with a thick-beamed awning and covered patio furniture arranged around a fire pit that looked more decorative than functional, especially this time of year. He led us off the patio and along the back of the house, then around the corner to the west-facing side.

A few strides later, he paused and motioned at a broken window. The point of impact was obvious, as cracks spider-webbed from it across the entire window. A few small pieces of glass littered the bare brown earth at the foot of the wall with a weathered adobe brick among them, but most of the glass remained still in the frame.

"Tempered glass? Interesting choice for a residential window," Mike said.

"This isn't my first run-in with vandals, I'm afraid." Reed circumnavigated the small debris field to stand on the other side and folded his arms.

Something about the brick drew my attention back to it. There was some sort of pattern on it, painted or drawn with marker. I edged closer, peering at it. It took a few moments for my eyes to register what I saw. What I'd mistaken for a pattern were words in unusually angular, blocky letters.

"Leave this place or die," I read aloud, then glanced at Mike. "I guess that's a pretty clear threat."

He nodded but straightened and addressed the victim. "Has anyone touched the brick since it was discovered?"

Reed shook his head. "No. As I said, this sort of thing has happened before. Well, not the death threat part, but the vandalism."

I tugged on Mike's sleeve. "I'd like to get a closer look at that thing." I motioned with my chin toward the brick.

Mike took out his phone and took a few pictures, then motioned for me to go ahead. I pulled a pair of nitrile gloves from my coat pocket and put them on, then crossed the safety glass to squat closer to the brick. I gave it a careful visual inspection but detected no magical residues, so I picked it up and turned it over. The same message was written on the other side, like whoever'd tossed it wanted to make absolutely sure the message was received no matter how it landed.

"When did it happen?" Mike asked, continuing the interview while I inspected the brick.

"Last night," Reed said. "I'm afraid I don't know exactly when. I was on the other side of the house. My groundskeeper discovered it this morning and alerted me."

"About what time was that?"

"Hmm. About eight-thirty."

Mike nodded. "Does your housekeeper live on the premises?"

"No. She usually arrives around six."

"And she didn't notice anything amiss?"

"She didn't mention anything. But she'd have little reason to be on this side of the house first thing in the morning."

Finding no trace of magic on the other side of the brick,

I stood and walked it over to Mike, holding onto it until he was ready to bag it. I pointed at the broken window. "What room is that?"

"A guest room. It's only used when I'm hosting a—oh dear, the retreat!" He placed a hand at the base of his throat. "I'm behind schedule. I've got fifteen guests arriving in under forty-eight hours, and there's still much to do. Is this going to take much longer?"

"I only have a few more questions, sir." Mike produced a large evidence bag from his inner coat pocket. "But we'll need to speak with the groundskeeper too." He opened the bag and held it out to me. I took it and slid the brick inside carefully before jotting down the date and my initials on the outside.

"That's no problem. He's around here somewhere," Reed said. "Alma can locate him for you on the radio. You don't need me for that, right?" He shifted his weight between his feet and darted an anxious glance in the direction we came.

"Nope," Mike said. "What kind of security do you have out here? Cameras, motion detectors, anything like that?"

"There are motion-activated floodlights and cameras outside, but I don't know all the details. Juan should be able to answer your questions about that. He installed everything."

"Juan?" I asked.

"The groundskeeper. Well, he's more of an all-around handyman." His eyes widened suddenly and he grimaced. "Ah, now I think of it, he might be off today. I mean, I think he took the rest of the day off. Family something-something. I'll have him give you a call."

Mike and I exchanged a brief glance. Odds were, Juan was an illegal, and Reed had just remembered.

"I'd appreciate that," Mike said. "We just want to ask him a few questions."

"Good, good." Reed's shoulders eased visibly. "Do you have anything else for me?"

"Just one more question," Mike said. "Can you think of anyone who might have a bone to pick with you?"

Reed breathed a heavy sigh. "Regrettably, yes. The Pueblo has made no secret of their desire to see me gone. If I were a betting man, that's where I'd start."

"Have you had run-ins with anyone in particular?" Mike asked. "Last count, a couple hundred people lived on the Tesuque Pueblo."

My estimation of Mike ticked upward some, not that it was particularly low. I wouldn't have expected him to know that little trivia nugget. At the same time, I was surprised how low that particular Pueblo's population was. The Pojoaque Pueblo, a few miles farther up Highway 285, was over one thousand strong. Of course, I only knew that because I'd done some research since my trip up there in December.

"Their Medicine Man's hot-headed grandson, for one. Most of their tribal council, the chief of police, some of their youths used my walls for target practice with BB guns last summer . . ."

"How about you make me a list and email it to me?" Mike produced a card from his pocket and offered it.

Reed took the card. "Yes, yes, that'll be fine. I've had a few issues with former clients over the years, too. And the Sons of Humanity were out here just last week, raising hell and throwing empty beer bottles over my gate. I filed a complaint about that with the state police."

Mike nodded. "We'll follow up with the state police on

that. If you think of anything else, give me a call. My cell's on the card."

I fell in step with Mike as Reed led us back to the back door and into the house, where he left us in the kitchen with Alma. Mike asked her a few questions while we politely sipped the tea she'd prepared, but she didn't have any more to offer than Reed himself had. She walked us to the front door after that, and we stepped out into the crisp February air once more.

"Well, that was . . . interesting," I said. "Why didn't you ask her to radio Juan?"

"It'll be easier to get the details on the security system from him on the phone. If Mr. Reed's sudden shift in demeanor was anything to go by . . ."

"He's an illegal?"

Mike nodded, and we started for the car. "Probably. And I don't want to deal with the paperwork."

"There's something else," I said. "Speaking of paperwork."

"Yeah?"

"If that guy is a witch, I'll eat my badge."

Mike lifted a brow at that but didn't respond until we were back in the car, buckling in. "Are you sure?"

"Positive. He may be in the registry, but he's not a witch." I probably should've felt some sort of kinship with him, but I didn't. I only felt like an imposter. He actually *was* one. "So, what's involved in transferring the case?"

"We can't."

"What? Why not? He's an ordinary guy who had an ordinary brick thrown at his house." I held up the bagged brick in question. "There was no magic involved. No magic crime, no witch, so why would it be our case?"

"He's in the registry," Mike said patiently, backing the car up to head back down the drive. "There has to be a reason."

"Um, yeah. He's a freaking con artist, Mike."

"What if he's like you?" He glanced over at me and arched a brow. "Do you register on witch radar?"

"I—I don't know. One of my special talents, apparently, is witch-sensing. Most witches can't tell a witch from a mundie until spells start flying." I didn't like it, but he had a point. I had no idea if I could sense a witch without magic. I was the only one I knew of. "But, now that you mention it, that's a pretty big loophole in the registry, isn't it? There's no penalty for falsely registering and no sort of 'witch test' to get in. You just fill out a form, get it notarized, and file it with the state."

"Who would voluntarily put their info in a publicly searchable database if not compelled by law? It's not like it comes with any special benefits."

"It's a wonder anyone signs up at all," I muttered, running a hand over my face. God knows I wasn't thrilled with the situation myself. But it was what it was. Maybe it was a good thing the state didn't police who was in the registry, or they might not have let me in. Lord knows my mother had taken pains to remind me that, as a null, I didn't have any sort of standing with the Circle, the alliance of powerful covens my family belonged to. Impersonating a Circle witch was a good way for a witch to get permanently bound—or disappeared. "So, we're stuck with him?"

"Think of it as an opportunity to practice the fundamentals of criminal investigation. We followed up on the report, we collected evidence and interviewed the victim and his household staff . . . What's next?"

"Donut break?"

"Obviously. But after that?"

I leaned an elbow on the door and drummed my fingertips lightly on the molded plastic covering it. "Hopefully some gym time, because all these donuts are going straight to my ass."

He laughed. "You'll have to work out on your own time."

I chuckled along with him, but not for the same reason. My own time. Between my full-time job at the hospital and moonlighting in Magic Crimes, I'd nearly forgotten what that was.

"Guess we'll have to drop the brick off for forensics and take a closer look at Reed's file, then. Get a better idea of past incidents and start a suspect list while we wait to hear from the groundskeeper about the security system and any possible video footage."

"Top of the class." He offered a fist and I bumped it, smiling because it seemed like maybe we were getting past what had happened the day before.

Might've been a little premature on that.

CHAPTER 7

I was with Mike until mid-afternoon, and when I got home, the apartment was blessedly quiet. I bypassed the couch, where Dan's nest of pillows and blankets remained. I'd learned early on in our cohabitation that tidying up behind him was a mistake. He'd had housekeepers cleaning up after him his entire life, and the last thing I needed was to set the expectation that I'd do it. This meant I ignored his mess in the living room unless I was expecting company, then needled him about anything I wanted him to pick up until he did it. Sure, it would've been nice if he'd taken some initiative, but . . . this was a temporary solution. Hopefully, it wouldn't be much longer until he was gainfully employed and out of my hair.

I toed off my shoes once I reached my inner sanctum— aka my bedroom—and closed the door before shimmying out of my jeans and flopping onto the unmade bed. Yeah, I know, it's a little hypocritical to be annoyed with my brother for not making his bed when I didn't make my own, but mine wasn't in the middle of the living room. I plugged my phone in and dropped it on the nightstand. I was just drifting off for a much-desired nap when the phone rang. Cracking an eye open, I glared at it before the ringtone registered. It was Matt. My annoyance faded, and rather than letting it go to voicemail, I answered.

"Hey, what's up?"

"Hey yourself. You working tonight?" He sounded far too chipper for—I glanced at the clock. 3:50 p.m.? Okay, I guess that was an appropriate time to sound chipper.

"Nope." I popped the P, just because it was extra satisfying. I love my nights off as much as the next gal.

"Sweet. I've got an extra ticket to one of those BYOB painting classes. Wanna come? I'll buy dinner, you bring the Pinot?"

"You know I don't have an artistic bone in my body, right?" I rolled onto my back and stared at the plain white ceiling.

"Oh, come on. It's more about drinking and chatting than actually painting. We haven't had a night out in a while. It'll be fun."

"You could probably talk me into it if I didn't already have plans."

"Barry?"

"Yeah. His roommate's band is playing again. Hexed. They're really good."

"Sounds like you're looking forward to the band more than the company. You tell him yet?"

I swallowed a sigh and forced some levity into my voice. "That I've got a girl crush on his roommate's girlfriend and her amazing voice? Oh yeah."

"You know what I mean."

"Yeah, I know." I let the sigh out this time. "I just haven't found the right time."

"What right time are you waiting for? Just tell him. Barry, baby, I'm a witch. Done."

I grimaced. Never had I ever called Barry 'baby.' "It's not that easy. Besides, Barry and I are just casual. He's moving back to Colorado at the end of ski season."

"Sure, unless you give him a reason to stick around . . ."

"Matt, I love you, but if you want the guy to stick around so much, *you* give him a reason."

"If only, honey bear. If only."

I rubbed my eyes. "Hanging up now."

"Wait! What time?"

"What time what?"

"What time is Barry picking you up?"

I sensed where this was going. "I'm not going to your painting class before my date, no matter how many smocks you layer on over my date night jeans."

He laughed. "How about just dinner, then?"

"Promise not to nag me about Barry?"

"Cross my heart. Pick you up at five?"

I glanced at the clock again. "Okay, but don't be late. Barry's picking me up at eight."

I set an alarm on my phone to make sure I didn't over-sleep, then curled up around a pillow and closed my eyes. Years of day shifts, night shifts, and swing shifts meant I could usually fall asleep pretty much anytime, day or night. The blackout curtains in my bedroom didn't hurt. But even the sound of late afternoon street traffic and the occasional door closing heavily somewhere in the building couldn't keep me from drifting off into a peaceful sleep.

The doorbell woke me ten minutes before my alarm went off, the sudden loud chime snapping me awake as if an air horn had gone off in my room. As a frequent day-sleeper, the doorbell was the bane of my existence, but I never had figured out how to disconnect it short of ripping it off the wall and cutting the cords. Can't say it hadn't been tempting now and then.

I rolled out of bed and got halfway down the hall before the goosebumps on my bare legs made me backtrack for pants. Answering the door without pants on is never a good idea, but in winter it's even worse. I stumbled back down the hall and peered through the peephole. Two women stood outside, distorted by the fisheye lens but not particularly threatening. The fact that they were still there after it'd taken me a solid fifty seconds or so to get to the door told me they probably weren't solicitors, but they weren't wearing uniforms either, and I wasn't expecting anyone.

I unlocked and opened the door, quickly taking in their matching outfits, dark braids, and pearly white smiles. Magic—or, rather the potential for it since they weren't actively casting—radiated from them like heat from a potbelly stove. There was only one reason I could think of why a pair of attractive twenty-something identical twin witches would be standing on my doorstep.

I rubbed my face and sighed. "Dan's not here."

I started to close the door, but one of them said, "Wait!"

Against my better judgment, I did.

"Emily Davenport?" the one on the left said.

"Who wants to know?"

The pair exchanged a knowing glance, then focused on me again. Lefty said, "Ms. Davenport, I'm Kara and this is my sister Kourtney. We were just in the area and wanted to stop by. Do you have a few minutes to talk about an exciting opportunity?"

I glanced between them. The only way I could tell them

apart was that Kara's lips gleamed with sparkly lip gloss. It wasn't much, but it was enough. "Whatever it is, I'm not interested. Sorry."

"Please, ma'am." The words tumbled so quickly from Kara's mouth that they about tripped over each other. "Thirty seconds of your time. For a fellow practitioner."

My eyes narrowed. I had no idea who these women were, but they seemed to know an uncomfortable amount about me.

When I didn't shut the door in their faces, Kourtney spoke. "First off, on behalf of the San Miguel Coven, we'd like to welcome you to Santa Fe."

I laughed. "You're a little tardy on that. I've been here for years."

The women exchanged another glance, twin brows furrowed. "Oh. My apologies," Kourtney said.

"We saw you were newly registered . . ." Kara said.

"Ahhh. I get it. So you're what, the witch welcome wagon?"

"Something like that." Kara shifted her weight and tucked her hands in the pockets of her puffy blue coat. "You didn't list a coven, but that's an optional field. Do you mind if I ask . . . ?"

I shook my head. "No. I mean, yes you can ask. But no, I don't have a coven. I guess I'm kind of a lone wolf. Witch. You know. Wait. Are you here to recruit me?"

Both pairs of shoulders bobbed. "Sort of. Maybe," Kourtney said. "With crime against witches on the rise in Santa Fe, it's not a great time to be unaffiliated. There's safety in numbers, and the San Miguel Coven is the largest coven in the city. We look out for each other, more of a family than a coven really."

It'd be hard to live in Santa Fe and not hear of the San

Miguel Coven, registered or not. They weren't lying about being the largest. The San Miguel Coven was the local branch of the Order of St. Bridget, which had risen in the national spotlight not long after witches were dragged out of the broom closet. They'd been around a lot longer, of course—not as long as the Circle, but a while. Decades. The Circle may have been the most powerful and intimidating organization on the continent behind the scenes, but the OSB was the public face of witchcraft in the United States, and the membership requirements weren't nearly as strict.

Once adopted as members of the OSB, law-abiding witches looking for safety in numbers didn't have to look any further. They could travel to any city with a branch coven and be welcomed like long-lost family. It was an attractive paradigm, especially for those who were forced out of conservative churches and other organizations when their witch status became known. Which isn't to say that it was a religious organization—far from it. But it did attract its own sort of fanatics.

"Gotcha. Well, thanks for coming by, but I'm not in the market for a coven right now."

Their faces fell like I'd canceled Christmas.

"Are you sure?" Kara asked.

"You don't have to decide right now," Kourtney added hastily. She pulled a business card from her pocket and held it out. "That's my personal phone number. You can call me anytime, day or night, if you have any questions about the coven or need help or just want to talk to someone who understands the plight of the modern witch."

I took the card after a brief hesitation, glancing at it before tucking it between my fingers. The OSB logo was stamped in one corner in gold foil, and it bore Kourtney's full name, email address, and phone number. "Thanks. Have a good night."

I closed the door and locked it, tucked the card in the back pocket of my jeans, and forgot all about it until, well, that's a whole other story. We'll get to that eventually.

CHAPTER 8

The music in the club was so loud I couldn't hear my own thoughts, but I didn't mind. There was enough pot smoke mingling with the cigarette smoke in the air that I'm pretty sure I had a contact-high. I didn't care about that either. The kick of the bass drum vibrated through my body, stronger than my own heartbeat and just as fast. We'd been on the packed dance floor, arms in the air and hips gyrating, since the beginning of Hexed's set. They were local favorites, and I'd recognized a few faces in the crowd from other shows I'd attended with Barry in the last couple of months.

Barry was a great dancer, which truth be told, bothered me a little. I mean, seriously. Other than having the misfortune to almost share a name with my cat, the guy had virtually no flaws. He was gorgeous, smart, funny, athletic, didn't take himself too seriously, had a good job, was understanding about my busy schedule, and knew how to have a good time. Best of all, he wasn't in the least bit clingy. But everyone has flaws, right? I knew if I looked hard enough, I could find one. I wasn't trying very hard. We hadn't even spent the night together. Maybe he hogged the covers, drank straight from the milk carton, or left the toilet seat up for all I knew.

As the heavy rock beat transitioned into a ballad, Barry caught my hand and drew me close. I curled my arms around his neck and leaned into him as we swayed to the sensual beat, grateful for the break but knowing I had only danced off a fraction of the calories from my dinner with Matt. The man knew my weaknesses better than anyone and hadn't even had to try very hard to talk me into an indulgent slice of triple chocolate cheesecake for dessert.

Barry's hands found my waist and slid around to my back, rucking up my Hexed T-shirt a bit. But as soon as his fingertips brushed my bare skin, he removed them and smoothed the shirt back in place. I'd been waiting for him to make a move for weeks, but he hadn't done more than hold my hand or kiss me goodnight. If he didn't do it soon, I was going to have to do it for him. Now that I thought about it, there was more than one way to burn calories.

On impulse, I curled my fingers in his hair and pulled his head down, kissing him right there on the dance floor. It was far from scandalous, but a deviation from our usual date routine nonetheless. I tasted mint on his tongue, like he'd been sneaking breath mints when I wasn't looking because that's the kind of guy he was. When he broke the kiss a few moments later, his pupils were huge and he wasn't breathing heavy just from exertion anymore. Neither was I. Score one for Team Emily. I winked at him and turned in his arms to put my back to his chest. His hands settled on my hips, and we danced some more, but the ballad soon ended, and we broke apart to applaud and cheer with the rest of the crowd.

In the brief lull between the crowd's adoration and the

next song, Barry's minty breath brushed my ear. "Want to get some fresh air?"

I nodded and we headed for the exit—with a quick stop at the bar for a bottle of water. Outside, the crescent moon was high, and the parking lot was packed. The air was also more than a little crisp, and I regretted not stopping by our table for our coats as gooseflesh broke out on both my arms almost immediately. Barry led me away from the door, down the cracked sidewalk a ways. Stopping on the edge of a pool of light from a nearby streetlight, he cracked open the bottle of water and offered me the first sip. We both drank.

He tilted his head. "Great show, isn't it?"

"Oh yeah, but it always—yeep!"

One minute I was standing on the sidewalk, and the next he had me up against the building, pressing a spine-tingling kiss to my startled lips. The brick wall at my back was cold, but the heat of Barry's body against mine kept the chill at bay. And the longer he kissed me, the more I forgot about the cold. He was like a bull who'd just seen a red cape, and I liked this new, aggressive side of him.

"You're so beautiful," he murmured against my lips, then pulled back a little to look into my eyes.

"You too . . ." I was too dazed to form a coherent thought.

He chuckled, and his thumb stroked my cheek. "You know, my contract is up in a couple months."

"Yeah." I shook off the sexy fog clouding my brain, struggling to follow his train of thought. Was he worried about me getting too attached if we slept together? Was that why he hadn't made a move yet? "Yeah, I remember. I know you're going back to Denver. You were up front about that."

"What if I didn't?"

"What?" The next shiver that ran down my spine was just the cold wall at my back. Right?

His thumb brushed my skin again as he gazed into my eyes. "Well, it's not like I have a wife and kids to get back to . . ."

I laugh-snorted. "That probably should've been one of my first getting-to-know-you questions, eh?"

His answering smile made me want to both kiss him again and flee, all at once. My heart raced. I didn't know what was wrong with me, but I wasn't sure I liked where this was going.

"I know there's not much work for ski instructors around here in the off-season, but I can always find something else."

"So you're thinking about staying in Santa Fe? Permanently?"

"Maybe." He shifted his hand, and his thumb brushed my lower lip. "What do you think about that?"

What did I think about that? It was a good question, and one I wasn't prepared for. I liked Barry a lot. Hell, less than a minute ago I'd been ready to climb him like a tree. But for the first time, I realized that part of what I liked about Barry was his expiration date. There was no expectation of more, no pressure to make a commitment. Was that what he was looking for now?

My phone buzzed in my back pocket, and a surge of relief ran through me. I didn't care if it was Dan wanting me to bring home a pizza or a telemarketer burning the midnight oil. Never before had I welcomed an interruption as much as I did at that moment.

Flashing him an apologetic look, I fished my phone out of my pocket and glanced at it. It was the hospital. Hope fluttered in my stomach, a first for a late-night phone call from work. I mean, maybe they just had a question about something, but it wasn't out of the realm of possibility that they needed me to come in.

"Sorry, I have to take this. It's work."

Barry nodded and stepped back. As soon as the heat of his body was gone, I began longing for my coat once again.

I put the phone to my ear. "This is Emily."

"Hi Emily, it's Wendy. Sorry to bother you on your night off." Her tone was anything but sorry. This is Steel Wool Wendy we're talking about. "But Rita is sick and needs to go home. Can you come in tonight?"

My eyes drifted to Barry, standing a few feet away with his back to me like that would give me a little more privacy for my unavoidably audible phone conversation.

In case you've ever wondered, I can confirm that it is, in fact, possible to feel guilty and relieved at the same time. "Oh no, I hope it's nothing serious. Yeah, I can do that. I'll be there as soon as I can."

"Thanks, Em. You're a peach."

I hung up but stared at Barry's back for a long moment with the phone in my hand. Guilt surged to the fore, and I bit my lip, wishing I could give him the answer he clearly wanted before I bailed. I just didn't know what *I* wanted, and that wasn't fair to him. Tucking my phone away, I touched Barry's shoulder and he turned around.

"I'm sorry, I—"

"Duty calls, I get it." He smiled and caught my hand, lifted it to his lips to brush a kiss across my knuckles. "Go grab your coat, and I'll walk you to your car."

I hurried away from him like the coward I was.

CHAPTER 9

When I retrieved my phone from my locker at the end of my—or, rather, Rita's—shift, I found a text from Tracy and two missed calls—but no voicemail—plus four text messages from Mike, all within the last hour.

7:22: You awake yet? We've got a call.

7:29: I'm coming over to pick you up.

7:50: Dan says you didn't come home last night. Where are you?

8:12: Found your car. I'll wait here.

Mike's last message was almost half an hour prior. Tracy's message was a simple "thanks" I didn't have time to overthink or follow up on just then. I changed out of my scrubs and into last night's date clothes quickly and headed outside, where I found my partner in the employee parking lot, his unmarked sedan parked next to my little red Corolla. Leaning against the front fender of my car, he lifted a hand and waved when he spotted me coming across the lot from the employee entrance. He had his "cop face" on, a stern sort of half-glower, like it was my fault that I hadn't kept him apprised of my whereabouts on my night off. My feet hurt, even after a shorter-than-usual shift, and I was just tired enough to have an extra spoonful of sass in my cup.

I lifted an eyebrow as I drew nearer. "Stalker much?"

"Stalk her? I barely know her," he deadpanned. "You look like shit. Get in, we'll get coffee on the way."

"On the way where?" I asked but walked around to the passenger side of his car nonetheless like he was some sort of pied piper for the caffeine-deprived.

"Crime scene." He met my eyes across the roof. "Nate Alan Reed was found dead this morning."

"No shit, really?"

He nodded, then disappeared from my view as he got into the car. When I joined him, he said, "Housekeeper found his body almost two hours ago. I don't know more than that, since I've been trying to track you down ever since."

"I can't carry my personal phone on the floor. So, shoot me."

"Too much paperwork."

Groaning, I buckled up and he backed aggressively out of the parking space. His posture remained tense, jaw set in a grim line as I studied his profile.

"Who pissed in your cereal this morning?"

"No one. I just—" He stopped himself and frowned, shaking his head.

I eyed him through narrowed eyes. "You just what?"

"I just don't like being behind the ball. We should be there already."

"Well, I'm sorry I got called into work I guess. But you don't need to know where I am every second of every day."

He grunted. "Someone should."

"What's that supposed to mean?" When he didn't

answer, I reached across the console and poked his leg. "Come on, man."

"Even your brother didn't know where you were, and you live with him. What if something had happened to you?"

"Dan knew I had a date, so he probably figured I got—" I gasped dramatically, putting a hand over my heart. "Michael Escobar. Were you—" Dramatic pause. "—worried about me?"

"Forget I said anything."

I grinned. "Oh no, there's no chance of that."

"You and your brother are infuriatingly alike at times."

"Ouch. Well, for what it's worth, I appreciate your concern. But I still won't text you the next time I go home with a guy or get called into work on my night off."

"Just tell your brother if you're not coming home, okay? It's called common courtesy when you live with someone."

"You're kind of cute when you're annoyed."

"Put a sock in it, Davenport."

We pulled into Nate Alan Reed's driveway about thirty minutes later. I was feeling a little more perky thanks to the coffee, but there hadn't exactly been any scintillating conversation along the way. I could tell Mike was still irked at me, but at least I'd had the presence of mind not to suggest he could've gone ahead without me. I was actually kind of grateful he hadn't, because that meant he was still committed to our partnership. Or maybe I was just reading too much into things.

An ambulance, a CSI unit, and two black and white SFPD cruisers littered the front drive. One of the cruisers was blocking the ambulance in such a way that suggested no one expected it to have to leave anytime soon. While Mike wedged his Buick in between one of the cruisers and the fountain, I fished my consultant badge out of my date night purse and slung the lanyard over my head. This wasn't the first time I'd had to go on a callout with Mike on short notice, so I'd made a habit out of bringing it with me everywhere.

We were met at the front door by a uniform with a tablet rather than the housekeeper. After checking our badges and signing us in, she waved us past. "Scene's in the back, but you can go through the house. It's down that hall and . . ."

Mike was already past her, striding with purpose in the direction of the kitchen.

I flashed the young woman a sympathetic smile. "We know the way, thanks."

I scurried after Mike, lengthening my stride to catch up. The house felt empty. It wasn't like we'd seen anyone but Reed and Alma on our last visit, but there had been a sort of warmth and welcoming that was strangely absent today. Speaking of Alma, I wondered where she was and felt bad that she'd been the one to find her boss's body. She'd seemed nice enough.

There was another uniform stationed on the back porch. He straightened away from the wall when we came outside.

"Where the hell is everyone?" Mike asked, frowning.

"Sweat lodge," the uniform replied. His shiny brass name tag read "Collins."

"Not for recreation, I assume," I said before I could stop myself.

Mike gave me a look over his shoulder, but Collins chuckled. "No, ma'am. That's where the body was found. It's thataway." He pointed. "Can't miss it."

I looked in the direction he pointed, and in the distance I could just make out a shape on the horizon. My aching feet throbbed a protest. "I don't suppose there's a golf cart around here somewhere . . ."

"You can wait in the car if you want." Mike lifted an eyebrow in silent challenge.

Rolling my eyes, I stepped off the patio and began the long march across the arid snow-patched landscape. I wasn't terribly eager to see Nate Alan Reed's corpse, but I was at least a little curious about what had happened to him. Now that I thought about it, I probably should have been alert for magical residues when we went through the house. I sharpened my focus and paid more attention while we walked.

A solid ten minutes later, we arrived on the scene. A perimeter had been cordoned off with police tape; they'd had to drive stakes into the ground to string it because there was nothing else within range to do it. The sweat lodge was a squat, domed structure in the middle of nowhere. It was covered with a patchwork of sand-colored canvas and animal hides, its flap of a door tied back.

Another uniform was stationed outside the lodge. He nodded to us in passing, and we ducked our heads to enter through the low opening. Inside, there was room to stand mostly upright. Mike had to hunch more than I did until we walked farther toward the center of the dome. The air hit me like a wall of heat and humidity despite ventilation flaps having been thrown open and the coals extinguished. I glanced up, noting the fiberglass poles that formed the frame of the structure, which was easily fifty feet in diameter. Big, for a sweat lodge.

The crime scene techs were taking pictures and dusting for prints, though there weren't many surfaces inside that looked like they'd hold them. More animal skins covered the hard-packed dirt floor here and there, and in the very center of the room was a fire pit ringed with fist-sized stones. The body lay nearby, curled on its side.

The air was stiflingly warm, humid, and smelled like Satan's butthole. If you've never smelled cooked human flesh . . . I don't recommend it. I resisted the urge to pinch my nose or wave my hand in front of it. If Mike could handle it, so could I. We wandered over to closer examine the body. The crime scene techs ignored us, probably intent upon finishing up and getting out of there as soon as possible.

At first glance, I'd thought the dead man was naked. But no, there was a loin cloth shrouding his nether bits. His skin was ashen gray and covered in a fine sheen of lingering perspiration. Or, at least I assumed it was lingering. As far as I knew, dead men did not sweat. I did, however, and I was certain that by the time we were finished, the shirt beneath my trench coat would be soaked through.

Putting aside my discomfort, I scanned the body and the area around it for traces of magic.

"No trace of magical residue on the body, but I'm seeing some around the fire pit . . . and there." I pointed at a ceramic bowl on the ground a few feet from the body.

Mike's attention lingered on the body for a few moments more, then shifted to the bowl. He stepped over to it and squatted down beside it, frowning. "Thought you said Reed wasn't a witch."

"He wasn't. I'm one hundred percent positive."

"So, someone else was here with him."

"Maybe, maybe not." I walked over to the fire pit. The coals had been doused with water, but when I held a hand over them, they still radiated heat. That somewhat explained the balmy temperature in the lodge despite the flaps that'd been thrown open to let some of the hot air out. "There's a stay-lit spell still active here." Something at the edge of the fire pit caught my eye, and I shuffled my feet a couple of feet over to take a closer look. Just outside the ring of stones sat a small leather pouch decorated with beads and feathers and strung on a leather thong. I fished a pair of nitrile gloves from my coat pocket—another thing I had begun carrying around everywhere, along with my badge—and motioned one of the crime scene techs over to take pictures of where it lay before I touched it. It wasn't until I picked it up and loosened the cord cinching the pouch closed that its contents pinged my magic radar. I shook its contents out into my palm, and a handful of obsidian stones tumbled out. Each was smooth and polished, but etched with a fire sigil.

"What'd you find?" Mike asked, watching me from the other side of the pit.

I straightened and walked over to him, holding out my hand. "Charms. Their resonance matches what I'm reading from the fire pit, so they're probably the source of the stay-lit spell. If we poke around in the coals, we'll probably find one of these in there." I glanced at the body. "I don't see any signs of a struggle or obvious wounds."

"Me neither, but we're going to have to roll him over to be sure."

The coffee I'd drunk on the way over sloshed in my stomach. "Ugh, do we have to?"

"We can wait for the M.E. But I think the cause of death is pretty clear."

Never—okay, rarely—one to back down from a challenge, I stepped forward and helped him roll Reed's corpse onto his back. The body was stiff, the heat having accelerated rigor mortis. "What do you think it is?"

"You're the medical professional. You don't recognize this?"

Frowning, I shook my head. "I'm a nurse, not a coroner. I specialize in living people who can tell me what they're feeling. I suppose if I had to venture a guess, I'd say heart attack." My eyes slid from the body to the clay bowl on the ground, recalling the traces of magic I'd seen there and the puddle of vomit beside the corpse. "Or poisoning."

"Perhaps. But consider the location the body was found."

I pointed at the bowl. "Well, if that didn't make him vomit, overheating might have."

Mike touched his fingertip to his nose.

"Heatstroke? You think?" I plucked the clay bowl from the ground with a gloved hand, bringing it closer so I could examine the wisp of magic clinging to it. Unlike the stay-lit spell, it was completely foreign to me. I might as well have been trying to read Arabic. I brought the bowl closer to my face and sniffed its contents. The thin liquid inside had a faintly bitter smell to it, but it wasn't anything I could place.

I set it back down, and one of the techs came over with a tube and swab to take a sample. He picked the bowl up with one gloved hand and started to bring the swab over to it, then stopped and lifted the bowl to his lips.

I lunged for him, knocking the bowl from his hand. It hit the hard-packed dirt upside down, spilling its contents.

"What the hell, man?" the other tech exclaimed, rushing over as if she thought flipping the bowl back over fast enough would keep its contents from soaking into the dirt.

"Don't touch it!" I held up my hands in warning while Mike and the tech stared at me in confusion. "The bowl is spelled, and it triggered even through his gloves."

"Gary? Are you okay?" Mike asked.

The tech who had been about to drink from the bowl blinked a few times. "What happened?"

I may not have recognized the spell, but I recognized what it'd done. "It's a compulsion spell. A compulsion to drink."

"Why didn't it affect you?" Mike asked.

"Good question. I'm not sure. Maybe it was keyed to humans."

"And now the evidence is all over the ground. Great," the other tech muttered.

"We can scrape the bowl for a sample," Gary said, but he didn't jump to do so.

"I'll do it," I said, taking the swab and tube from him.

"How are we going to check it into evidence?" the other tech asked. "We have to pick it up somehow."

"There must be some tongs around here somewhere for handling the hot rocks," Mike said, then glanced at me. "I guess we can rule out natural causes."

I grimaced but nodded as I squatted to turn the bowl over and collect a sample of its contents. There was no question in my mind. Nate Alan Reed had been murdered.

CHAPTER 10

Perched atop a hard wooden stool in the middle of Nate Alan Reed's kitchen with an untouched glass of water before me, I quietly observed his distraught housekeeper on the other side of the island. Alma kneaded dough like her life depended on it, only stopping to brush the occasional tear from her cheek with the hem of her apron. It'd probably throw the mix off if it landed in the dough.

She'd been up to her elbows in flour when we returned to the house and gave us two options: wait until she was finished, or talk to her while she worked.

"Like I told the other policeman," she said between sniffles, "I assumed he was asleep in his room when I got here."

"What time was that?" Mike asked. As usual, I let him take the lead, merely observing in case I caught something he missed—as unlikely as that was.

"Six. I make a pot of coffee and I get the bread started before I make breakfast, so it's ready when Mr. Reed rises."

"What time is that, normally?"

"Seven-thirty."

Mike tilted his head, studying the housekeeper thought-fully for a moment. "And this morning?"

"When he didn't come to breakfast, I checked his room and he wasn't there either."

"What time was that?"

Her hands stilled. "I—I'm not sure."

"Best guess?"

She folded the dough over again and pushed with the heels of her hands. Once. Twice. Three times. "I don't know. I just—I didn't want the breakfast to get cold. So I looked in on him, and he was gone."

Mike scribbled in his tiny notepad. "What about last night? What time did you leave?"

"A little after eight." She didn't have to think too long about that.

"Did you say goodnight to Mr. Reed before you left?"

Her dark eyes lifted, gone wide with shock. "Oh no, of course not. He doesn't—" She pressed a floured hand against her aproned midsection. "—*didn't* like to be inter-rupted during his meditation time. We said our farewells earlier, as usual."

"What time was that?"

"I suppose around seven, after the *puta* departed."

"*Puta*?" I asked, unable to stop myself. Not that the slang wasn't in my lexicon, but more out of curiosity about what "bitch" she was referring to.

Alma muttered under her breath, loud enough for me to tell it was in Spanish but soft enough that I couldn't make out her words.

"Ms. Gonzalez?" Mike prompted.

"Señor Reed's girlfriend, Miss Ashley." She wrinkled her nose. "They had an argument."

Ahh, so there was some enmity between the housekeeper and Reed's girlfriend. "What was the fight about?" I asked.

Her lips tightened and she eyed me. "I would never eavesdrop on Señor Reed. I heard the shouting and decided it was a good time to run the vacuum."

"Do you know Ashley's last name?" Mike said. "We'll need to contact her."

The sound of a rising commotion elsewhere in the house filtered into the room, drawing my attention to the doorway. A woman's voice grew louder and more distinct.

"Well, I guess you'll have to arrest me, then! Nathaniel! Nathaniel! Come tell this bitch to let me in!" There was a pause, then the low hum of a more metered voice, followed by a more shrill, "Nathaniel!"

"That," Alma said, "would be Miss Ashley." She gave the dough a final firm knead, then balled it up and tossed it into a large oiled ceramic bowl. "Iverson is her last name." Grabbing a towel, she wiped her hands and then covered the bowl before moving around the island to head deeper into the house.

Mike and I exchanged glances, then slipped off our stools and followed the black-clad woman to the front door, where a rail-thin brunette in designer everything looked down her thin nose at the uniform guarding the door.

"No, I don't *live* here, but—there! Thelma! Come tell this woman I'm allowed in."

Alma leveled a dead-eyed stare on the brunette from a distance. "I always thought *you* would be the death of him."

Ashley furrowed her brow, blue eyes darting between all parties present. "What—what are you talking about?"

"You'll have to find some other gullible rich man to sink your teeth into," Alma said. "Señor Reed is dead. And for the last time . . . my name is *Alma*." Having said her piece, the housekeeper walked back the way we'd come, slipping past me on her way to the kitchen.

As for Ashley, well, she stood there with her mouth open in shock and her eyes blinking rapidly. "What? No, that's not —that can't be—" Her eyes darted between the three of us who remained, and then she let out a wail and crumpled to the floor.

The uniformed officer took a knee and put a hand on Ashley's back.

"Abrams," Mike said, "would you escort the lady to the living room please?"

Officer Abrams nodded and spoke quietly to the distraught woman, urging her to stand. She turned toward the officer and wrapped her arms around her, nearly pulling her down onto the floor.

I caught Mike's eye and quirked a brow. He motioned over his shoulder with his head before turning to trek back to the kitchen. I went with him, Ashley's noisy sobs echoing behind us. We found Alma there as expected, washing her hands at the sink.

Mike took his notepad back out and scanned his notes, then picked up where he left off without missing a beat. "So, you said goodnight to Mr. Reed around seven, but you left closer to eight?"

"Sí."

"And he was alone in the house when you left?"

"Sí"

"Did you arm the security system?"

She scoffed. "Sí, of course."

"How long have he and Ms. Iverson been seeing each other?"

Alma shut off the water and grabbed a clean towel to dry

her hands, her expression thoughtful. "Oh, I suppose about a year."

"You said you always thought she'd be the death of him. What did you mean by that?"

"Miss Ashley can be demanding. Their relationship was . . . troubled. Señor Reed, he was such a kind and gentle soul. I never understood what he saw in her. But I always worried she'd drive him into an early grave. He was not a spring chicken, you know. And when they fought . . ." She grimaced, hands automatically folding the towel into a precise rectangle for hanging. "It was a good time to vacuum."

"How often did Mr. Reed make use of his sweat lodge?" Mike asked.

"Oh, quite often. Though, more commonly when he has guests. It is unusual for him to sweat alone, though he does so now and then."

"Did he mention anything to you last night about planning to use the lodge?"

Alma shook her head. "No, no, señor." She looked out the window, worrying her lower lip between her teeth, then shook herself. "I should put the roast back in the deep freeze since I won't be cooking it tonight." Turning, she hurried toward the refrigerator.

"What made you think to check the lodge for him?"

The housekeeper stilled with the refrigerator door open and the roast in her hands, her back to us. "I . . . he wasn't anywhere else. I wasn't sure where else to look?"

"It's quite a hike out there. When did you say you found Mr. Reed's remains?"

"Seven-thirty."

"That's when you said you discovered he wasn't in his room."

"Wait," I said, a thought suddenly occurring to me. And of course, popping right out of my mouth. "The 9-1-1 call came in at 7:01."

Mike shot me a look, and I clamped my hand over my mouth. Meanwhile, Alma put the roast back in the refrigerator and closed the door. She leaned forward and rested her forehead against the stainless steel appliance, shoulders quaking.

Mike walked around the island and approached her, then put a hand on her shoulder. "It's okay, Ms. Gonzalez. I know you've been through a lot today, but if we're going to get down to the bottom of this, we need you to tell us the truth. You didn't find Mr. Reed's remains, did you?"

The housekeeper turned, her face once more wet with tears. "It was me. I swear it. I just—I misremembered the time, is all."

I leaned against the island, watching this unfold with interest. It was better than a true-crime documentary. Reed had lived alone. If the housekeeper hadn't found his body, who had?

"But you have a routine, don't you?" Mike said, his tone quiet but firm. "Six o'clock arrival. Seven-thirty breakfast . . ."

More tears flowed down Alma's face. "Please, señor. I am an old woman. I was mistaken."

"The handyman!" I blurted.

Mike tossed an unreadable look over his shoulder. I wasn't sure if I should cringe or pump my fist, so I snapped my mouth shut. Mike turned back to Alma, who trembled now, her eyes wide with terror.

"No," she said. "No, no. It was me. I found Mr. Reed. I saw the smoke out the window while I was cooking, and—" She broke off, sucking in a big gulp of air.

"I need you to think long and hard about what you're doing, Alma," Mike said. "We already know you've been lying. The question is why. The way I figure, you either killed Mr. Reed yourself and are trying to cover it up, or you're trying to protect someone."

"He didn't do anything! Juan is a good boy," she choked out between sobs.

I pushed off the counter and joined them, motioning for Mike to back off a bit. My heart ached for her. She'd lost her employer, whom she obviously cared for, and hadn't held up well under police scrutiny when she'd tried to lie to protect her friend. I pulled a slightly crumpled tissue from my pocket and offered it to Alma, waiting patiently while she mopped her cheeks and blew her nose with a shaking hand.

"Detective Escobar and I have little interest in Juan's legal status. All we want to do is find out what happened to Mr. Reed. You want to know that too, right?"

Alma nodded, however reluctantly.

"Now, you say Juan is a good boy. I believe you. If so, then he has nothing to fear from us. We're going to need access to the security system data even more now, so we're going to need to talk to him anyway. If it'd make you feel better, you can sit in on our chat."

She lifted her chin slightly, sniffling yet, but with hope in her dark eyes. I glanced past her to Mike, who gave me a slight shake of his head. But I was in too far now.

"Juan, he-he doesn't speak much English. I can translate?"

Mike's brow furrowed. "I—"

"Sure," I said, ignoring my partner's pointed look. "Is he here now?"

She nodded, rubbing her nose with the tissue. "Sí. I will get him."

After Alma hurried off, Mike gave voice to the frustration in his eyes. "You know as well as I do that we don't need a translator," he said in Spanish.

I shrugged. "So, if she leaves things out or alters details in the translation, we'll know. And that's valuable information. Besides, you'd be surprised what people say when they think you don't understand them."

Mike narrowed his eyes briefly, then chuckled, his features relaxing. "You're smarter than I give you credit for."

"That's kind of a backhanded compliment, but I'll take it."

CHAPTER 11

I took us the better part of an hour to get back to Reed's girlfriend. The interview with Juan yielded little fruit. Nothing he nor Alma said or did raised any further red flags for Mike or me. The kid had arrived about twenty minutes before the housekeeper to check the coyote traps Reed had instructed him to put out the previous week after a few recent sightings. Along the way, he'd noticed smoke coming from the sweat lodge and found it odd. When he went to check it out, he'd found the body and alerted Alma, who'd called the police.

Everything seemed to check out, though we'd know for sure when we had a chance to review the security footage and logs. We had no particular reason to suspect Juan. He may have been in the country illegally, but that didn't make him a killer. Reed had paid cash and was willing to look the other way about his status.

When we finished up and migrated to the living room, we found Ashley Iverson perched on the edge of Reed's brown leather sofa, clutching a tissue in one hand and Officer Abrams's hand in the other. Mascara was smudged around her eyes and ran in watery tracks down her cheeks, and her nose was red and puffy. Nonetheless, she was an ethereal beauty. And young enough to be Reed's daughter, easily. There was something about her eyes; they drew me into their clear blue depths, enough so that I had to blink and double-check she wasn't a practitioner. There was definitely some sort of charm spell going on, with her eyes as a focal point, but I couldn't quite locate the source.

"I apologize for the wait, Ms. Iverson," Mike said.

"It's okay," she said, then drew an unsteady breath before continuing. "I'm sorry, this is all just so . . . so sudden. I'm still processing. Nate was my—my—"

"Boyfriend?" I said. That was what Alma had said, after all.

Ashely scrunched up her cute button nose. "He hated that term. What we had was deeper. Spiritual. He was my . . ." My tired brain threw in a few unflattering options while she floundered for words. Meal ticket? Father figure? "Soul mate."

Deciding that one good con artist deserves another, I dropped into an overstuffed armchair. Something jabbed into my butt, and I shifted to pluck it out. It was the corner of a remarkably pointy throw pillow. Weren't these things supposed to make a chair more comfy, not less?

"I'm sorry for your loss," Mike said, settling on the other end of the sofa. "I'll take it from here, officer."

Officer Abrams didn't acknowledge Mike's words until Ashley released the death grip she had on the woman's hand and quirked a fragile smile. "Thank you for sitting with me, Rashida." Abrams's eyes lingered on Ashley a few moments more, then she blinked slowly and got to her feet.

"You're welcome," she said, a little breathily. "If you need anything else, I'll be right over there." She motioned toward the foyer, then turned and walked away, flexing her fingers a bit as she made for the door.

Ashley divided her attention between me and Mike, blue eyes swinging between us. "This is a nightmare. Why would someone want to kill my Nate?" Her eyes welled with tears once more.

"That's what we're here to find out." Mike scooted closer to her, not quite taking Officer Abrams's spot at her side, but nearly. "When was the last time you spoke with Mr. Reed?"

Ashley dabbed at her eyes with the tissue, then leaned over and tossed it onto the coffee table where a dozen or more crumpled tissues already lay. She tugged a fresh one from an earth-toned box and twisted it between restless fingers. "Last night. I—I was supposed to stay the night, but we had an argument."

My ears perked. I'd all but forgotten Alma's mention of a fight. A glance at Mike told me he hadn't, or his cop face was really good. Honestly, it could've gone either way. He didn't notice my glance, leaning forward in his seat and watching Reed's girlfriend like she was the most interesting person he'd ever met. Hanging on her every word. I winced, wishing I'd had a chance to warn him about the spell. The more eye contact he made, the harder it'd be for him to shake off. We were going to have to work out some hand signals or something. My warded coat could shield against targeted spells, but this sort of thing was more insidious. It couldn't have been strong, or I wouldn't have been able to resist it either. I wondered if Mike was sensitive to such spells. Some minds were more vulnerable than others.

"What was the fight about?" Fortunately, Mike hadn't completely lost track of what he was supposed to be doing. Yet.

She grimaced. "What do most couples fight about?

Money. It seems so unimportant now. But I can't stop thinking about it. If only I'd been here, maybe he'd still be alive."

"Don't beat yourself up, ma'am. You can woulda, shoulda, coulda yourself all day long, but it won't make it any easier." Mike inched closer and placed a hand on her knee.

I cleared my throat. "Detective?"

It took a solid two-count for Mike to tear his eyes away from Ashley and look over at me in obvious annoyance. I glanced pointedly at his hand. He quickly withdrew it and put a little more distance between himself and the interviewee.

"You said your fight with Mr. Reed was over money. Can you be more specific?" Mike asked.

Reassured that he was back on track, I resumed searching for the charm. It had to be a charm. I could still feel the lure of her from six feet away like she was the goddamn Queen of New Mexico, but it wasn't particularly hard for me to resist. I wondered if she'd used the charm to win—and keep—Reed's favor, or if she'd thrown it on this morning on her way to come make up with her lover. I avoided her eyes, since they were clearly the focal point of the spell, but started at the top of her head and began working my way down.

Her earrings? No, the tiny studs were too small, and gemstones didn't lend themselves to rune etching—which is how 99% of charms are created. The runes act as a focal point for the spell, which soaks into the gouges left behind on whatever the charm was crafted of. The runes glow when the charm is active, but it's not always obvious if it's crafted in such way that the rune faces inward. The smaller the spell, the weaker the glow, but this wasn't a small spell.

Wherever it came from should have been obvious, even if the rune was against her skin or tucked inside a pocket. My eyes lingered on a wide silver cuff bracelet circling her slender wrist. There was a large oval-shaped turquoise stone in the center, but I didn't see any traces of magic around it either.

"He wanted to postpone our vacation. We were supposed to leave next week for Aspen," Ashley said in the meantime.

"Did he say why?" Mike asked.

"Blah, blah, business trip, blah." She curled her fingers around her bracelet, blocking it from my view. I flicked a glance up and found her eyes focused on me. Guess my scrutiny wasn't exactly subtle.

I cleared my throat. "I feel it's only fair to warn you that using magic to influence a police officer is an arrestable offense."

"I-I'm sorry." Ashley yanked the bracelet from her wrist, and I felt the spell snap like a crisp piece of bacon, just not as satisfying. "I forgot I'd put it on."

I glanced at Mike, who blinked rapidly and gave his head a shake as the charm's effects dissipated. I stood and crossed the short distance between my chair and the sofa, holding out a hand.

"May I?"

Ashley licked her lips nervously but placed the bracelet in my hand. "Am I in trouble? I really did forget."

I turned the bracelet over, studying the back of it, but found no etching on the back. Interesting. The stone itself must've contained the rune, then it was set in the bracelet with the rune concealed by the band—unless the spell itself was invisible. Dan knew how to do that, but it was far from common knowledge.

"It's a charm spell," I said for Mike's benefit. "Pretty sneaky. Not technically illegal the way compulsion spells are, but . . . borderline. Especially since it's specifically crafted to be difficult to detect, too. That costs a pretty penny. So, which is it, Ms. Iverson? Friends in high places or low ones?"

Ashley's full lower lip quivered. "I—" Her eyes darted between me and Mike, and then she shook her head, frowning. "Isn't finding Nate's killer more important than where I legally obtain charms?"

"All information pertaining to the case is important, and you appear to have a history of using magic charms to influence the victim." I glanced at Mike who gave me an infinitesimal nod. We were on the same page, thinking about the charms we'd found in the vicinity of Reed's body. Not to mention the spelled bowl—which definitely was illegal.

Her blue eyes went cool. "I didn't kill Nate! I love him!"

"No one's accusing you of anything, ma'am," Mike said. "We're just collecting facts."

"It's interesting that you assume he was murdered, though," I couldn't help but point out.

"I don't think I want to say anything else without an attorney present."

Oops, my bad.

"You're certainly within your rights to request that, Ms. Iverson. But please forgive my partner. She's . . . new."

Indignation flared, but I kept it in check. He was right, and I'd been wagging my tongue when I was supposed to be observing. The woman's charm use had rubbed me the wrong way, and I'd been combative ever since I brought it up. Leaning over, I set the bracelet on the coffee table and withdrew to my previous seat.

Ashley sighed heavily but nodded. "I'm sorry too, I just —I'm not myself today. This wasn't at all what I expected this morning. You have to understand. Nate and I, we've been together for almost a year. That was the reason why canceling our trip made me so mad. It was supposed to be an anniversary celebration." She dabbed at her eyes once more. "I bought that last night, hoping I could talk him out of his business trip. That's all. I normally wouldn't resort to such a tactic, but it was very important to me. He is—was— very important to me."

"Where did you buy the charm?" Mike asked, scribbling a note on his notepad.

"Prince Charming."

His pen stilled. "Sorry?"

"That's the only name I have for him, sorry. A friend introduced me to him a few years ago. Hang on, I have his card."

She stood and crossed the room to where her handbag lay discarded on a table near the doorway. Prince Charming. I'd never heard of the guy, but it wasn't like I knew all the witches in town. I'd spent most of my time avoiding them since I moved into the area.

Ashley produced a plain white business card from her wallet and held it out to Mike. "He's in Taos. It's a bit of a drive, but . . ."

Out of our jurisdiction, I thought at first. Then I remembered the task force. Maybe not?

Mike took the card from her and snapped a picture of it with his phone before offering it back to her.

She took a step back, quickly shaking her head. "No, no I'm not going back there. It was a bad idea. I see that now."

"Alright." Mike tucked the card in between the pages of his notepad. "You said Mr. Reed was planning a business trip? Do you know where he was going or what the business was?"

"Florida. He didn't say what it was, just that it was important. I was too angry to ask for details. But there's probably something in his calendar. He lives by his calendar. Lived. God, this is going to take some getting used to. Why him? Why?" Her shoulders shook, and a few more tears ran down her cheeks, leaving little round dots on her silk blouse as they dripped off her jaw.

Her grief had seemed genuine up until that point, but now she was laying it on pretty thick. I half expected her to press the back of her hand to her forehead and swoon, but she remained on her feet.

"I understand, ma'am," Mike said, standing. "We'll get out of your hair, I just have one more question."

She sniffled but nodded. "Yes?"

"Where were you last night between the hours of seven p.m. and four a.m.?"

Her posture stiffened and she lifted her chin. "Home, asleep."

"Alone?" I asked, getting to my feet as well.

She narrowed her eyes. "If you have any other questions for me, I'm going to insist on my attorney being present."

"Let's go, Emily." Mike turned and headed for the foyer.

I trailed along behind him with a smirk. "That was a no, right? That sounded like a no to me."

CHAPTER 12

W hen we got back to the station, Mike had me read through his notes on the vandalism case. Fortunately, he'd already gone through the incident reports Reed had filed over the years with state, county, and local law enforcement. It was a thick file. I wondered if Dan would be quite as interested in being a cop if he knew how much tedious paperwork and reading it involved. Patience had never been one of his few virtues.

"Well, on the upside, I guess the vandalism case gives us a jump start on a suspects list," I said, looking up from the tablet.

"You'd think, but they're probably unrelated."

"What makes you say that?" I half-sat on the edge of his desk, tucking my ankle below my knee. "I mean, less than twenty-four hours after someone threw a brick at his house, he was murdered."

Mike leaned back in his chair, lacing his fingers behind his head. "Well, the thing about death threats is that they're threats. The person behind them usually doesn't want to kill the target. They want to scare the target into doing what they want. They couldn't have expected him to pack up and move in twenty-four hours. Besides, murders usually go down two ways. Well, three, if you count involuntary manslaughter. But really more like two. Planned, or in the heat of the moment. If you were planning to murder someone, would you throw a brick at their house the day before?"

"Ahh, I get it. Probably not, because I wouldn't want to draw attention to myself."

"Exactly. Or alert your would-be victim of what was coming. Unless you're a very special kind of psychopath who wants to terrorize them first."

"Well, we probably shouldn't rule out special kinds of psychopaths this early."

"True, padawan." He sat up in his chair and pulled the thumb drive Juan had given him out of his pocket and plugged it into his computer.

"Time to review the security footage?"

"Yup. This could take a while. You want to head home and grab a nap, maybe a change of clothes?"

I looked down at my date night scoop-necked T-shirt and skinny jeans and chuckled. "You trying to tell me something, partner?"

"Just that I've kept you up well past bedtime, and you worked last night."

A fresh wave of fatigue washed over me at the reminder. I rubbed a hand down my face. "Yeah, and I have another shift tonight. I wish your magic still worked on Steel Wool Wendy. Maybe you should try asking her out to dinner."

"What?"

"You're single, she's single, I'm just saying . . . maybe she'd be more a little more flexible if she was getting laid."

He chuckled. "I'm not going to prostitute myself with your supervisor so she lets you out of a shift here and there."

"Shame. If you change your mind, let me know. I've got her number." I stood and stretched, and something in my back popped that felt briefly painful and then a whole lot relaxing. "Aw, crap. My car's still at the hospital."

"Take mine." He pulled a set of keys out of his desk drawer and tossed them my way.

I missed, and they fell to the desktop with a noisy clatter. "Won't you need it?"

"That's my personal car. It's in the back lot. Shouldn't be hard to find. Might need gas."

Far be it from me to look a gift horse in the mouth. Borrowing Mike's car and sleeping in my own bed sounded two hundred times better than trying to grab a nap in an interrogation room or jail cell. I swiped the keys off the desk into my hand and turned the keyless entry fob over. A shiny Jeep logo adorned the back. "Okay, thanks. I'll bring it back in a few hours with a full tank."

I left the station in Mike's gunmetal gray Cherokee with the facts of the case—what we knew of them, anyway—spinning around in my head. Nate Alan Reed, a self-styled shaman and mystical self-help guru, had been compelled to drink some sort of concoction and then died in his sweat lodge, most likely of poisoning or heat stroke. He was survived—as far as we knew—by his housekeeper, his handyman, and his girlfriend. The guy was loaded or at least lived like he was, so I couldn't help but wonder who would benefit most from his death.

The bottom line? We had a lot of digging to do, and I hated leaving Mike to do it alone. But the dull throb in my head and the ache between my shoulders told me if I didn't, I'd regret it. Plus, in nursing, there was a very real possibility I could kill someone if I didn't get some sleep before my next shift.

This was definitely one of those times where I needed to take care of myself so I could take better care of others. That's why it was all the more frustrating when the screech of the fire alarm woke me from a dead sleep about ninety minutes after I fell into bed. My eyes snapped open, and I blinked at the ceiling in confusion for a few seconds before lurching out of bed and flying across the room to the door. The smell of smoke registered seconds before I grabbed the door handle, so I had the sense to tap it quickly to see if it was hot.

It wasn't, so I flung the door open. Smoke poured into the room, and I got a lungful of it, which set me to coughing as I headed down the hallway. I saw no flames, just smoke, and I wasn't sure where it was coming from until I got to the living room and heard cursing coming from the kitchen.

I rounded the corner to find my brother waving a towel at the oven—which was wide open, smoke pouring out of it —and there, yes there, I finally caught a glimpse of flame.

"What the hell, Dan? Put that out!"

"I can't find a fire extinguisher!"

"You're a witch for fuck's sake! Can't you just . . ." I waved my hands helplessly. I sure as hell couldn't.

"Oh. Right." A glowing nimbus sprang up around him, and the flames flickered and went out. He tossed the towel over his shoulder and looked at me. "Sorry, I kind of for—" He coughed. "Forgot it was in there."

"Help me open the windows so we can air this place out. And, for future reference, the fire extinguisher is under the sink." Eyes watering, I made my way through the apartment to open what few windows I had. It was still bloody freezing outside, and the rush of cold air into the room reminded me that I hadn't worn pants to bed, just an oversized T-shirt worn soft over the years. I think it might've been Matt's at one time. That didn't stop me from rounding on my brother in a fury while the alarm continued to screech in the background. "What the hell is wrong with you?"

Dan had transitioned from waving the towel at the oven to waving it at the screeching box of doom. "I set the timer, but it didn't go off," he shouted back, forehead crinkling.

"Since when do you even know how to use an oven?"

"I know how to use an oven!"

I pointed toward the kitchen. "The evidence says otherwise!"

"What are you now, a lawyer?"

"And a judge, jury, and executioner if you don't take the damn battery out of that thing until the smoke clears."

He looked from me to the alarm and back again. "It has a battery?"

God save me from spoiled rich kids. Never mind that I'd been one too until I left home. At least I'd done it to better myself. Dan had gotten himself disowned, though that was more about my mother overreacting than it was his fault. Grumbling regardless, I stalked over to the dining table, grabbed a chair, and dragged it underneath the alarm. I climbed onto the chair to search for the battery compartment, sure the damn thing was shattering my eardrums from the high-pitched squeal at close proximity. I finally figured out to twist the whole thing and remove the cover so I could get to the battery.

I yanked it out and enjoyed several seconds of peace while my ringing ears recovered before a noisy pounding sounded on the door.

"I'll get it!" Dan made a beeline for the door.

"Wait, I—"

Dan flung open the door, and more cold air blew into the room, raising a whole flock of goosebumps all down my bare legs. I stood there paralyzed in horror, arms still in the air, oversized T-shirt riding up with my sushi-printed panties peeking out in front of the pair of firemen standing outside the door. How the heck had they gotten here so fast? They looked ready for action too. One even had an axe. But the most horrifying thing of all was when the warm brown eyes of the one in front met mine and recognition washed over me.

Well, fuck.

CHAPTER 13

I climbed hastily off the stool and tugged my T-shirt down for good measure. I hadn't seen John Warren in weeks. Truth be told, I'd been avoiding him a bit. Well, there was no avoiding him now. It might seem far too coincidental that the one firefighter I happen to be acquainted with shows up at my door when my brother sets fire to a casserole, but that's kind of how my life works. I've learned to take it in stride. Mostly. That didn't mean my face wasn't on fire. I hoped they didn't take the hose to me.

"Sorry, gents, false alarm," Dan said. "We just had a little problem with the oven."

"Mind if we take a look?" John asked, all business while his partner raked me over with his eyes. Maybe *he* needed to be hosed down.

Dan stepped aside and motioned for them to enter.

"Emily," John said in passing, giving me a nod.

"John," I squeaked, then cleared my throat and coughed a little, hoping I could claim smoke inhalation as the cause.

A smarter woman probably would have retreated to her room to find a pair of sweats, but strangers in my space have always put me on edge, so I tugged my shirt down a little more and perched on the edge of the sofa while the firemen checked to make sure there was no further threat in the kitchen. Dan followed along with them, and I heard a quiet hum of exchanged words and manly chuckles before they all came filing back out again.

"Looks like everything is under control," John said, lingering while his partner continued toward the door. "Be sure you put that back up once the smoke clears out." He motioned at the smoke detector casing and battery still clutched in my hand. "It could save your life someday."

I shot a baleful look at my brother. "I'm pretty sure it just did."

"So dramatic." Dan rolled his eyes.

John met my eyes and smiled. "Don't worry, it happens to everyone sometime."

I blinked in confusion, watching him as he headed for the door. A glance in Dan's direction showed him looking far too innocent for my liking. I stood, giving my shirt another tug. "Wait! I . . ."

John paused and turned back, arching a brow beneath his hat.

"Thanks for dropping by. I'm sorry I haven't called. Or, more specifically, returned your calls."

His lips curved in a faint smile. "It's okay. You don't have to explain yourself. You two have a nice rest of your day." He glanced in the direction of the kitchen. "Maybe order a pizza. Just a thought."

"Great idea," Dan said, taking out his phone as if he planned to do that.

All I could do was watch as the two firemen exited my apartment, closing the door behind them. Maybe John didn't think I needed to explain myself, but it sure felt like I did. At least I had enough sense not to go rushing out after him in my underwear. The fire department showing up at my door was more than enough of a scene for one day.

"I don't know what you see in Barry. That guy is way hotter," Dan commented as soon as the door had shut.

I opened my mouth, a sharp reply on the tip of my tongue, but his mention of Barry made something click in my brain. "Where's the cat?"

"Probably hiding under the bed."

"My door was closed. Barrington!" You'd be surprised how long it can take to locate a nine-pound cat in a 600 square foot apartment, but it took us the better part of ten minutes to locate Lord Barrington who—as Dan had suspected—was under the bed. He must've run into my room after I opened the door. Thank god there hadn't been an actual fire, I thought while coaxing him out, because I'd forgotten all about him in the heat of the moment.

Pun not intended.

Too wired for sleep by then, I padded out into the living room in my now sock-covered feet. I'd put pants on too, in case you were curious.

Dan sat on the couch, flipping through channels. I curled up on the other end, pulling the blanket from the back of the couch around me.

"Pizza should be here in ten," he said, reminding me of two things: that he'd probably been in my wallet without permission again, and that John had been the one to suggest pizza on the way out—while giving me a decidedly knowing look I was too mortified to examine at the time.

"What did you say to them?" I cast a sideways glance at my brother. Usually, my suspicions are one hundred percent warranted, and this time was no different.

He shrugged, which only made me more suspicious.

I leaned over and poked him. "Tell me."

"I don't remember."

"I don't believe you."

"You've got good instincts. Can we just leave it at I was embarrassed and I didn't want my bros to know it was me?"

"Okay, let's bypass the bewildering and unlikely notion that John and his work buddy are somehow your 'bros' and move straight to the part where you told them it was me?" Annoyance welled in my chest, but it was an all-too-familiar feeling these days. I embraced it because it might help me stay warm while the house aired out.

"I didn't! Specifically."

"What, specifically, did you tell them?"

"You're like a dog with a bone sometimes, you know that?"

"Do you want to find out if my bite or my bark is worse?" I snapped my teeth at him.

He eyed me dubiously but sighed. "Something about some women not belonging in the kitchen."

I stared at him for a long moment, mouth agape. "Seriously? I may not be a world-class chef, but I've never set anything on fire. Anything."

"Congratulations." He went back to flipping channels, jabbing the button on the remote more forcefully than necessary. I watched him in silence for a minute, thinking about how annoyed I got when he used my credit card without permission to buy food, and how the only thing he ever seemed to make on his own was a sandwich. Here he was, trying to turn over a new leaf, and I was giving him a hard time about it, probably ensuring he'd never try again. Which, to be fair, might have been a good thing considering how the first attempt had turned out. Still, it wasn't very sisterly of me. I kept falling back on old habits, being combative rather than supportive of his efforts to become a functioning adult who couldn't throw money around to make everyone do everything for him.

I wiggled my foot out from under the blanket and extended my leg across the couch to nudge his leg. "If you want to learn how to cook, I can show you a few things. Or Matt's really good at it. I bet he'd love to teach you."

"I just wanted to do something nice for you," he said, staring ahead.

"Really?"

"Yeah. I mean, you work really hard. I'm not blind. And I appreciate you letting me stay here while I figure things out."

My face heated again, but this time from shame. My throat felt tight, and not from the aftereffects of the smoke. I spent a lot of time doing things for other people, but it was actually kind of rare for someone to do something for me in return. Part of that was my fault because I held people at arm's length, afraid to open myself up to being hurt or rejected. I swallowed and looked down at the blanket tucked around me. "Thanks, Danny."

"Also, Tracy's coming over."

Oh. So, his motivations hadn't been quite so pure. Just like that, the warm fuzzies evaporated. I had a momentary twinge of horror at the thought of someone coming over to the place while it was in disarray, but glancing around, I found that Dan had picked up a bit. The blanket draped across the back of the couch rather than unfolded in a pile on the cushions hadn't even registered when I'd grabbed it.

Standing, I folded the blanket and tossed it over the back of the couch again and headed back to my room, finally giving Tracy's text message a second thought on my way down the hall. Being awake to talk to her in person while she was there might've been a good idea, but sleep felt way more important in the moment.

"Em?"

I flapped a hand over my shoulder. "Have fun. I'm going to try and sleep again. I need to be back at the station in a few hours."

"You don't want any pizza? I paid for it myself, for the record."

"Maybe later, assuming you don't set fire to the microwave too." For the record, I hate microwaved pizza. A fresh wave of annoyance washed over me.

"Ha-ha, very funny," he said.

"Yeah, I'm a riot," I muttered to myself, too distracted by renewed fatigue and annoyance to wonder where he'd gotten money from if not my wallet.

CHAPTER 14

When I arrived at the station late that afternoon, Mike was still behind his desk—or behind his desk again, I suppose. It's hard to tell at a glance. He looked up from his computer when he noticed me heading his way and cocked his head, studying me with insightful brown eyes.

"You're one of the few people I know who somehow manages to look less rested after a nap."

"Probably because it was interrupted by the fire department." I gave his keys a light underhand toss.

He caught them and dropped them back in his desk drawer. "Did your cat get stuck in a tree?"

"Worse. Dan nearly set the apartment on fire." I flopped into the chair on the other side of his desk.

"Uh-huh."

"I'm not joking! There were flames shooting out of the oven."

"Did you get any sleep at all?"

"Yeah, a little. But enough about me. Where are we at on the case?"

He swiped a pen from his desk and leaned back in his chair, fiddling absently with the pen while he spoke. "There's nothing on the security recordings from the night of the murder, just Reed going out the back door and never coming back. We did get a good shot of the perp who threw the brick the night before, though."

"Show me?"

His chair squeaked as he sat upright again, dropping the pen and leafing through the papers on his desk until he found a few printed stills to hold out to me. I shuffled through them, pausing to study each in turn. They were a bit grainy and gray-washed as nighttime security footage tends to be. The first was a front shot of a man in dark clothes with a bandana covering the lower half of his face, carrying a brick. The second was obviously from the same camera, but of the back of the man as he walked the other direction. The brick was nowhere to be seen. The third was a blow-up of the back of the man's neck. A tattoo of some sort peeked out from behind a braid that hung down this back. Thick jagged lines in a radial pattern spread from whatever was in the center. I squinted but couldn't make it out.

"This is it?" I shuffled through them again, looking twice for identifying features.

"Yup. Only one of the cameras caught him, so he must've approached the property from the side rather than head-on. Otherwise, the front gate or back door cameras would've spotted him."

"The property isn't fenced, is it? Just that low wall at the front?"

"Yeah. And that's more decorative than anything. Easily hopped by an average adult."

I nodded and handed the stills back to him. "Any idea who he is?"

"Actually, yes." He turned his monitor so I could see it. On the screen was an arrest record, complete with the usual front and side view mug shots. On the side-view, a tattoo wrapped around from the back of the man's neck. It looked similar to the one on the security cam footage. I leaned forward in my chair, squinting to read the details from where I sat a few feet away.

"Noah Chavez, arrested six months ago for trespassing on Reed's property," Mike said. "He and a few of his buddies from the Tesuque Pueblo decided to crash some sort of closing ceremony for one of Reed's private retreats. Reed didn't press charges, so he was released after a few hours."

"And now he's giving death threats? That escalated quickly."

"The two have a bit of a history. There were incident reports filed by the state, Pueblo, and county authorities over the last few years."

I gave a low whistle. "So, definitely a person of interest."

"Yup."

"So, why aren't we heading out to talk to him?" I sat back in my chair.

"Waiting on the green light from the Pueblo police. We can't just waltz into the Pueblo and start asking questions, unfortunately."

"Alright. So, in the meantime, what else do we have?"

"Autopsy is still pending. I got the lab report on the substance in that bowl . . ." He frowned at his cluttered desktop and lifted a few papers, hunting around.

"Is everything okay, Mike? You seem unusually scattered this afternoon."

He found what he was looking for and tossed the report

down in front of me, then leaned back in his chair and scrubbed his fingers through his hair, leaving it sticking up oddly in places. "This is a bit of a high-profile case. I've been getting all sorts of phone calls from the media since the story broke, and wouldn't you know it . . . apparently the vic was a personal friend of the mayor."

"That's rough. Is that going to make things easier or harder for us?" I scanned the first page of the report, which was a summary of the findings. I whistled. "Mescaline. That's peyote, right?"

"Yup," Mike said.

I glanced up, blinking. "To which?"

Mike spread his hands and sighed. "All of the above? Take your pick."

"Easier, harder, and peyote. Gotcha. That's a controlled substance, right?"

"Schedule I, same as heroin and LSD."

"How hard is it to come by?"

"Legally or illegally?"

I chuckled. "Both?"

"Well, it's legal in Denver. Less so around here. The state has an exemption for religious use and cultivation for religious use, but it's still not legal to sell. There's a small number of growers and sellers in Texas, but they're tightly regulated and only allowed to sell to members of the Native American Church."

I laughed. "Native American Church? Very funny. I'm a white girl, but I'm not that gullible."

He held up three fingers. "Scout's honor."

"Huh. It sounds like something an Indian trickster made up to fool the white man."

"Maybe it was, since it allows them to buy peyote legally for 'religious' purposes. And I'm sure some do have legit religious purposes. Traditions run deep for a lot of folks. But there are just as many Natives as there are others out there just chasing a good time." His phone vibrated, and he paused to glance briefly at the screen before pushing back his chair and standing. "Let's continue this in the car. I got the green light from the Pueblo."

"Okay." I stood and waited while he gathered up the paperwork scattered on his desk and shoved it all into a file folder, then put the folder in his file drawer and locked his desk. "How do you know so much about peyote, anyway?"

"I wasn't always in Magic Crimes, you know. I used to be in Narcotics."

"Oof. I bet that made you popular around here." Santa Fe County has to be one of the capitals of recreational pot use.

He shrugged, holding the door open for me as we exited the squad room. "Being popular has never been high on my list of priorities."

Considering his voluntary department change, I nodded. "Clearly. So, Reed's cultural co-opting extended to hallucinogens."

"Maybe. We don't know yet if it was his or if the killer brought it with them. And that bowl was spelled, remember? If he drank it, it wasn't of his own volition."

"Right. So, is there a chapter of the Native American Church in Santa Fe?"

"Nope. Used to be one in Taos, but they got in trouble a few years back over a marijuana growing operation. The Church would have us believe that was just a few bad apples, but I dunno."

"Speaking of Taos," I said, pausing while we both got in the car. "When are we going to go talk to Prince Charming?"

"The only thing on the card was an email address. I gave it to IT to see what they could do."

"Did they roll their eyes?" I knew enough about tech from listening to Matt rant over the years to know that there was little anyone could do with a random email address—even the cops—no matter what Hollywood would have us believe.

"A little. But I figured it was worth a shot. I can't just email him."

"Why not?"

"Because if he's selling borderline illegal charms, he's probably not going to respond to an email from a santafenm-dot-gov address."

"Hey, why don't I have one of those yet?"

"Focus, Emily."

"Right. Well, we could create a fake email address. Or, hey, what if I reach out to him instead, posing as a buyer? A friend of Ashley Iverson . . ."

"Hmm." He mulled the suggestion over while he backed aggressively out of the parking spot and then accelerated toward the parking lot exit. At least he hadn't dismissed the idea out of hand. "That could work. Once you make contact, you can set up a meet and we can ask him a few questions." He glanced at me. "But don't go off half-cocked."

"Who, me?" I widened my eyes, but I'm not good at the innocent look.

"Yes, you. Make contact, see if you can set up a face-to-face. But that's it. No meetup without me. Got it?"

Have I mentioned I hated it when he ordered me around? I kept my eyes out the window but muttered something vaguely affirmative. As if I would've set up a meeting without him. I was smarter than that. That was something Dan would do.

"Davenport?"

"Got it," I snapped, tightening my grip on the door handle when he made a hard right. The way he drove, all of his rights were hard, and the lefts weren't much softer. I stewed for a minute or so, then drew in a calming breath and turned my attention back to the case. "Okay, so what else do we have besides Pueblo Guy?"

"I spoke to his attorney about the will. He's still trying to get in touch with next of kin, so there's nothing he can share with us yet."

"Did he say who the next of kin was?"

"Sister in California. I've got a call out to her too."

I ticked that mental checkbox and considered what else we knew. Mike was rarely content to just volunteer information, always nudging me to think like an investigator. "Anything interesting on the calendar?"

"Yeah, he had a court hearing scheduled next week in Jacksonville."

"Ahh, the business trip he had to cancel his vacation for?"

"Most likely. I made a few calls. It was a family services hearing. Apparently, the guy owed a quarter of a million dollars in back child support."

"Wow. How many kids?"

"Dunno. But it sounds like the ex-wife might have a legitimate reason to want him dead."

I tapped my chin thoughtfully. "Maybe. I mean, she can't get money from him if he's dead."

"No, but assuming he's worth as much as his house suggests and his kids are in his will, he might've been worth more to her dead than alive." He shrugged.

"Okay, so we have the angry girlfriend, the offended Pueblo man, the scorned ex-wife, anything else?"

"I was able to track down the incident report from the night Reed—Hirshman, whatever—mentioned the Sons of Humanity were throwing beer bottles over his gate. The state police were able to identify both of the culprits from the security footage: Hunter Thomas and Javier Morales. Morales was on parole at the time of the incident, so he's serving out the rest of his sentence now."

"Heck of an alibi. What about the other guy?"

"Still around town somewhere, as far as I know. The vic didn't press charges, so he's still a free man. Lucky, too. With his rap sheet, the judge probably wouldn't have gone easy on him."

"Did this guy ever press charges, or just file reports?"

"Only if there was property damage and the perp refused to pay for repairs."

I shook my head. "I don't get it. He just let people harass him for years and didn't do anything about it. Maybe if he had, it might not've been so bad."

"Or it might've made it worse. It's hard to say."

"Fair enough. Anything else?"

"Oh yeah. I saved the best for last."

Smirking, I gestured for him to get on with it.

"Six months ago, one of his former clients sued him over medical bills and emotional distress he claims resulted from —wait for it—unsafe operation of a sweat lodge."

"No shit, really?" I smacked his arm across the console. "Way to bury the lede!"

He chuckled. "That's not all. The case was dismissed."

"Wow, just . . . wow. So, you're saying our vic died from sweat lodge syndrome after making someone else sick in a sweat lodge? That's almost too poetic. So why are we heading out to the Pueblo instead of talking to this guy?"

"He's not local. I asked the Albuquerque PD to pay him a visit."

I nodded and gazed out the window as silence settled between us, thoughts of the case swirling around in my head. "Hey, do you have Prince Charming's card on you?"

"There's a picture on my phone." He made no move to reach for it, not that I expected him to. Cops who get in trouble for distracted driving tend to get a suspension rather than a strongly worded lecture.

I leaned over and snagged his phone from the dash mount and pulled up his photo library. The picture was the most recent one, so it was easy to find. I sent it to myself, then resisted the temptation to swipe through his pics—after all, he hadn't objected to me getting into his photos, so he either didn't have anything interesting in there or trusted me not to snoop—and switched the phone back to the GPS app before sticking it back in the mount.

We still had twenty-plus minutes ahead of us, so I figured I might as well be productive. Pulling out my own phone, I opened up my email and started composing an introduction to the charm dealer.

CHAPTER 15

The trip out to the Tesuque Pueblo Tribal Police Department may have been a solid thirty-minute drive from the SFPD, but at least it was mostly highway. We pulled up in front of the fairly nondescript building just off exit 175 a little after four p.m. The plain beige building was somewhat at odds with the sleek police cruisers parked out front. It reminded me a little of those guys who live in shitty hole-in-the-wall apartments but drive Ferraris.

We met up with a tall, barrel-chested older man in the lobby who introduced himself as Officer Tsosie. We exchanged friendly handshakes, then it was back out to the car. We followed Tsosie's cruiser out of the parking lot and down the narrow asphalt ribbon that wound through the Pueblo. Dirt roads branched off from it, and the view was mostly snow-dotted brown earth, scraggly trees, crumbling adobe, and the occasional trailer. Despite the fancy police cruisers and brand new casino, this was not one of the richer Pueblos. Its residents were mainly farmers and artists —potters, sculptors, and painters. The casino was a relatively recent addition at this point, and still in the process of earning back what it'd taken to construct it.

When we finally turned down one of the dirt roads and drove toward a trailer set well back from the road, I'd completely lost my sense of direction and wasn't sure where we were in relation to anything. Despite the vast tract of land the Pueblo occupied—something like 17,000 acres—the population was fairly condensed. Just like any town, the farther out you got from the center, the farther apart the houses were.

The trailer that Noah Chavez occupied was painted green and white and had seen better days, but concrete steps ran up to a more recent screened-in porch addition. A newer model pickup truck was parked off to one side, and there was a shed beyond the truck whose doors were open, but I couldn't quite see inside it from our angle of approach. Officer Tsosie pulled up beside the parked truck, and we parked behind it.

I followed the officers toward the front door, though my eyes were drawn to the shed. Who left their shed door open, unless it was for something other than storage? A workshop, maybe? As my roving eyes returned to the building in front of me, I thought I saw the blinds in the front window twitch but chalked it up as my imagination. It was quiet out here, a sort of quiet you don't get even in a small city like Santa Fe. Peaceful. A dog barked in the distance, and the air was crisp and smelled of wood smoke.

On the porch, Officer Tsosie knocked on the front door and we all stood around while no one answered. My eyes roamed the wooden porch furniture curiously. It looked homemade, and I spotted runes carved into the wooden backs of the chairs, swirling lines that looked like smoke in the abstract. The unwary eye might think the design purely decorative, but I knew a fire-resistance ward when I saw it. The whole porch might burn down—unless there were runes tucked away where I couldn't see—but the two chairs and low table perched on it would be left standing regardless.

"His truck is here, so he must be here," Tsosie said, turning from the door to look in the direction of said truck.

A moment later, the door opened and a willowy young woman looked out through the screen door. "Afternoon, Billy." Her dark eyes darted past him to Mike and me, narrowing slightly.

"Afternoon, Maria. Your brother around?"

"Nope, sorry."

"You sure?" Tsosie glanced out the screened porch window again. "His truck is here. Maybe he's in the workshop?"

She shook her head, then lifted her chin. "Who're they?"

Before Tsosie could answer, a soft noise I couldn't identify drew my attention back down the porch stairs and to the sight of a man coming around the corner of the trailer. His dark eyes met mine and he froze, glancing between the figures gathered on the porch and the conspicuous tribal police car parked beside the pickup. I thought I recognized him from Noah Chavez's mug shots, but I wasn't one hundred percent sure.

I nudged Mike with my elbow, but the perp took off running. As he whirled, I caught a glimpse of a distinctive tattoo peeking out around the sides of a thick black braid.

It was definitely our suspect, and he definitely didn't want to talk to us.

"Noah, wait!" I sprinted for the stairs. The screen door slammed against the side of the house as I shoved it open and ran after him. Thundering footsteps followed me across the porch and down the steps as Mike and Tsosie joined the pursuit.

"Stop, police!" Mike called, probably out of instinct more than anything. After all, he had pretty much zero jurisdiction here.

Glad I'd put on sneakers on my way out the door this afternoon, I ran after the guy like he had a batch of fresh, pillowy sopapillas under his arm. He started off running toward the truck but must've noticed our car parked behind him because he suddenly veered off and headed for the road.

"Noah!" Officer Tsosie's booming voice called from behind me. "What's the rush, man? We just want to ask you a few questions!"

I glanced behind me and found Mike catching up while the older officer lagged behind. At least Mike wasn't hollering after me to wait in the car. I would've been hard-pressed to listen. Noah turned left at the end of the drive and headed in what I thought was the direction of the main road. Maybe we would've been better off chasing him in a car rather than on foot. I altered my trajectory to be less of a chase and more of an intercept course, figuring I'd be able to get over the low adobe wall along the front of the property without much difficulty. Kind of like Noah probably had to access Reed's property without being caught on camera. There was a certain poignancy to that.

My plan worked. I gained steady ground, and Noah was right in front of me on the other side of the wall when I got to it. I threw myself over it and opened my arms wide. In my head, I'd executed a brilliant flying tackle and would pull him to the ground neatly, buying just enough time for Mike to catch up.

What actually happened was: My eyes were glued to

Noah, so I misjudged the height of the wall. My foot caught on it, and while I went over the wall it was less a flying leap than an awkward tumble. I did manage to wrap an arm around Noah's leg on the way down though and clung to it like my life depended on it as I hit the ground, shoulder-first. His other foot skidded on the dirt, and he flapped his arms for balance but couldn't quite halt his momentum. He toppled over and landed beside me, cursing and struggling to try and free his leg.

"Let me go, you crazy bitch!"

I'd been called worse. "It's over, Noah. My partner is right behind me, and when Officer Tsosie catches up we've got some questions for you."

"I don't have anything to say! I don't know who you are or why you're here."

"Then why did you run?"

He didn't have an answer for that and continued to squirm and kick until Mike caught up to us and restrained him properly. I gratefully let go of Noah's leg and rolled onto my back, taking a moment to catch my breath and stare up at the gray sky. I sat up and got to my feet in time for a crash course in proper handcuffing technique before Officer Tsosie arrived.

"What'd you have to go and do that for?" Tsosie grumbled as he hauled Noah to his feet. "Detective Escobar here just wanted to ask you a few questions, but now we're going to have to take you to the station, and I'm going to have to explain to the chief why the medicine man's grandson was brought in in cuffs—again."

To his credit, Noah did not use magic to try and escape, though he surely could have. Neither Mike nor Officer Tsosie had any—and of course, neither did I. Noah definitely had the upper hand, but he submitted to the authorities with quiet dignity, chin raised high and dark brown eyes defiant.

"Alright, let's go." Tsosie tugged him back down the road toward the front drive. "I told you to leave that crazy white man alone," he muttered. I was just downwind enough to pick it up.

"He fouls the land with his presence," Noah said, shoulders back and head held high. A man of conviction, if not the best judgment. "He usurps our traditions and uses them to make money."

"Says the man who sells cheap pottery and rain god sculptures to tourists at the flea market," Tsosie replied. "I don't think you've got too many stones to throw."

Noah snorted. "Selling crap to tourists is also one of our long-standing traditions. At least I know enough not to profane our most sacred rites."

"In his own way, Mr. Reed was kind of in the same business. Selling crap to tourists," I said.

Noah glared at me over his shoulder like it was all my fault he was in this mess. Which, my aching shoulder reminded me, was partly true. But he held his tongue the rest of the way, and once he was settled in the back seat of Tsosie's cruiser—with his sister making herself noticeably scarce—the officer turned back to us.

"Follow me back to the station, and you can ask him all the questions you want. I've known Noah his whole life, and I'll admit he's a bit of a hot-head, and he doesn't make great decisions when he's been drinking. I wouldn't put it past him to throw a brick at that white man's house, but murder . . . I don't think he's got it in him."

"For his sake, I hope you're right," Mike said.

I nodded toward the house. "What about the girl? She lied to us. Maybe she knows something."

"I'm sure she was just trying to protect her brother," Tsosie replied. "Which isn't a good look for her, but . . ."

Mike nodded and held out a hand. "Let's not kick the hornet's nest any more than we already have. If we need to talk to her later, she shouldn't be hard to find. I appreciate your assistance, officer."

Tsosie shook Mike's hand before offering a handshake to me too. I swallowed my surprise and shook his hand, then stepped back and walked with Mike down the driveway to our car. When I got there, I reached for the door handle, but a hand on my back stopped me. I turned to face Mike, resigned to another lecture about overstepping my bounds.

Instead, he clapped a hand on my shoulder and squeezed. "Nice work."

Tears sprang to my eyes—not because of the sentiment, but because he'd just squeezed the shoulder I'd landed on. "Thanks."

"You okay?" He frowned, eyes narrowing in scrutiny.

"Yeah, I just landed a bit badly. It's fine."

He hastily removed his hand, brows drawing together. "Shit, you need an ice pack or something? I should have a chemical one in the first aid kit."

"It's fine. If that changes, I'll let you know." I rolled my shoulder and bit the inside of my cheek to distract myself from one pain with another. Yeah, it definitely wasn't fine, but I wouldn't admit it just then.

For a moment, I thought he might fight me on it. In the end, he nodded and walked around the car to get behind the wheel. Breathing a sigh of relief, I joined him in the car and cranked the heat up while he backed down the drive.

"Do you think Noah killed him?" I asked.

"Nope." He popped the P definitively.

"What makes you so sure?"

"Did you hear what he said?"

I thought back. "Yeah. But I'm not sure what you're getting at."

"'He fouls the land with his presence,'" Mike quoted. "Fouls. Present tense. I doubt he even knows Reed is dead."

CHAPTER 16

B y the time we got back to the tribal police station and sat down with Noah, he was disinclined to talk. Tsosie sat in on the session, leaning against the wall with his arms folded across his barrel chest. Every now and then, Noah glanced in his direction, but the officer merely stood there in silence, observing. I wondered if the officer had advised him to keep his mouth shut on the way.

After several minutes of patient questions met with stony silence, Mike took out his phone and fiddled with it a moment before tossing it on the polished wooden table. It landed in front of Noah with a dull thud. He frowned as he leaned forward and looked down at the screen. Mike had pulled up the photo of Noah walking past Reed's security camera, holding a brick.

A muscle in Noah's cheek twitched, and he looked up at Mike again. "That could be anyone."

Mike leaned forward and swiped to the photo of the man departing, then again to the blown-up image showing the tattoo. "Looks a lot like yours, don't you think?"

It took about five seconds for Noah to process the fact

that he wasn't going to wiggle out of this. "Fine. I did it. But you and I both know the old fuck is too soft to press charges. So, why are you even here?"

Mike sat back in his chair once more. "You're right. Mr. Reed won't be pressing charges. He's dead."

Noah's wide eyes flew to Tsosie who remained impassive.

"His body was found this morning," Mike said. "So, given that you've just confessed to threatening to kill him less than forty-eight hours ago, Mr. Chavez . . . Where were you last night between the hours of seven p.m. and four a.m.?"

Noah shoved back his chair and jumped to his feet, slamming his palms against the table top. "I didn't kill him!"

"But you threatened to kill him." Mike idly rubbed his thumb against the edge of the table.

"But I—I wouldn't actually do it!" Noah's frantic eyes shifted to Tsosie. "Tell them, Billy! You know me."

Tsosie spread his hands. "I already did, son. But Detective Escobar can't just take my word for it. So answer the man's question. Where were you last night?"

Noah wet his lips and collapsed in the chair, rubbing his forehead. "I ate dinner with my grandparents, and then I went home to work in my studio."

"What time did you leave your grandparents, and what are their names?" Mike took out his notepad and scribbled a note. I liked that he was a pen and paper guy, even though there were about a billion phone apps for note-taking.

"About six-thirty. They eat early."

Mike looked up from his notes when Noah stopped there. "And their names?"

"I . . . do we have to involve them in this?" He glanced at Tsosie.

The older man shifted uncomfortably. "Probably best if

we didn't. That's outside the timeframe anyway, so it's not like they'd be giving you an alibi."

Relief flooded Noah's face, at least briefly. "I-I was alone last night. I puttered in the studio for a couple hours, then watched a movie and went to bed."

"Is there anything else you can tell us that might help our investigation? Anyone you might know who also had a beef with the deceased and might have been willing to follow through on your threat?"

"Are you asking me if I hired someone to do it? Come on, man."

Mike chuckled. "I don't imagine you'd admit to it if you did. But no, I'm just wondering who else around the Pueblo might've wanted the guy gone."

"Um, everyone?"

Tsosie cleared this throat. "He's not being smart, detective. Well, not *just* being smart. Mr. Reed was not well-regarded on the Pueblo. Pretty much anyone here would've been happy if he'd moved on, but I can't think of anyone who would've resorted to murder to get rid of him."

"He claimed to have Tesuque blood in his ancestry," Noah said, lips twisting in distaste. "He went so far as to try and register as a member of the Church, but he had no proof. He's just a pretender. Hell, he isn't even a witch."

"How did you know he wasn't a witch?" I said, surprised into not holding my tongue.

"One of my sister's friends is dating his butler or some-thing. He told her the guy uses charms to trick people into believing he has magic."

"Butler?" Mike asked. "Do you have a name?"

"I don't remember. He's a young guy. Hispanic."

"Juan?" I said, knowing full well that Juan wasn't Reed's butler but also that Reed didn't have a butler at all. As far as we knew, his only employees were the housekeeper and the scrappy young handyman.

He shrugged. "Yeah, maybe."

The interview paused while Mike scribbled a note, then circled back to something else Noah had said. "You mentioned the Church. Is there a branch of the Native American Church in the Pueblo?"

"Yes," Noah said.

I wondered if the local churchgoers had access to peyote, legally or otherwise. But even I knew it was a bad idea to ask outright. Mike was always telling me not to tip my hand about the facts of our cases in front of suspects. On this occasion, I actually remembered.

"Are you a member of the Church?" Mike asked.

"Yeah. But what does that have to do with anything?"

Mike shrugged. "You're the one who brought it up."

"Because—you know what, never mind. Are we done here?" His eyes swung between Mike and Tsosie.

Mike pushed back his chair. "For now, yes. Though I'm going to have to ask you not to take any sudden trips out of town."

"I'm not under arrest?" Noah said, blinking.

"That'll be up to whoever inherits his damaged property, I suppose."

Tsosie nodded. "In the meantime, why don't you focus on your art and stay out of trouble."

Noah sprang to his feet and nodded. "No trouble here, no sir."

We bid farewell to Noah Chavez and Officer Tsosie and left the station proper.

"Still think he's innocent?" I asked as we settled in the car for the trip back to town. "He may have access to peyote, they have a long history of antagonism, and he obviously hates the guy." With all that said, I was still on the fence myself. We had nothing concrete on him other than the video, and threatening to kill someone is a whole world away from actually doing the deed.

"We don't have a lick of evidence that points his direction other than the threat he made. I still don't think he did it, but we can't fully rule him out either. Not this early. Anyone in the NAC could potentially have access to peyote. I think we need to take a closer look at the Tesuque chapter, since the Tesuque were the ones with the biggest beef with the guy."

"So, check the website, see if there are regional or local contacts listed?"

"Bingo. But I'll take care of that after I drop you off at your car so you can get ready for work."

Right. Work. I nodded absently and gingerly prodded my shoulder. It was getting stiff, which wasn't a good sign. I really should've taken him up on that ice pack, but I hadn't wanted to make a big deal out of it. Hadn't wanted to seem fragile when Mike already treated me like glass half the time. If I went in a little early, I could ice it before my shift and take an anti-inflammatory. One of the good things about working in a hospital was easy access to first aid supplies.

CHAPTER 17

"Tell me when it hurts." Russell pressed his fingers into the soft tissue just behind my shoulder joint, and I sucked in a hissing breath through my teeth.

"Now."

"Hmm." He walked his fingers around the joint while I bit my lip, determined not to cry out.

Why does every medical assessment usually involve a doctor poking the thing that hurts and seeming puzzled when that makes it hurt more? I'd made it almost an hour into my shift when Russell noticed that I was favoring one arm, but it wasn't until about the halfway point that he persuaded me to let him take a look. That's how I ended up on the wrong side of an exam table when what I'd really wanted was another ibuprofen and a nap.

The rattle of the curtain opening drew my attention from the shooting pain the doctor's theoretically gentle fingers provoked and to the startled, familiar face peeking into the exam room. She yanked the curtain closed again quickly.

I chuckled. "It's okay, come on in Suzi. I'm decent."

"No, no, it's okay!" she said from the other side of the curtain. "Gracie said you were back here, but I didn't—she didn't . . ."

I winced because the appearance of Russell's wife hadn't stopped him in the slightest. He was still focused on his task, jabbing my tender flesh with suddenly bony fingertips and all the gentleness of a man with hammers for hands. "You're welcome to come in. This is mostly for Russ's benefit."

The curtain fluttered and she peeked inside, curiosity alight in her pretty brown eyes. "How so?"

I started to shrug but thought better of it. "I told him it was no big deal, but you know how he is." I glanced down at my shoulder, which had a big purple bruise where I'd hit the ground earlier. Russell had asked me to trade my scrub top for a gown so he could examine it, so it was bare for the moment.

"Ohhh. Gotcha." Suzi slipped inside and closed the curtain behind her. "You were late, so I thought I'd come see if you forgot or were held up."

I blinked owlishly at her for a moment before realization dawned. "Oh shit. I totally lost track of what day it was. I'm sorry." Suzi and I had been getting together for coffee every couple of weeks. She kept weird hours the way Russell and I did. She was self-employed and tended to adjust her hours to whatever shift her husband was working so they actually got to see each other and have meals together like a normal couple. And after I'd discovered she had something of a psychic twinkle but otherwise not a lick of magic . . . I was intrigued and wanted to get to know her better. She'd become a trusted friend and confidant. I'd even started opening up to her a bit about my background.

"It's okay. Don't sweat it. May I ask what happened?"

"I tackled a fleeing suspect."

She tilted her head. "Slipped on ice, eh? It happens to the best of us."

I rolled my eyes rather than correct her. It wasn't like I was out to impress either of them, but I wasn't a great liar, and sometimes telling the truth is just easier. Instead, I shifted my attention to her husband. "What's the verdict, doc?

"No amputation necessary, at least." He drew the gown back up over my shoulder and tied the shoulder tie loosely. "Range of motion is good. It's bruised and tender, but as long as you're not feeling any shooting pains down your arm I'd say just keep up with the ice and ibuprofen and baby it the rest of the night. If it's worse tomorrow, don't be a hero. Let me know, and we'll get some imaging done. Okay?"

"I told you it was no big deal." I hopped down from the table.

"Doctors and nurses are the worst patients," Russell said with a shrug and a smile, ambling over to Suzi and pecking her lips. "I'd better get back to work. See you later at home?"

"Of course. I'll just wait outside while you get changed, Em." She flashed me a smile, then exited stage left while Russell held the curtain open for her.

Grateful for a lack of audience while I struggled back into my bra and scrub top, I did it as quickly as possible and —I thought—in silence. But when I drew the curtain back a couple of minutes later, Suzi regarded me with sympathetic brown eyes. At least she didn't say anything about it. In fact, she didn't even try to make small talk as we made our way through the hospital to the cafeteria. It wasn't until we sat opposite each other at one of the smaller tables along the wall that the silence between us was broken.

"So, how've you been?" She toyed with the tea bag string dangling over the rim of her beige plastic mug.

I tore into my packaged sandwich and transferred it to the plate I'd nabbed from the salad bar. "Fine, you?" It was an automatic response, and she picked up on that.

"You don't look fine, girl."

"It's not that bad, really. I can move it, see?" I rolled my injured shoulder and tried not to wince.

"That's not what I'm talking about. Well, not just what I'm talking about." She wound the string from her tea bag around one finger and bobbed it in the watery brown liquid a few times. "You look tired. I can see it in your eyes, and your energy's off."

"You can sense energy around people?"

"Don't change the subject. But no, it's just a figure of speech."

"Oh." I took a bite of my sandwich, a little disappointed that there wasn't another layer to Suzi's abilities I hadn't been aware of. Though speaking of energy, there was something off about her too, but I couldn't put my finger on it. "Well, I probably look tired because I *am* tired. It's been a freaking long couple of days."

She cupped both hands around her mug. "Tell me about it."

So, I did. Starting with Dan wanting to be a cop and ending somewhere around the time Mike dropped me off in the parking lot a few hours back. It felt good to talk to someone about it, even though she didn't do much more than listen. Suzi was a good listener, kind of like Matt. I realized somewhere along the way that I hadn't heard from Matt since my date with Barry, but upon reflection . . . that was slightly more than twenty-four hours ago. It felt like a lot longer.

"Wow, that is a pretty freaking eventful couple of days."

I smiled thinly. "Just another day in paradise."

"So you're on the Reed case, wow. That's been all over the news. It's astonishing to me that enough people believed in that whack-job to hold a candlelight vigil."

"You didn't hear it from me, but the mayor's one of them. He's leaning hard on the captain, but fortunately, that shit hasn't rolled downhill. Yet." I knocked on the table, which probably only bore a passing resemblance to wood, but it was all I had handy.

Suzi took a thoughtful sip of tea. *Tea.* It finally hit me. Suzi always had coffee when we got together. I took another bite of my turkey sandwich and studied her more carefully. That was when I noticed it. A tiny spark, something I'd never sensed from her before. Magic. I almost dropped my sandwich, and it wasn't until Suzi said my name—twice—that it finally penetrated.

"Sorry. What?"

"I said, how long do you plan on doing this? Moonlighting with the police department while working full time at the hospital."

"Um, I dunno. But enough about me. Let's talk about you."

"Me?" She chuckled and shook her head. "Compared to you, I'm Little Miss Boring. Work's been steady. I got a new client this week . . ."

"Are you pregnant?"

Her mouth dropped open, and she stared at me for several long seconds with wide eyes. Then she glanced around quickly before leaning over the table a little. "Shhh. I haven't even told Russ yet. How did you know?"

"You're drinking tea."

An anxious laugh spilled from her lips. "Oh my gosh, do you go around asking everyone drinking tea if they're preggers?"

"Well, no. But you always have coffee. And there's something else."

"What?"

I sat back in my chair and rubbed the back of my neck. "This is going to sound crazy, but . . ."

"But what?"

"I think your baby has magic potential."

Suzi startled, knocking her cup over. Hot tea slid across the table toward me in a rush, and I barely scooted my chair back in time to avoid getting a lap full of scalding hot liquid as it cascaded over the edge of the table in a brown waterfall. We both grabbed for the napkins, but there were only a few that I'd grabbed from the communal dispenser on the table with the forks, knives, and spoons before we sat down.

Suzi vaulted from her chair. "I'll get some more." She hurried off while I used the napkins to dam my side of the table, trying to keep more from ending up on the floor. Fortunately, the tea had only flooded the table around my plate, missing the plate itself but leaving it like an island in a pale brown sea.

Once everything was cleaned up and we were again seated across from one another, Suzi sat back in her chair and stared at me for several minutes while I finished the first half of my sandwich.

While I took the top piece of bread off the other half of the sandwich and rearranged its contents so the turkey was more evenly spread, I broke the silence. "You're probably wondering how I could possibly know the baby is a witch."

"The thought had crossed my mind. Along with how it possibly could be. I'm not, Russ isn't . . . and I swear it's his. There hasn't been anyone else. I would never, *never* betray him. Oh god, is he going to believe me?"

Tears welled in her eyes, and I reached across the table

to put a hand over hers before they could spill free. "Hey, take a deep breath. Okay? It's totally possible for two regular joes to have a witch child. It's rare, but it happens. Hell, it's even possible for two witches to have a talentless child. That's how I came about, remember?"

"But you're not completely talentless."

"Neither are you."

Her troubled eyes slid away from mine before she closed them. A single tear leaked from one and dripped down her cheek, but she turned the hand beneath mine over and curled her fingers around mine.

"Look, we don't know why you have prophetic dreams, but I've told you before that I think it's a strong suggestion of witch blood in your family somewhere. It's just a bit . . . diluted."

She nodded and lifted her eyes once more to meet mine. "I need to tell Russ. We need to figure out what to do."

A gnawing sense of unease rose in my stomach. Was she saying what I thought she was saying? That she might terminate the pregnancy just because the baby wasn't— well, normal? And if she did, wouldn't it be kind of my fault? I was all for a woman's right to choose, but this felt . . . wrong. On a fundamental level. I peeled my tongue off the roof of my suddenly dry mouth. "What do you mean?"

"We'll need help, right? If the baby is a witch, how will they learn to control their power if we can't teach them?"

The fist squeezing my stomach loosened its grip as relief flooded through me. I deserved the discomfort for jumping to conclusions. "Eventually, yes. But you'll have time. A few years, at least. Magic manifestation is a later stage of child-hood development. You won't have to worry about levitating bassinets or anything like that."

Suzi loosed a gusty sigh and slumped back in her chair,

releasing my hand along the way. "Thank god. Okay, this—this is doable. I'll just tell Russ and explain what you explained to me, and you'll back me up, right? Oh, wait. Shit. Russ doesn't know, does he?"

She wasn't wrong. Although I had registered, I was still keeping my witch status on the down-low at the hospital. I mean, my supervisor knew that I was doing some consulting work with the police, but she didn't know all the details of the situation. No one I worked with did, and I liked it that way while recognizing that it was a stolen season. They'd find out eventually, and I'd go from being Emily the nurse to Emily the Other. I can't say I wasn't dreading that day, but I wasn't immune to the pleading look in her eyes either. The poor woman was pregnant with a gifted child and all she needed was an ally. How could I refuse? "He doesn't. But I guess it's okay if he does. Just ask him not to spread it around, okay? For now."

She nodded quickly, then looked down at her empty cup. "I'm going to get some more tea, and we can talk about something lighter for a while."

She was up and off before I could reply, leaving me alone with the remains of my sandwich. I sipped my water and picked at the sandwich a bit, mulling over the fact that I'd just sensed magic in an unborn child. How weird was that? I wondered if there'd been others. I mean, I'd been around pregnant witches before. It would've been hard to distinguish the child's magical signature over the mother's. But I also wondered if I'd encountered a mundie carrying a witch before and assumed she was a witch. If I focused, would I be able to tell if a pregnant witch was carrying a gifted or ungifted child? If so, that was definitely not something I wanted getting out. Sensing a person's magical gifts wasn't something most witches could do, after all; it was one of my conduit powers.

I'm pretty sure if my mother had known I would be born without a scrap of magic, I never would've seen the light of day.

CHAPTER 18

The rest of my shift was uneventful, and I emerged from the hospital to find that a cold front had blown in and fluffy white flakes were falling from the sky. Judging from the liberal dusting outside, they had been for some time. Fortunately, de-icer had been sprinkled on all the walks outside, so I didn't have to worry too much about slipping on the way to my car.

"Emily!" a voice called from behind me.

I stopped and turned, spotting a woman in a pale pink blouse and gray skirt hurrying down the path toward me, clutching a piece of paper in one hand. She wore a hospital badge but wasn't someone I recognized, and she'd clearly dashed out here in haste; she wasn't wearing a coat. I suspected she was already regretting it. "What's up?"

Her cheeks were flushed a soft pink from the cold by the time she caught up with me. "This came for you." She thrust the paper at me, which turned out to be an envelope. I took it, puzzled. It was a letter addressed to me, care of the hospital, from a local address I didn't recognize.

"Thanks, I—"

The woman was already hurrying off, fat flakes of snow dusting her shoulders and hair. Couldn't blame her. I wouldn't have been eager to stand around out in this weather either, not without proper attire. I turned my attention back to the envelope, tearing it open as I started across the parking lot. Inside was an honest-to-goodness letter, not hand written, but still . . . I couldn't remember the last time I'd gotten an actual letter from someone, much less at work.

Dear Nurse Davenport,

You may not remember me because we only met briefly and I'm sure you see dozens of patients every day, but I wanted to take a moment to thank you. We had to bring our daughter in to the ER a few days ago, and—

I didn't get any further before the sound of a revving engine brought my eyes up from the page in time to see a sky blue grocery-getter bearing down on me, traveling way too fast down the row of parked cars to be looking for an open spot. I had mere seconds to react, and I spent a few precious ones staring in shock. There was no time to dive out of the way, so I did the only thing I could think of: I jumped. Instead of being hit dead-on, I tumbled over the hood of the car and hit the windshield. Someone screamed —it might've been me. The driver braked, and I rolled back down onto the asphalt in front of the car, landing hard but fortunately not directly on my injured shoulder. Blinking, I lay there in confusion for a moment, expecting someone to come running from the car to apologize, but no one came. I was dimly aware of someone shouting. The engine revved again and the car jerked toward me again, but only for a second as the driver hit the brakes once more.

I pushed myself up to my knees, my shoulder screaming in protest, then got to my feet. Shooting pain in my ankle warned me I'd given it a twist, but I did my best to ignore it and shot the driver a glare and the bird as I limped out from in front of the car. What I saw when he glared back nearly stopped me in my tracks. He wore a look of complete and utter hatred, lips twisted in a sneer as his contemptuous eyes attempted to burn holes right through me. My thoughts spun as I tried to place his face, but he was a complete stranger to me. Once I was out of the way, he rolled the car forward and the likewise unfamiliar woman in the passenger's seat rolled down her window and spat at me. The bubbly glob of saliva landed well short of my sneakers.

"Go back to hell, witch!" she shouted, and then the driver gunned the engine again and the car took off down the aisle, fishtailing as he took a hard right and booked it for the exit.

I stood there for a long moment, shaking like a leaf. That was no random encounter. They knew I was a witch, and it's not like I was wearing a scarlet W on my chest. Had they found me in the registry, like the Jehovah's Witchnesses that'd turned up on my doorstep the other day? My eyes fell on the thank you letter where it lay on the asphalt, dropped in the scuffle and ground into the slushy pavement by my assailant's tires. I became vaguely aware of someone calling my name. Grasping my shoulders. My injured one howled a protest, and I made a noise like a wounded deer as the world briefly whited out.

"Emily! Emily, are you okay?"

I blinked a few times, and when my vision cleared, I looked up at the worried face of Andy, one of the hospital's EMTs. He had his arms around me, having caught me as I teetered. He must've just gotten off too, or maybe he was arriving for a shift. I couldn't recall if I'd seen him the previous night.

Eventually, I gathered my wits about me enough to pull away and respond. "I—Yes, I think so."

"What the hell was that? We should call the police. I got the guy's license plate."

My eyes darted around, but fortunately, it didn't look like anyone but Andy had witnessed the event. "No," I said quickly. Calling the police meant making a scene. "No, it's okay. I'm fine."

"You're not fine, that guy tried to run you over! It was no accident, I saw it with my own eyes. Are you hurt? That was quite a tumble you took. Did you hit your head?" He lifted an index finger in front of me. "Follow my finger with your eyes."

I grabbed his finger and pushed it away. "I didn't hit my head. I think I twisted my ankle a little, but I'm fine. Really."

"Well, let's get you inside anyway. Someone needs to check you out."

"Andy, really, I—"

"You're still on hospital property, Em. It's a liability thing. You have to come inside."

I grimaced. "Really, I'd rather just forget the whole thing happened."

"The police or the check-out. Your choice."

Sighing, I closed my eyes and rubbed my forehead with gloved fingertips. "Come on, man. One thing leads to another, you know. The police are obligated to notify the hospital, and vice versa."

"Damn. I was hoping you wouldn't think of that." His mouth turned up in one of his Labrador-like smiles. "At least let me give you a proper screening for head trauma. To ease my conscience, if nothing else."

"Fine, fine."

I moved away from him and stooped to retrieve my letter

from the ground, then limped with him over to where his rig was parked in an adjacent lot. Fortunately, his partner was still on break and not lurking around the ambulance. I didn't want to have to explain any of this to anyone. His examination took around five minutes, during which he pronounced me not concussed—something I could've told him, since I hadn't hit my head—and my ankle not broken. He wrapped it for me and made me promise to put some ice on it when I got home, which I did before limping to my car.

I thought that'd be the end of it, but I was very, very wrong.

CHAPTER 19

It's always alarming when a door opens as you're about to put your key in the lock. I stood on the doorstep with the key poised in the air for a moment, blinking at my brother. He hadn't developed psychic powers, in case you were wondering. Rather, he was dressed in a pair of running shorts and a hoodie.

"Hey, sis! I was just headed out." He slipped past me onto the landing, leaving the door open in his wake. "Lock the door behind you, eh?"

"What are you doing? You're going to freeze to death in that getup."

"It's a little brisk, isn't it? No matter. I'll warm up. This place has nothing on Boston winters, anyway." He commenced jogging in place.

"You don't jog. And is that my hoodie?"

"I do now. Gotta get in shape for the physical exam. Mike says there's an endurance run and an obstacle course."

He really was serious about this cop thing, apparently. I expected he would've become distracted by something else by now. "You've been talking to Mike?"

"Yeah, yesterday morning when he came by looking for you. Congrats, by the way. Barry's a lucky guy." He flashed me a rakish grin and winked.

"I didn't—that's none of your business."

My brother gave a carefree shrug. "If you say so. Anyway, sleep well. I'll see you later." He turned to jog off in the direction of the stairs.

Shaking my head, I stepped inside the apartment and started to shut the door before something occurred to me. I moved back outside as quickly as my tweaked ankle would allow and stopped at the railing, leaning over to call after him as he jogged down the stairs, "What do you plan to do about the application fee?"

"Already taken care of!" He waved jauntily as he hit the ground floor and started off down the sidewalk.

I went back inside, this time shutting the door behind me, wondering where Dan had gotten the money for the application fee. Was that something else he'd talked to Mike about? Was Mike eager enough to work with a real witch to back my brother and leave me high and dry? Or had his gal pal Tracy floated him some cash? Hector would love that. Crap. I still hadn't replied to her one-word text. But what would I say anyway? I'd extended the olive branch. It was up to her to decide to take it if she needed it. Maybe she didn't need it. I hoped she didn't.

Too tired for such heavy thoughts, I limped into the kitchen to make a couple of ice packs—one for my ankle and one for my shoulder—and flopped on the sofa to ice up. The smell of smoke lingered in the air, but the living room was still pretty tidy. Dan had folded up his bedding and left it at one end of the sofa, and his clothes were presumably corralled in his suitcase or stuffed in a closet somewhere, out of sight and out of mind.

My phone vibrated in my pocket, and I pulled it out to glance at the screen.

Barry: How's your day going?

I set the phone aside, face down, without unlocking it so he wouldn't know I'd even read it. An inbound tide of guilt lapped at my feet in the process, both for the way I was avoiding him and the way I'd left things hanging on our interrupted date. He deserved better. Still, I didn't have it in me to pretend that everything was peachy—and I definitely couldn't tell him about how my day was actually going. I'd text him later, I told myself. Spoiler: I didn't.

Fatigue pressed me deeper into the sofa, but every time I closed my eyes I saw the car speeding toward me. I was pretty sure I'd have nightmares about it for weeks—which I did—and in those nightmares, I wouldn't have jumped. The car would've slammed into me, crushing flesh and bone, sending me flying across the icy parking lot, probably breaking both my legs. Would they have spat at me and hurled insults as I lay in agony on the cold hard ground in a pool of my own spreading blood?

I shuddered. What was I going to do? I hadn't understood why Reed would decide not to press charges against the people who'd harassed him, but now that the rat tail was in the other cauldron . . . I kind of got it. My knee-jerk reaction had been to let it go, in big part because I was still living with one foot in the broom closet and it'd happened right outside my workplace, but also because growing up I'd been conditioned to accept thinly veiled ridicule—and not so thinly veiled ridicule—for being a null.

I was going to have to figure out how much I was willing to take and where I'd draw the line. Because I may have developed the ability to be polite, smile, and turn the other cheek as a defense mechanism in my formative years, but that'd only get me so far when insult literally became injury. Eventually, I would have to stand up for myself, protect myself, because I couldn't rely on someone else to do it for me.

I must've dozed off because I woke with a start when the door slammed shut behind Dan. A quick check of the clock on the entertainment center told me barely forty-five minutes had passed.

Dan headed for the kitchen to grab a bottle of water but soon returned to flop on the sofa beside me. "What happened?" He motioned at my bandage-wrapped foot, which was propped up on the coffee table with the ice pack under my ankle. Said ankle had gotten nice and numb, though the plastic bag I'd put the ice in had leaked a bit, and I could feel the wet towel under my bare heel.

Part of me didn't want to talk about it, but he'd probably find out the truth eventually anyway. I sighed. "Some jackass almost ran me over in the hospital parking lot."

"That sucks." He cracked open the bottle and took a sip, then offered it to me.

I waved it off. "Yeah. What sucks even more is it wasn't an accident."

"What makes you say that?"

"Because his girlfriend—or whoever—rolled down the window, spat at me, and told me to go to hell. Or, rather, to go back to hell."

Dan draped one sweaty arm along the back of the sofa. "Been there. Well, sort of. Anyway, who was it?"

"I have no idea."

"But they obviously knew you . . ."

"I'm pretty sure I've never met either of them before. I think it was more about me being a witch than me being, well, me."

He was quiet for a moment. "But how would they know that, if they didn't know you?"

"The registry. It's the only thing that makes sense. The other day a couple of recruiters for the San Miguel Coven came by to invite me to join up. They're the local OSB chapter."

Dan grimaced. "You're not thinking about signing up, are you? Those guys give me the creeps."

"I wasn't, but now? I dunno. I've never been in a proper coven before. I'm sure there are benefits. Personal injury lawyers, maybe."

"Yeah, if you can look past the brainwashing. Hell, for all you know, they were behind the attack! Trying to scare you into joining."

"Don't be ridiculous." But what was it one of the twins had said to me? Something about crimes against witches being on the rise? It hadn't struck me as a threat, but . . . no. I was not going to go full conspiracy theorist on this one. I wiggled my foot out from under the ice pack and set it on the floor gingerly. "I knew that some people watched for new registrants to pop up, but . . . ugh. Guess I should've bought a private mailbox or something rather than using my home address. Let this be a lesson to you when you register."

"But this attack, you said it was at the hospital?"

"Yeah."

"So they must've done some research on you."

I eyed him. "If you're trying to make me feel better, it's not working."

"Sorry, just thinking out loud. Did you tell Mike?"

"No. I don't want to be that person, the one that goes running to her cop friend because someone makes trouble for her. You know?"

"Trying to run you down in a parking lot is a dangerous type of trouble to make. You should report it."

He wasn't wrong. I let my head drop onto the back of the couch and sighed, staring at the ceiling. "I'll think about it."

"Good. 'Cause you know I can't keep my mouth shut to save my life, and Mikey's my bro. We've got a gym date next Thursday."

I snorted. "Loose lips aren't the best quality for a police officer, you know."

He elbowed me. "I'm gonna be a badass police officer. Just you wait."

I made a noncommittal noise and hauled myself off the couch before stooping to collect my phone and half-melted ice packs. "I'm going to bed. Don't wake me up unless the house is on fire again. And, for that matter, don't set the house on fire again."

CHAPTER 20

M y alarm woke me up a few hours later, and muscles I'd barely known I had groaned in protest when I rolled over to turn it off. Flopping onto my back, I lay there for several minutes trying to convince myself to get up. I felt like, well, like I'd been hit by a car. I was stiff and achy all over, but I had too much to do to lie in bed the rest of the day.

Eventually, I talked myself into sitting up and grabbed my phone off the nightstand to check for messages. Steel Wool Wendy had left me a voicemail asking me to come in a little early so we could "chat" before my shift. That never boded well. I'd been planning to drop by the station once I was ambulatory and check in with Mike, but he would've texted if there had been any major developments. I figured I might as well get the "chat" with Wendy out of the way first.

Once I determined that my ankle would hold my weight and had not, in fact, swollen to elephantine proportions, I grabbed a shower, got dressed, popped a few ibuprofen, and headed to the hospital. All the way there, I wondered what she wanted to talk to me about that was so important. I hoped it didn't have anything to do with the incident in the parking lot that morning, but I couldn't think of any other reason why she'd want to talk to me.

I figured I'd get a lecture. Maybe a reprimand. And I'd have to fill out a bunch of paperwork and get a physical to document any injuries that'd arisen from the incident. Still, I did my level best not to limp my way through the front door. It helped that the ibuprofen was starting to kick in, and moving around had eased the aches that'd settled into my muscles while I slept.

Wendy wasn't too hard to find. I just followed the trail of nurse's tears and scowling orderlies until I caught up to her in the break room.

"Hey boss lady, you wanted to talk to me?"

The buxom Latina looked up from her phone, surprise flitting across her face briefly. "Oh, hi, Emily. I didn't expect you so early."

"I had some spare time this afternoon." I shrugged my good shoulder. "What's up?

No sooner had I spoken than the break room door opened again and a couple of pediatric nurses wandered in. I nodded politely to them, but Wendy ignored them entirely.

Standing, she strode toward me. "Let's find somewhere a little more private."

That boded even less well. I tried to keep my expression neutral and nodded. "Whatever you say, boss."

Wendy didn't have an office per se, so she pulled me into a vacant on-call room for our little heart-to-heart. "Thanks for coming in."

"What's up?" I sat on one of the narrow beds and tried to play it cool.

She sat across from me on another bed, smoothing her

scrub bottoms over her thighs in a hesitant, stalling manner that was very unlike her. "There's no easy way to do this, I'm afraid. I have to let you go, Emily."

I blinked. "Let me go . . . You're firing me?"

"I—yes, that's it." She grimaced like she didn't like the term. "I'm sorry."

"If this is about yesterday, I know what I did was wrong. I should've filed a report. I was just really shaken up and I didn't want to cause a fuss."

She tilted her head. "I'm not sure what you're talking about, and it's probably better that I don't. This isn't about any particular incident."

"Then what's going on?" I tried to keep my voice on an even keel, but it felt like the walls of the small room were starting to close in. Hell, it felt like my whole life was spinning like a plate on a spindle.

"It's recently come to our attention that you're a practitioner."

The statement hung in the air like a fart in church while I stared at her in equal parts disbelief and horror. "You're firing me because I'm a witch? That's not—you can't do that. That's discrimination."

"No, of course not. But you failed to inform the hospital of your practitioner status. You're in breach of contract, so I have to let you go. I'm sorry, Emily. Lord knows I'd keep you on if I could without legal being all over my ass. I know we haven't always seen eye to eye, but you're one of my best. You're welcome to use me as a reference. I'll have your back. And you've got this new job with the police department . . . I'm sure you'll land on your feet."

I was stunned into silence by some combination of the absurd reality I found myself in and Wendy's uncharacteristically sympathetic demeanor. The woman's nickname was well-earned, and everything about this was so out of character for her. Not the firing—I mean, she'd once fired a nurse in front of everyone for mixing up lab orders one too many times. Wendy took no prisoners. She was hard, but she was also fair. The fact that she wouldn't let me get away with tweaking my schedule on the fly according to the police department's needs wasn't just because she wanted to make things hard for me. It was that she didn't want to make things hard for everyone else who'd have to pick up the slack. I got that, on some level.

This? I didn't get this. Maybe she was being honest, or maybe she was flattering me because she didn't want me to make a scene, or maybe . . . maybe she was scared of what I might do. Everyone here had seen firsthand what unstable witches could do, after all.

She was right to be concerned—just not about me. I couldn't lash out with magic even if I'd wanted to.

I'm not sure how long I sat there in a daze. It didn't even occur to me to ask how they found out. My work at the hospital was more than a job to me. It was a lifeline. The people there had become something of a surrogate family to me, and now they were rejecting me just like my birth family had. This was exactly why I hadn't told them about being a witch to start with.

"I—I guess I should go, then." Blinking back tears—of sadness or rage, I wasn't sure—I stood.

Wendy joined me on her feet. "I have to accompany you to clean out your locker, and I'm going to have to ask for your badge."

I looked down at the piece of plastic clipped to my shirt, and the emotions swirling in my stomach solidified as anger. Protective, familiar anger. I unclipped the badge and tossed it at her, grimly satisfied when it smacked her chest and she fumbled to catch it. "Mail my stuff to me."

I stalked out of the on-call room and didn't look back when she called my name. I marched down the familiar halls and out of the building without saying a word to anyone. When I got to my car, I yanked open the door and threw myself inside, then forced myself to take a few deep, calming breaths so I was able to insert the key in the ignition rather than stab it. I could practically hear Matt's voice in my head, pleading with me to not drive angry.

If they didn't want me here, fine. That just meant I had plenty of time to focus on the case, and I needed to prove to Mike, now more than ever, that I belonged on his team.

CHAPTER 21

I headed to the station to report for duty. If anything could help me forget about my income being three-quartered, it was burying myself in our high-profile investigation. It was probably too much to hope that the PD would take me on as a full-time consultant now that my schedule had freed up, and even if it did, I wasn't sure the pay would be enough to keep me afloat. Either way, I didn't want to talk about it, so I didn't bring it up with Mike.

Because not all my luck was bad, I got an email back from Prince Charming shortly after I settled in to work, so we packed up and headed for Taos to meet up with him. The hour-and-a-half drive up there was beautiful as always, with the snow-capped Sangre de Cristo Mountains growing ever closer as our route continued to the northeast. For a while, the highway ran alongside water-carved canyons that might have nothing on the Grand Canyon but are still beautiful on their own. I couldn't help but smile when we passed a winery I'd visited once with Matt. I still had a bottle of wine from that trip in my pantry that I'd been hesitant to open—not because it wouldn't be delicious or I couldn't come up here and buy more, but because of the memories wrapped up in it that I didn't want to let go of.

The scenery and Mike's quiet company helped to settle me by the time we crossed into the Taos city limits. Santa Fe is well known for its artistic community, but Taos turns that up to eleven. It was originally founded as a trading outpost back in the 18th century, but by the 19th century, it was a full-blown art colony. Now they have three art museums, numerous historical sites, and countless artists in residence —quite a feat for a town with a population of fewer than six thousand souls. It's a mecca for the visual and performing arts, and I've been up there a few times since I settled in New Mexico, but it's not an insignificant drive.

As we stepped inside the coffee shop where we were set to meet Prince Charming, the warm, coffee-scented air wrapped around me like a fuzzy blanket. My nostrils tingled, and for a moment I almost forgot the true nature of our errand as we drifted toward the counter. My eyes drank in the decor, which featured lots of earth tones and dark wood. It was pleasantly decorated, though—oddly—none of the artwork appeared to be for sale. There were a few shelves of bagged coffee beans, mugs, and other coffee-related items for sale, though. Chalkboards hanging over the counter displayed the specials and prices, written in a tidy but decorative script with floral embellishments. Someone had clearly had fun decorating the board around the menu items. Two young women worked behind the counter, one preparing drinks while the other manned the register. Both wore tank tops and jeans, and their arms bore numerous tattoos. One had dark purple hair, the other orange, and they gave each other good-natured sass as they worked.

While we waited our turn behind a man ordering

several complicated drinks, I finally thought to look around and see if I could spot the man we were there to meet. We were a little early, so it didn't surprise me that I didn't see anyone that fit the bill. He'd described himself as six feet one with dark hair and said he'd be wearing a red University of New Mexico T-shirt. There were a handful of patrons scattered amongst the tables, but no one wearing a red shirt.

When our turn came, we ordered our drinks and then selected a table to sit at while we waited for them to be prepared. I shed my coat and settled in, stretching one leg out under the table to take the weight off my ankle while my eyes wandered around the room some more, part people-watching and part taking in previously missed details. Mike sat quietly across from me, and when my eyes drifted past him at one point, I noticed he was studying me rather than our surroundings.

"What?" I asked.

He shrugged. "You tell me."

"Tell you what?"

"We just spent an hour and a half in a car together, and you barely said a word other than to ask me to turn up the heat."

"I was cold."

He shook his head and shifted on his chair, leaning back and tapping the broad tips of his fingers on the tabletop. His eyes drifted to the door as it opened, but it was only the arrival of a pair of women in yoga pants and sweater tunics.

"Mike, house blend!" one of the baristas called. Then, seconds later, "Emily, large mocha extra whip and a cinnamon roll!"

Yes, I'd decided to eat my feelings. Don't judge me.

I started to rise, but Mike waved me back down and wandered off to fetch our order. The front bell chimed again, and I twisted in my seat to look that direction. This time it was a tall dark-haired male witch with a close-cropped beard and a red UNM T-shirt peeking out between the halves of an unzipped brown leather jacket. I raised a hand to get his attention, and he smiled as he headed in my direction. The name "Prince Charming" conjured up a lot of ideas, but this guy looked like he'd been plucked out of Aladdin more than Cinderella. His skin was dusky, his eyes an intriguing olive green, and his medium-length hair was rather curly. If pressed, I would've placed his age around thirty-five.

He caught my eye and smiled as he approached my table. "Please tell me you're Emily."

"Guilty. Thanks for meeting with me." I stood and offered him a hand, which he took in both of his and bent over it. Thankfully he stopped short of actually kissing it.

His dark eyes shimmered with warmth as he looked up at me from beneath his dark lashes. "The pleasure is mine."

Mike came to my rescue, noisily setting down my giant plated cinnamon roll before placing a huge coffee mug more gently next to it. You could've fit two of the big cinnamon rolls inside the coffee mug, it was so large. Practically a coffee bowl.

Prince Charming glanced at Mike, then at me, lifting a dark brow as he released my hand with obvious reluctance. I opened my mouth to make introductions, but Mike beat me to it.

He offered Prince Charming a hand. "Detective Mike Escobar, Santa Fe PD."

The witch hesitated only briefly before shaking Mike's hand. "You're a long way from Santa Fe, detective." *And out of your jurisdiction* hung unspoken in the air.

"Sure am. But I thought it best to be upfront with you, in

the interest of open communication. Should I call you Prince? Or Mr. Charming?"

"Whatever suits you, I suppose. I think I'm going to need a drink to go with this conversation."

"What'll you have?" Mike said. "My treat."

"Oh, you don't have to—"

"I insist." Mike pulled out the chair opposite mine and pointed at it.

Charming sat obediently. "Dirty chai with a double shot, two percent, extra foam."

Mike nodded and wandered off to place his order while I joined Charming at the table and picked up my fork.

"Are you a cop too?" he asked, eyeing me as he shrugged off his jacket and let it hang off the back of his chair, half inside out.

"No, I'm a nurse." I could still call myself that, right? I did have the degree and the registration, if not the employment. A wave of what I can only describe as grief washed over me, but I stuck a bite of the cinnamon roll into my mouth before I could dwell on it, cheered by the burst of cinnamon and sugar on my tongue.

"A nurse?" Charming looked from me to Mike and back again in obvious confusion.

"I'm also a witch, and I do some consulting with the police on the side. I'm sorry about the deception, but we didn't think you'd want to meet if you knew who we were."

He leaned back in his chair, crossing an ankle across his knee. "Why's that? My business is perfectly legal. I'm a licensed charm dealer."

"I'm going to go out on a limb here and say that 'Prince Charming' isn't your legal name. You don't exactly have a storefront either, and the charm you sold Ashley Iverson was . . . not technically illegal, but pretty borderline."

"I'm not sure what charm you mean."

"You took this meeting when I told you Ms. Iverson referred me, so you know who she is."

"I have a lot of clients." He shrugged, the corners of his mouth twitching upward. "Many women find my charms irresistible."

Mike returned with Charming's drink and snagged a chair from a nearby table so he could join us. "What'd I miss?"

"I was just explaining to Mr. Charming here why we were circumspect about setting up this meeting, and he was playing dumb about Ms. Iverson's fancy charm."

"Ah, I see." Mike nodded. "Well, here's the thing, Mr. Charming. The woman says she got it from you, and we're interested in what other charms you might have sold her or her ex-boyfriend."

Charming winced. "Guess the charm didn't help her make up with him after all?"

I speared a piece of cinnamon roll on the tines of my fork and pointed it at him. "So you do remember it!"

"We'll never know if it would've helped," Mike said. "I called him her ex because he's dead."

The witch choked on a slurp of espresso-laced tea and began to cough noisily, drawing the attention of pretty much everyone in the coffee shop. I passed him a napkin while Mike leaned over and pounded him on the back a few times.

"Nate Alan Reed is dead?" Charming said when he'd recovered enough to speak.

"As a doornail." I popped another bite of the cinnamon roll into my mouth, and the sugary goodness melted on my tongue. They'd even warmed the thing up for me. It was divine. "You knew him?"

He quickly shook his head. "Only by reputation."

"We found some charms at the scene of the crime and wondered if you might be able to identify them." Mike pulled an evidence bag from his pocket, the one that contained the stay-lit charms from the fire pit. He set it on the table.

"Why do you need me to identify them? You've got her." Charming gestured at me with his head.

"Sorry, I misspoke. We were wondering if they might be something you sold to Mr. Reed or Ms. Iverson."

Frowning, Charming reached for the plastic bag and held it up so he could examine its contents more closely. "Yeah, these are mine. I never met Reed, but his girl is a regular."

I filed that away, wondering if Reed's girlfriend had been supplying him with the charms he'd used to help fake it as a witch. He wouldn't be the first. I once heard the cautionary tale of a woman out in California who'd used charms to pass as a witch for a while. No one would have cared if her last name hadn't been Sandoval. The Sandoval Coven is another one of those long-established Circle covens. When the Circle came knocking, she disappeared for six months for "rehabilitation" and spent the rest of her life in a psych ward, doped up on a potent cocktail of the best science could offer just to stop her from screaming all the time. I shuddered at the thought. My mother was fond of cautionary tales like that.

"We're going to need a list of every charm you've sold her," Mike said, snapping me out of my thoughts.

Charming's eyes darted between the two of us. "Is Ashley a suspect?"

"Maybe," I said. "We need to know what else she might've had access to."

Charming considered this for a moment, then nodded.

"Okay, I can do that. But I can't believe she'd kill him. She was crazy about the guy. Crazy to hold onto him, anyway. Most of the stuff she bought was fairly innocent. I think she just liked the convenience of things like these." He tossed the bag lightly down on the table again. "Stuff any witch can do, but it's novel to someone without magic, you know?"

"Like what?" Mike asked.

"Firestarters, light globes, minor levitation, water purification, male enhancement . . ." He glanced at me as he trailed off, then cleared his throat. "Not that I've ever needed to resort to that to satisfy a woman, of course. My charms are all-natural."

"Of course," I said mildly.

"You can—you know what, I don't think I want to know," Mike said.

I bit my lip to keep from laughing, but Charming smiled broadly. "It's not about making it bigger," he said. "It's about making it feel bigger. It's an air magic trick. You just—"

"Don't need details about your kinky sex magic," Mike finished for him, holding up a hand.

"Pssh. That's not kinky. Kinky is—"

"We're getting off-topic here," I said, trying to steer the conversation back into more comfortable waters for all parties. "Unless, of course, you were selling kinky sex charms to Ms. Iverson."

"Nah, that's not really my thing. Then again, maybe it should be. I bet there's a market for it." He stroked his beard thoughtfully.

"Can you email me the list of charms you sold to Ms. Iverson? You've got my address," I said.

"Yeah, sure."

Mike shifted in his chair, leaning an elbow on the table.

"Let's talk for a moment about that compulsion charm you sold Ms. Iverson."

Charming's face shut down, jaw firming and lips tightening. "That wasn't a compulsion charm. I don't do that kind of magic."

"What would you call it, then?" Mike asked. "What exactly was it doing?"

"Ensorcellment. I call it the Charming Special. It's actually one of my newer charms, but it's selling like hotcakes. It makes the wearer fascinating to the opposite sex. Or the same sex. Or both sexes—that'll cost you, though."

I was far from the foremost scholar on magic, my education being more theoretical than practical, but even I knew there was a very fine line between compulsion and ensorcellment. "Now you're splitting hairs."

"Not at all," he said with a smile. "Compulsion imposes the will of the caster on the target. That's illegal. Ensorcellment just makes the caster much more interesting. Sure, it might mean that the target will do what the caster asks, but it doesn't take away their free will. It won't make them do anything that is against their nature."

I shook my head. "You can't cast a spell that changes how someone acts toward you without somehow influencing their mind."

"The letter of the law is compulsion—" He swiveled his head toward Mike. "—right, detective?"

Mike gave him a curt nod, but he looked like he'd swallowed a bitter pill.

"Ensorcellment is harmless." Charming twisted in his seat to access the pocket of his jacket and pulled out a tiny plastic zipper bag that was barely two inches square. You know, the kind that jewelers and drug dealers—and I guess charm dealers—buy in bulk. He held it up. Inside was a slim silver ring with a small opal stone. "See for yourself."

He set the sealed charm on the table and slid it over toward me. I eyed it like it contained a viper and slid it back using a napkin as a buffer. "I saw Ashley's charm in action, thanks. What I couldn't see was the spell itself, or really any indication that the charm existed aside from its effect. Why don't you show me?"

"Afraid I can't." He sat back in his chair and swigged another noisy slurp of his coffee.

"You mean won't."

"No, I actually can't."

I rolled my eyes. "I'm not after your trade secrets, Charming." I leaned on his name, a little heavy on the sarcasm.

Mike leaned forward, his head tilted slightly. "Who's your supplier?"

"Wait, what?" I glanced between the two of them. Mike had made an intuitive leap I hadn't seen coming.

"That, I could tell you." Charming rubbed the back of his neck. "But I won't."

"Wait, wait, wait. You're telling me that you're selling borderline illegal charms that were made by someone else, using spells you don't even know yourself?" My voice must've gone up a bit because Mike's foot nudged me under the table and I doubted he was trying to play footsie.

Charming shrugged. "Business is booming. I don't have the time or the energy to make every charm I sell myself. So I do what any savvy businessman does. Outsource."

I opened my mouth, then shut it again as synapses started firing in my brain, connections snapping together where nothing but trailing ends had existed moments before. There was only one witch I knew who could make spells invisible. One who had recently come into some money, no less. The idea of my little brother—with his aspirations of becoming a police officer—fencing barely legal charms should've been completely ridiculous. But it was just absurd enough to be true.

CHAPTER 22

Dan didn't answer my text, but since my car was parked at the station, I figured he wouldn't get far before I got home. I told Mike about my suspicions on the way back from Taos, and he agreed to let me talk to Dan on my own since the charms he'd peddled—if he'd peddled them—weren't technically illegal. Plus, they were only tangentially related to the case. We still didn't know where the bowl had come from, but we hadn't wanted to ask Charming about it directly until we got the list of items he'd sold Ashley Iverson. I doubted he'd list it even if she had bought it, on account of it being very illegal, but sometimes it's important to keep particular details close to the vest.

Once we got back into town, we headed for our next stop—the address on file for Hunter Thomas, one of the Sons of Humanity who'd had a recent run-in with the victim.

The Terra Vista Apartments didn't have much terra or vista to them from where I stood, unless you'd count a green-tinted pool with a thin sheet of ice across the top to be particularly scenic. I didn't. The whole place had a tenement feel to it. The walls were in desperate need of power washing, and concerning stains darkened the cracked concrete walkway here and there. Bits of trash fluttered around in the wind like urban tumbleweeds.

I let Escobar do the knocking, and he had his badge ready to flash when the door opened. If the door opened. I could have sworn I saw the curtains in the window twitch after the knock, but no one answered right away.

"Maybe we should come back la—"

The door finally opened, just far enough for a pair of suspicious brown eyes to peer out. The pupils were blown wide, despite the bright sunlight on our side of the door. Whatever they were on, I hoped it was good.

"Didn't order no pizza," a husky female voice slurred.

Mike displayed his badge, and the woman's eyes widened. She tried to slam the door shut, but Mike had already moved his foot to prevent it. "Sorry to bother you, ma'am. I'm Detective Mike Escobar, Santa Fe PD. This is my partner, Emily Davenport. We'd like to speak with . . ."

The woman abandoned the door and fled into the darkened apartment. Mike and I exchanged a glance and then he sighed heavily as he unholstered his gun.

"Wait out here." He started to push the door open but paused long enough to give me some side-eye. "I mean it."

I nodded and he moved inside, gun held at the ready, while I stood obediently on the front stoop, hands tucked in pockets, feeling more than a little bit conspicuous. And, oddly, not the least bit annoyed about being left behind. They say you should never judge a book by its cover, but considering the outside of this place, I was more than a little wary of what might be on the inside. The neighbor's door opened long enough for someone to peek out, then closed again when I glanced in their direction. Yes, please ignore the *gringa loca*—crazy white chick—outside. Nothing to see here, move along.

It wasn't long before Mike called me inside. I glanced left and right, then crossed the threshold and squinted in the low-lit room. I closed the door behind me to keep what little heat there was trapped inside. I found my partner in the kitchen, standing beside a squirming and cussing Hispanic woman on the floor. Her wrists were cuffed behind her, so she wasn't getting much traction.

"Feisty, eh?" I commented, lifting a brow. She was currently accusing him of some rather indecent acts with a dog, in Spanish.

Mike chuckled. "Apparently. Now, ma'am, I just want to have a little talk with you. I don't care how much heroin you're hiding in your toilet."

She kept right on cussing, right up until the front door slammed open, courtesy of a well-placed kick that splintered the doorjamb and sent bits of wood and dust flying. I turned just in time to see the outline of a figure in the doorway, backlit by the afternoon sun. Then I was flying through the air, tackled to the ground by Mike as a shotgun blast exploded and a load of birdshot went pelting through the air where I'd just been standing. Apparently, they really didn't like cops in this neighborhood.

The woman in the kitchen was screaming in Spanish; I could almost make out what she was saying around the ringing in my ears.

"Stay down!" Mike shouted, close enough to my ear that I managed to make it out. I did my best to become one with the filthy, disgusting carpet—seriously, it was bad enough that I noticed it even in the heat of the moment. My concerns about the interior of the apartment had been completely warranted. This carpet made me want to dive into a pool full of isopropyl alcohol. I thought I might not feel clean again until every inch of my body was scrubbed and sterilized, my clothes burned just to be safe. That kind of filthy.

There were more gunshots. I'm not sure how many. I'd never been that close to a gun discharging before. I was scared out of my mind, and I kept thinking, *This isn't how I want to die.*

Fortunately, it wasn't my day to die. The whole thing was over in seconds, and Mike's weight lifted off me, his hands checking my coat for holes before he rolled me over and looked down at me with concern etched on his face.

"Emily, are you okay? Emily!"

I nodded quickly, if belatedly, as bile rose in my throat. I hadn't vomited at a crime scene in weeks, but there I was struggling not to hurl. It wasn't just that the carpet was that vile, it was the clash of terror and relief, titans of adrenalized emotion warring within me. It was over, and I was going to be okay.

Once he assured himself I was unharmed, Mike picked himself up and hurried over to check on the man lying just inside the doorway. He kicked the shotgun away and knelt to check the guy's pulse. As I sat up, I saw the blood soaking the man's white T-shirt.

"He's alive," Mike said.

Instinct kicked in, and my nausea vanished. I was on my feet in an instant and across the room in a flash, sore shoulder and bum ankle or no. "Call an ambulance."

The man's pulse was slow, and he'd already lost a lot of blood. There were two blood-ringed holes in the front of his shirt, one in his chest and one in his abdomen. I enlisted Mike's help in rolling the man onto his side so I could check for exit wounds. He did so with his phone clamped between his shoulder and his ear, rattling off details to dispatch.

I tuned him out, focusing on my task. There was only one exit wound on the man's back, which meant there was still a bullet in him. Namely, the one higher up on his chest. I cursed inwardly, hoping that it was tucked away somewhere it wouldn't do much more damage.

Rocking to my feet, I ran into the kitchen, looking for something—anything—I could use to put pressure on the wound. A kitchen towel hung from the oven door handle, but it was so small and threadbare that I dismissed it immediately. My eyes fell on the woman on the floor, who glared up at me with some mixture of anger and fear.

"Where are your towels?" I asked in Spanish.

She rattled off an answer, and I found the drawer in question in short order. I rushed back into the living room with the towels and shoved one under the unconscious man so it was wedged between the exit wound and the floor and used the other two to put pressure on his wounds.

"Is there anything I can do?" Mike asked, having finished up his call by then.

I grabbed one of his hands and brought it to the lower towel. "Pressure here." I shifted my hands, putting pressure on the chest wound with one so I could monitor the guy's pulse with the other. But when my fingers searched for his pulse again, they found none. "Dammit!" I moved to begin chest compressions, hoping I wasn't just moving the bullet around in his chest, shredding tender tissue. But if I didn't pump the guy's heart for him, he definitely wouldn't make it.

I paused after a couple of minutes of compression and breath cycles to check for a pulse and found one. It was thready, but it was there. Forty beats per minute. I sank back on my haunches and took over for Mike, applying pressure

to both wounds. Neither had bled all the way through the
folded towels yet, which was a good sign.

Now that I had a breather, I studied the guy's face. "It's
him, isn't it? Hunter Thomas."

"Looks like him." Mike patted the guy's pockets with his
free hand. Lucky for us, he was a carry-your-wallet-up-front
guy. Mike managed to get his wallet out and fumbled with it
one-handed in search of ID. "Yup. Hunter Charles Thomas."

"Why the hell did he open up on us?" Now that I'd
brought the subject up, anxiety welled up from my stomach
and I glanced uneasily at the open door. No one had come
to see what was going on, even after the gunshots.

"Guilty men have the most to lose . . ." He shrugged.

"He didn't do nothing!" the woman in the kitchen
screamed. I'd forgotten all about her. "Did you kill him, you
fucking pigs? Help! Hellllllp!"

Something nagged at the back of my mind as I kneeled
there on the grimy floor waiting for backup to arrive, like a
distracting background in an online video or a low-hanging
branch tapping against a window. Tap. Tap. Something
about Hunter Thomas. I studied him in silence, wondering
if maybe I recognized him from somewhere, or if I'd
forgotten some first aid protocol or another—as unlikely as
that was. Then it struck me with sudden clarity, the faint
shimmer of power at his core.

I gasped. "He's a witch."

"What?" Mike looked from me to Thomas and back
again.

"You heard me!"

"I did, but that doesn't mean it makes any damn sense.
This guy is an anti-witch activist. And that's putting it
mildly. He's been arrested for multiple counts of aggravated
assault, vandalism, and criminal mischief against witches."

"I know, Mike. I read his rap sheet just like you did."

"Jesus." He pushed his fingers through his hair and rocked to his feet, began pacing the tiny living room. "Do you think he knew? Is that even possible?"

"No." I thought for a minute. "Well. Maybe? I mean . . . technically it's possible. Magical talent manifests during childhood. Until then, it's just latent potential. I've never heard of a witch failing to manifest that potential. But it is possible to bind a witch's power so they can't access it. So, theoretically, a child coming into power could be bound, and might never know what they're missing."

"Can you tell if he's bound?"

I shook my head. "It's not something I can sense, no. Remember when Dan was bound? I had no idea until he told me. Anyway, that's just a theory. There could be a lot of explanations for him turning against his own kind. We won't get an answer until we talk to him."

That was assuming, of course, we'd get the chance. The truth of that hung unspoken in the air until the ambulance and its crew arrived a few minutes later. Fortunately, we were on the wrong side of town for any high probability of it being a St. Vincent's rig. I recognized the EMTs who arrived to take over for us, whose nametags read Rausch and Garcia, but didn't know them well. They rushed in to take over for me and Mike, and I began to give them the rundown while they prepped the guy for transport.

"Caucasian male, gunshot wounds to the chest and abdomen. One bullet still inside. Heart stopped briefly, but CPR brought him back. Pulse forty and thready, breaths eighteen."

Rausch glanced up at me, then did a double take. "You're a nurse, right? St. Vincent's?"

"Yeah," I croaked out. My mouth was suddenly dry. It

didn't seem like the right opportunity to reveal to any of them that I'd been fired earlier in the day.

"He's lucky you were here," Rausch said.

My hands started to shake. They were covered in blood, so I didn't want to tuck them in my pockets. I was going to miss this. The adrenaline rush of a fresh trauma, the relief and satisfaction when my skills, training, and experience saved the day—or at least contributed. The sense of fulfillment that came from helping people. The world seemed to blur around me as I stood there. I followed Mike's instructions and answered questions as other cops arrived on the scene and the EMTs took off with our suspect. I was there, but I wasn't there. Checked out, emotionally and half mentally, shrouded in a sort of numbness that's not uncommon for someone who's been through a traumatic event.

Eventually, I became aware of Mike repeating my name, and I blinked, focusing on him where he stood in front of me. "Yeah?"

"Time to go. You okay?"

"I was fired today." I have no idea why I blurted that out. The words just came out on their own, and I couldn't take them back.

He blinked. "What?"

"Nothing. Never mind. Where are we going? The hospital?"

Mike put his hands on my shoulders. "What do you mean you were fired?"

"I was let go. They're moving in a different direction . . ."

"I know what being fired means, Emily. Why on earth did they fire you? I've seen you in action. You're a damn good nurse."

I stared into his eyes, torn between warm fuzzies from

his compliment and the swirling nausea the conversation provoked. "Because I'm a witch."

"They can't fire you because you're a witch." His fingers tightened on my shoulders, and I winced because one was still a bit tender. He loosened his grip immediately, murmuring an apology.

"I didn't tell them I was a witch."

"You didn't . . ."

I bit my lip. "I know we probably need to go to the hospital, but—"

"No." He shook his head. "There's nothing we can do there but sit around with our thumbs up our asses. After this shitshow, we've got a mountain of paperwork waiting for us. I can send a uniform to read him his rights when he gets out of surgery."

His hands dropped from my shoulders, and we headed for the car, side by side.

"But Emily?" He cast a sideways glance in my direction.

"Yeah?"

"We're not done talking about this."

"Not even if I tell you I was the victim of a hit-and-run this morning?"

Do I know how to distract a guy, or what?

CHAPTER 23

Once we got back to the station, we spent several hours filling out paperwork and being interviewed. It turns out, there's a lot of red tape involved when a police officer fires their gun, not to mention shoots someone. I also filed a report about the hit and run at the hospital, at Mike's insistence. After all, I had nothing left to lose. The cat was out of the bag at the hospital. What were they going to do, fire me again? It turns out, the car they'd tried to run me down with had been reported stolen earlier in the day. I vowed if and when the culprits were found, I would not hesitate to press charges. Enough was enough.

Eventually, Mike was called into the captain's office. I hung out at his desk with his phone, waiting for some word from the hospital about Hunter Thomas. He was still in surgery the last time we checked in, but at least that meant he was still alive. We both very much wanted to talk to him.

When Mike came back twenty minutes later, he wore resignation like an ill-fitting suit.

"What happened?"

"Administrative leave."

I shot to my feet. My wrapped ankle twinged and threatened to roll, but I held it together. "What? He shot first! He tried to kill us!"

Mike stepped closer and put a hand on my shoulder. "Easy there, Em. This is standard procedure. It'll only be a few days while they dot the I's and cross the t's."

"We've got an active murder investigation. Wait. What about me? Am I—" The horrifying thought of being let go from both of my jobs on the same day flashed through my mind.

"I'm the one that fired the weapon, so . . . just me." He squeezed my shoulder, which was still a bit sore from my tumble yesterday. I winced, and he quickly removed his hand. "But they'll be reassigning the Reed case, I'm sure. We can't just pause that investigation for a few days. The trail will go cold, and the mayor's still breathing down the chief's neck."

"It wasn't very warm to start with," I muttered, then sighed. "So I'm going to have to work with someone else? Who?"

"Don't know. You'll probably hear about it before I do." He picked up his phone, glancing at the screen before tucking it in his pocket. "Anyway, I've got to head out. If I hear from the hospital, I'll pass it along. Otherwise, I'll see you in a few days."

I watched him until he turned a corner and disappeared from sight, then sat there staring at his desk for a while. Now what? I had limited access to the police department's computer system, so I logged myself in and pulled up the digital copy of Reed's case. It was up to date as far as this morning, so I updated it with what we'd learned from Prince Charming. Then I put a call in to the hospital to check on Hunter Thomas. While I was on hold, a shadow

crossed Mike's desk and I looked up to find Detective
Anderson looming over me.

It wasn't hard for him to loom, or even intentional most
of the time. He was a tall drink of water whose dark
eyebrows were the only hair on his shaved head. He always
seemed to be smirking, and it wasn't a great look for him.
We'd crossed paths numerous times, both in the field and at
the station. He worked in missing persons and was one of
many SFPD cops who didn't think witches deserved their
own investigation team. Mike and I weren't super popular
around the department.

"Can I help you with something, detective?"

"Yeah. I'm going to need the Reed case file. Print it out
and bring it to my desk." He turned and started to walk
away.

"I'm not your secretary," I called after him.

"Close enough, *partner*."

His words finally caught up with me. The Reed case file.
Anderson had been assigned to the Reed case. I was going
to have to work with that narrow-minded asshole.

"Ms. Davenport?"

I'd all but forgotten I was still on hold with the hospital.
"Yeah, I'm here."

"Mr. Thomas is out of surgery and stable, but still recov-
ering from general anesthesia. He'll be in post-op for a few
hours, and then he'll be moved to a regular room."

"Great, thanks for the update." I knew from experience
that the police wouldn't be able to talk to him until he was
in a regular room and awake. Until then, a uniformed officer
would stand guard. Officially, Thomas was under arrest,
even though he needed to be read his rights when he
regained consciousness. The uniform would handle that
before me and Mi—Anderson got there.

I hung up and sent the case notes to the nearest network printer, then headed over to retrieve them and walk them to Anderson's desk. Missing Persons occupied a corner of the squad room, where the four detectives' desks were pushed together. Three of the four were present, standing around with mugs of coffee and chatting. They went silent as I walked up, all eyes on me.

I held the fresh printouts out to Anderson. "I'm not sure why you want printouts when you can just pull up the case on the computer. It's kind of a waste of paper." Never mind that Mike had a hard copy of it all—minus today's additions —locked in his desk.

"Call me old-fashioned," he said, taking the thick stack of paper from me and setting his coffee down on the edge of the closest desk. "Thanks, sweetheart."

I bristled. "My name's Emily."

"Right, right," he said absently, riffling through the papers, his gray eyes moving back and forth as he scanned the pages. "What's the current status? Who are the suspects?"

"Um, well, there's the girlfriend—though we're pretty sure she didn't do it. A Pueblo man who threatened to kill him twenty-four hours before he was killed, a Sons of Humanity skinhead who vandalized his place recently . . ."

Anderson's jaw tightened. "Escobar put that one in the hospital, yeah? The skinhead."

"Yeah." I studied him carefully, uncertain how to interpret his reaction. He seemed unhappy, but I wasn't sure why. "Why'd they put you on this case, anyway? I would've expected it to go to someone in homicide."

"Just lucky I guess," he muttered, but he didn't sound very happy about it.

"Hunter Thomas is out of surgery, but it'll be a few hours

before we can talk to him. That'll give you time to get caught up. I'm going to go home and, uh, feed my cat. You can call me if you have any questions."

He waved me off, turning to walk around his desk and drop into the chair without another word. Clearly, I was dismissed, and it didn't make me like the guy any more than I had to start with. The other two missing persons detectives gave me knowing looks before retreating to their own desks, leaving me standing there until I decided the most dignified exit was a silent one.

I turned and most definitely did not huff my way to the door.

CHAPTER 24

I was completely unprepared for the glorious aromas filling my apartment when I walked in the front door. The living room was empty, so I followed my nose into the kitchen, where I found Matt standing in front of the stove in the "Dinner is coming" apron I'd gotten him for Christmas one year but he always conveniently forgot to take home—not because he didn't like it, but because it gave him an excuse to come over and cook. I'm not sure why he thought he needed one; I was always happy to have him.

"That was fast, did you—oh, hi, Em." He flashed me a smile, tapping the wooden spoon on the side of the pot to knock off the excess before setting it in the spoon holder.

The scent of rich broth, fork-tender pork, green chile, and spices had managed to supplant the lingering smoke smell entirely. I slipped past him to get a bottle of water from the fridge. "That smells amazing. Pozole?"

"Yup. I was going to make a batch of beer bread to go with it, but what the hell happened in your oven?" He folded his arms across the stylized wolf head sporting a chef's hat on his chest.

I sighed and twisted the cap off the bottle, leaning back against the counter across from Matt. "Dan happened. How bad is it? I've been afraid to look."

"Not you're-gonna-need-a-new-oven bad, but . . . it might eat into your security deposit."

"Shit. I didn't even think of that." My shoulders slumped. I didn't *want* to think about it, either. Money was something I didn't want to stress over right then. I had plenty of other things to stress about. "Where is my walking train wreck of a brother, anyway?"

"I sent him out for bread, on—"

"—account of the oven," we finished together.

I smiled at him, but his brows pinched together and a line appeared between them. "You look like you've had a very trying day."

"I have. I really have."

He glanced over his shoulder at the simmering pot of stew. "I've got plenty of *thyme*."

I sighed and sipped my water, trying to decide how much I wanted to confide. He'd hear it all, eventually, but some of it stung more than others.

Matt unfolded his arms. "Wow, must be serious. You didn't even chuckle."

"What?"

"At my joke. Time, thyme, I mean I didn't expect you to know that pozole doesn't actually call for thyme—though it does take a fair bit of t-i-m-e."

That did finally draw a chuckle. "You are such a nerd."

He pushed up his non-existent glasses with his middle finger, then stepped over and wrapped an arm around me, steering me toward the kitchen table. "Come on, tell me all about it."

"I don't even know where to start."

"It hasn't even been forty-eight hours since the last time we spoke. So, how about we start there?" He pulled a chair out for me, and I sat quietly while he rounded the table to settle opposite.

"That might be too far back. The last two days feel a lot longer than they probably have been. But let me see if I can sum it up. Barry's looking for a commitment, I'm up to my eyeballs in a high-profile murder investigation, and I fucked up my shoulder tackling a suspect. Dan tried to burn the place down—though I guess you already knew about that— but on a related note the firefighters caught me in my undies, and one of them was John Warren. It turns out I can sense magic in unborn children, I was the victim of a hate crime this morning and tweaked my ankle, then I got fired this afternoon, was shot at, had to resuscitate the shooter, was reassigned to work with Detective-fucking-Anderson while Mike's on admin leave. Oh, and I think my brother's hawking barely legal charms to a charm peddler in Taos."

Mike blinked owlishly at me a few times. "That's a lot to unpack."

"Tell me about it." Still, just saying it out loud took some of the load off, a sort of psychological purging if you will. I leaned my elbow on the table and planted my temple against the heel of my hand, slumped in my chair.

"I'm not sure where to start," Matt admitted, leaning back in his chair and idly scratching his jaw. His ankle bumped mine under the table, a comforting gesture from afar. Fortunately, it was my good ankle.

I wished he were close enough to hug. Matt gave great hugs, and there was a part of me that wanted to be held and comforted no matter how much of a strong, independent woman I was. I sighed and closed my eyes, listening to the pot simmer quietly on the stove behind me and letting the pozole's soothing aroma wrap around me like an olfactory blanket.

"Why were you fired?" he asked.

That surprised me. I figured he'd start with Barry or John since meddling in my personal life was one of his favorite pastimes—which was only slightly preferable to Dan treating it as a spectator sport.

"They found out I was a witch, and I didn't check the witch box on my intake paperwork."

A sympathetic wince crossed his face. "Did you tell them you didn't know you were a witch when you were hired?"

"Now that you mention it . . . no. It didn't cross my mind. I was just so floored. Wendy caught me completely off-guard. I thought she was going to yell at me because I didn't report someone trying to run me down in the parking lot."

"Someone tried to run you down in the parking lot?" He straightened further in his seat.

"Yeah, that was the aforementioned hate crime. I never should've registered. It's brought me nothing but trouble, I swear."

Matt leaned over and took my hand, folding his long, warm fingers around it and rubbing soothing circles on my wrist with his thumb. "I'm sorry you've had to deal with that. I didn't think people would actually come after you like that."

"Me either. But there's nothing I can do about it now. Maybe get a dog. A big one."

"I don't think Lord Barrington would appreciate that, and you'd have to pay another pet deposit. Speaking of money, if you need any help—"

"I'm fine for now. I appreciate the offer, and I'll let you know if it changes, but I have enough in savings to keep a roof over my head for a couple of months at least, and I'm still drawing a small check from the police department for my consultant work. Maybe Dan will get a job and start contributing, that'd help too." My mind briefly went to the monthly "allowance" I got from my parents, ten years of which sat untouched in a bank, quietly gaining interest. But no. That was a last resort. If that.

"Are you going to fight it?"

"Fight what?"

"Your dismissal. It has to be some sort of discrimination, doesn't it?"

He had a point. I studied the pattern of the wood grain on the table while I mulled it over. "I'm not sure. I mean, New Mexico is an employment-at-will state after all."

"Yeah, but there are laws protecting people from being fired because of their race, gender, sexual orientation, or disability. If witches aren't included in that, they should be. I mean, what are they worried you're going to do to someone? Magic them healthy?"

"I wish." I shook my head, but his words had merit. "I'm not sure I'm up to becoming the poster child for equality. Hell, I'm not even sure I could afford it if I wanted to. But you've got a point, and I'll think about it."

He squeezed my hand. "Again, I'm willing to help. Also, it might be that pushing back is all you need to do. Get in HR's face and tell them that you're not going to go quietly, that they're engaging in discriminatory practices and you're willing to take them to court over it."

But was I? I wasn't sure. I'd been shocked, then angry, and now I was just hurt. "I'll think about it," I repeated.

"Dan said you got a letter from your mom, too. Do you want to talk about it?"

"Talk about it? I haven't even opened it. Hell, I'm not even one hundred percent sure where it is."

"You're not even a little curious what she has to say?"

"Not even a little bit. It's been ten years, Matt. Ten years." I couldn't stop the bitterness from creeping into my voice because, at the end of the day, she was my mother. The one person in this life who should love me unconditionally. But she thought I was a null. I knew now that I wasn't, that telling her could change how she felt about me, how she treated me. The thought alone twisted my stomach. I deserved better. "Whatever it is, I don't want to hear it."

"Okay." Matt stood and rounded the table to wrap his arms loosely around my shoulders and kiss the top of my head. He said nothing more, but I soaked in his love and support like a sun-starved house fern.

Then Hurricane Dan blew in, shattering the peaceful moment. The door slammed shut behind him, and the plastic bag in his hand crinkled gratingly as he shifted it between his hands while he removed his coat.

"As requested, one loaf of bread–bakery, not pre-sliced. But I still think you're crazy. White sandwich bread is where it's at." Dan tossed the grocery bag our way.

Matt caught it and pulled out the loaf of bread inside. It was one of those round artisan loaves, the top crusted with seeds. "Are you sure you two are related?"

"Sometimes I wonder," I murmured, eyeing my brother while Matt took the bread into the kitchen with him. I wasn't sure how I wanted to broach the subject of the charms. Should I just ask him outright, or try to catch him in a lie?

Dan tossed his coat over the back of a chair, then dropped into said chair and draped an arm over the back of it. "How long until we eat?"

"Just have to heat up the bread," Matt said.

Dan's focus shifted to me. "How's the murder-solving

business?"

"Could be better. We've got some leads, but it takes time. Speaking of which, can I pick your brain?"

Dan shifted in his seat, leaning forward with interest. "Absolutely!"

"The victim's girlfriend had a fancy charm she'd recently bought from a dealer in Taos. It was made in such a way as to be virtually undetectable."

He looked away, suddenly finding Matt's kitchen activities very interesting. "Huh, that sounds like some powerful mojo."

"Or the technique, perhaps, of someone who knows how to make spells invisible."

Dan's eyes jumped to me, wide and full of outrage. "Dear sister, are you suggesting that I had something to do with that?"

"Actually, yeah, that's exactly what I'm suggesting. Did you? And before you answer, let me remind you that lying to a police consultant is a criminal offense."

"It is not."

"Okay, but lying to your sister could get you looking for another couch to surf."

He sighed dramatically and slumped in his seat. "You're such a hardass."

"Better a hardass than a dumbass."

"Play nice, kids," Matt called from the kitchen.

I shot him a glare over my shoulder, but he had his back turned. It wouldn't have done any good anyway.

"Before I answer, was the charm used in conjunction with a crime?" Dan asked.

"Unknown. But that's kind of a risk you take when you deal charms, becoming an accessory after the fact."

He rolled his eyes. "I didn't sell anything dangerous."

"But you did sell something."

"Yeah. Tracy introduced me to this guy. Said he was looking for unique shit, not just your standard firestarters or pimple concealers, and he was willing to pay well for it. And someone keeps nagging me about paying my share, so I figured it'd be a good way to earn a few quick bucks without resorting to flipping burgers. He supplied the materials, I supplied the spells."

"Did you create an ensorcellment charm for him that would make someone irresistible to whatever gender they wanted to be irresistible to?"

"If so, sign me up for one of those," Matt said with a chuckle.

"I may have sold him a few of those," Dan replied.

"What else did you make for him?"

"A few loaded dice, tattoo concealers, walk-softlies, hair straighteners, oh, and I enchanted a few bottles of nail polish so they'd change color periodically."

The last one gave me pause. "What? Who wants color-changing nail polish?"

"He said he could sell it as mood nail polish." Dan shrugged.

"And you were okay with that? You know what? Never mind."

"Most of his stuff is what he says it is, or at least what I saw of it was. He's not a complete con artist."

My ears perked at that. "You saw his stuff?"

"Ugh, not like, his stuff-stuff." He glanced past me into the kitchen. "Not that there's anything wrong with that."

"Daniel." I slapped the table lightly with an open palm. "Focus."

"I met him initially at a coffee shop, but when I dropped off the goods he showed me his workshop."

"What kind of stuff did he have?"

"Why, are you in the market for something? You know, all you have to do is ask and I—"

"What about a bowl? Did he have a bowl?"

His brow furrowed. "Um. I don't remember seeing one. Usually, charms are small, but I guess in theory you could charm a bowl to keep its contents warm. Oh! Dude, I should suggest we spell some coffee mugs. Who doesn't want a self-warming coffee mug? He could even order some with his logo on them."

"Does the guy even have a logo?" Matt asked, setting a bowl of steaming pozole in front of me.

I barely noticed, and that's saying something because my stomach had been rumbling loud enough to wake the dead since I walked in the front door. Matt and Dan chatted around me a bit, but my mind was too far away from their friendly banter.

A bowl like the one we'd found at the crime scene wouldn't be something a dealer just had sitting around. It was the kind of thing you'd need to special order if you couldn't create it yourself, and there was little chance Charming would tell us even if he had created it.

I shook the thoughts off when Matt's hand landed on my shoulder, giving it a warm squeeze on the way to his seat with his own bowl in his other hand. He smiled at me, and I smiled back automatically as I dipped my spoon into the stew and brought it to my lips for a taste. As the spicy broth rolled across my tongue, I boxed up all of my lingering thoughts and emotions about the case and the turns the day had taken and shoved them into the back of my mind, intent on enjoying good food and good company. It'd all be there when I got back to it, but for now, it was enough to just . . . be.

CHAPTER 25

Since I wasn't working night shifts for the time being, I made myself sleep at least part of the night in an effort to flip my schedule. I'd probably need a nap during the day, but it was a start. My body ached even worse when I got up —the day after is always the worst. But at least my shoulder felt a bit better and my ankle bore my weight without a hint of a twinge. After a few more ibuprofen and a hearty breakfast at the café, I dropped by the police station with an extra to-go cup of coffee for my temporary partner. I found Anderson at his desk and set it before him with a smile and a flourish, determined to make nice.

"I wasn't sure how you took it, so it's black." I produced a handful of sugar packets and creamer cups from my pocket and deposited them beside it.

He looked at me in confusion, but pulled the cup toward him and took off the lid. "Thanks. What brings you in?"

I leaned a hip on the edge of his desk and sipped my own brew. "The case, of course. What's on the agenda today?"

"I didn't call you." His brows drew tighter together. "But

thanks for the coffee." He sniffed it and took an experimental sip before reaching for a sugar packet.

"I'm your partner." I flapped my badge at him.

He chuckled softly. "You're a consultant. When I need to consult, I'll give you a call."

"I see." I mulled this over while I took another sip of coffee, watching him pour three sugar packets into his own cup and then look around with a frown as he realized he had nothing to stir it with. He ended up grabbing a pencil from a cup on his desk to use, and that didn't seem sanitary at all. I suppressed a grimace. "Are you going to talk to Hunter Thomas today? He's probably awake by now. I could tag along."

"That's not necessary."

"Are you sure?"

"Already talked to him. He's got an alibi."

"Oh. Okay." Disappointment flared. I'd been looking forward to talking to him, both to find out if he might've been involved in Nate Alan Reed's death and to maybe get some idea of how a witch ended up a card-carrying member of a human supremacy group. I knew a few things about what it was like to be a witch and want to keep it on the down-low, but I didn't hate all witchkind because of the shitty hand I'd been dealt. And this guy, from all accounts, really hated witches. "Have we heard anything from the Albuquerque PD about lawsuit guy?"

"Yup. His alibi is solid too. He was seventy miles away when the murder took place."

"And the ex-wife?"

"Furious that she's not getting her money anytime soon because few of Reed's assets were liquid and his will is going to be tied up in probate for a while, but she was definitely in Florida at the time of the murder."

"I guess ruling suspects out is progress." I fidgeted with my cup, frowning. "So, there's nothing at all I can help with? I mean, I got coffee and everything. Put me to work."

He looked at me, then at the coffee, then back again. Sighed. "If you've got nothing better to do, I guess you can ride out to the Pueblo with me."

"Which one?" A trip to any Pueblo sounded better than sitting around the house with my brother.

"Tesuque. They're holding our murderer until I get there to pick him up."

I blinked. "Wait, what murderer? We have a murderer?"

"You should know, you were at the interview. Noah Chavez, remember? Death threat, no alibi . . ."

"Of course I remember him. But we didn't have any evidence linking him to the crime. Did something new come in?"

He smiled an all-too-smug smile for a man who was swooping in on a case someone else had done most of the legwork on. "Remember that magic bowl from the crime scene? It was one of his."

"What do you mean?"

"It had his maker's mark on the bottom and his finger-prints all over it."

My thoughts spun. I remembered Noah being an artist, but if pottery had been mentioned, it'd slipped past me. Still . . . "That's kind of circumstantial, don't you think? I mean, the guy sells his work openly at the Tesuque market. Anyone could've bought it from him."

Anderson pushed to his feet and grabbed his coat. "And yet, when you put it with the death threat, access to peyote via the NAC, and his acknowledged animosity toward the victim, well, we've got motive, opportunity, and means. Open and shut."

I wanted to argue with him, but my case was no stronger —maybe even weaker—than the one he was building against Noah Chavez. I may not have been convinced of his guilt, but I wasn't fully convinced of his innocence either. I also had no alternative theories to offer.

"So, you coming or not?" Anderson asked as he put on his coat.

"Yeah. Yeah, I'm coming."

To say the drive out to the Tesuque Pueblo Police Station was awkward would be putting it mildly. After my third attempt at making conversation fell flat, I gave up trying and spent the rest of the trip staring out the window and listening to the country music quietly drifting from the car's speakers. Country music wasn't my go-to, but at least it wasn't auto-tuned to hell.

We pulled up outside the tribal police station just after eleven and headed inside to pick up our—or at least Anderson's—man. Officer Tsosie brought a handcuffed Noah Chavez to the lobby after the appropriate transfer of custody paperwork was signed. The handcuffed man hung his head, his unbraided hair hanging limply around his face. While Anderson swapped out the handcuffs, Noah lifted his head and met my eyes. He had a kind of shell-shocked look about him, like he couldn't believe this was happening, and my internal scale tipped slightly toward innocent. "Help me," that look seemed to say. Sure, he could have been acting, but I wasn't convinced he was. Either way, when Anderson gripped his arm and steered him toward the door, he shuffled along.

I turned to follow, but Tsosie caught my arm. I met his somber eyes and inclined my head in silent question.

"A minute, Ms. Davenport?"

"Sure."

He released my arm but waited for the door to swing shut behind Anderson and Noah before speaking. "What happened to that other detective? Escobar."

"He's on administrative leave." I didn't think Tsosie really needed to know the details of yesterday's incident, which was for the best since thinking about it made my stomach twinge uncomfortably. My patchy sleep the night prior had been haunted by dreams about staring down the barrel of a shotgun. About what might've happened if Mike had been just a fraction of a second slower in tackling me to the ground. I wasn't sure if that was better than dreaming about being hit by a car or not.

Tsosie grunted and looked out the glass door. I followed the direction of his gaze, observing Anderson guiding Noah to the backseat of his unmarked sedan.

Tsosie blew out a heavy sigh. "I said it when you were here before, and I'll say it again. That boy is not capable of murder."

"The evidence suggests otherwise." I chewed on my lip. The evidence wasn't as strong as I would've liked. I couldn't shake the feeling that Anderson was just eager to make an arrest and get the case off his plate.

Tsosie faced me once more. "You've got to help him, Ms. Davenport."

"What?"

"Noah. My hands are tied. It's out of my jurisdiction. My boss signed off on the transfer, but it just doesn't feel right to me. He said Noah's fingerprints were found at the crime scene. Is that true?"

"Yes." I hesitated to say more, unsure what was appropriate to share. But Tsosie was sworn to uphold the law just like any other cop. "There was a spelled bowl at the crime scene with peyote remnants in it. We think the killer used it to force the victim to drink peyote. Noah's fingerprints were on the bowl."

"Shit." Tsosie glanced sharply out the window again.

"But . . ."

"But?" His eyes snapped back to me.

I looked out at the car. Anderson stood outside behind the open driver's door. He met my eyes and tapped his watch, motioning toward the car with his head. "But the bowl was Noah's. That is, it bore his maker's mark. You said that the victim had plenty of enemies on the Pueblo. What about Noah?"

"That boy isn't being framed, ma'am. He's being railroaded. I can't believe the chief signed off on this. This is classic American justice. Find the brownest suspect, and he's the one that did it." He shook his head, frowning hard.

His words struck me. Was that what this was? The thought had never occurred to me. "I don't know Detective Anderson well, and I'll admit he seems keen to close this case quickly, but I don't think the color of Noah's skin has anything to do with this." The fact that he was a witch? Maybe. I kept that thought to myself. "I've got to go. They're waiting for me."

He gripped my arm lightly. "Please, Ms. Davenport. I know you might not believe me, but if I'm right, the real killer is still out there."

"I'm just a consultant, officer. There's not much I can do, but I'll do what I can."

"That's all I ask." He released my arm and fished a crumpled slip of paper from his pocket, then snagged a pen from the nearby reception desk and scribbled something on the back of it before handing it to me. "This is my cell number. If there's anything I can do, you just let me know. Okay?"

I tucked the paper in my pocket and nodded, then

headed outside into the brisk afternoon air. I knew better than to broach the subject of Noah being racially profiled with Anderson while Noah was in earshot, so it was another long, quiet car ride back to the station. My thoughts flitted around in my brain like schools of colorful fish, darting this way and that, never landing in any one place for long. I thought about the weak evidence against Noah. I thought about Anderson's obvious disdain for Mike, myself, and the Magic Crimes department. I thought about the pair of haters that'd tried to run me down yesterday just for being a witch. I thought about Officer Tsosie's conviction that Noah was innocent and hoped there was someone who would advocate for me like that if I ever ended up in the backseat of a prejudiced policeman's car.

I shadowed Anderson during the booking process, claiming I hadn't observed it before. I had, but really what I wanted was an opportunity to speak with Noah. I got it when Anderson got a phone call and had to step away for a moment.

"Keep an eye on him," he told me gruffly before taking a few steps away with the phone to his ear.

I nodded to Anderson, then shifted my focus to Noah, who sat dejectedly on a nearby bench, handcuffed to a chain bolted to the floor.

I sat beside him. "Officer Tsosie is pretty convinced of your innocence."

"I don't think his opinion really matters in this case."

"True enough." I glanced at him. "But mine does. If there's anything else you can tell me, anything at all that might exonerate you, now's your chance."

He sighed. "I've told you everything. I broke the guy's window. I threatened him. But I was just trying to scare him, trying to get him to leave. I didn't kill the guy. I swear. I could never do something like that. Never."

His eyes met mine briefly around the dark curtain of his hair, pleading with me to believe him.

"You want to be booked in too, Davenport? Two's as easy as one." Anderson interrupted, his caustic tone bringing me to my feet.

"Orange isn't my color." I stepped away from the bench, tucking both hands in my pockets. My fingers encountered the receipt in my coat pocket, and I pinched it between my fingers. Noah's predicament would weigh on my conscience forever if I didn't do something. One way or another, I had to figure this out.

And I knew exactly where to start.

CHAPTER 26

I banged on the door for the third time. It was no delicate rapping of knuckles. Each time, I'd knocked a little louder until I'd escalated to pounding my fist on the door hard enough to rattle it in its frame. I knew Mike was home. His Cherokee was parked in the driveway.

Finally, the door flew open.

"Jesus Christ, Davenport. What's the emergency?" He stood there wearing a towel around his waist and nothing else, his tousled hair still wet and stray droplets of water clinging to his dusky skin.

If it had been anyone but Mike, I might've paused to enjoy the view. "It's after noon. Why are you just now showering?"

"It's not like I had to rush out of the house this morning."

I pushed past him into the house. I'd never been to Mike's place before. I'd had to check the department directory for his home address before I left the station. I glanced around briefly. It was tidy, which I appreciated. Tastefully decorated too, which gave me pause. I knew he was single, but I suddenly wondered if there'd been a Mrs. Escobar at some point. Or another Mr. Escobar, for that matter. But you can't assume a guy was gay just because he had matching furniture and a lap blanket thrown over the back of his couch. Then again, Matt and I had been together for years before he came out. It's a wonder I didn't assume all men were gay until I found evidence to the contrary.

"I need the keys to your desk."

"Okay . . ." He shut the door and turned, gripping the knot in his towel. "Can I put some pants on first?"

"Oh. Yeah, sure. I—I'm sorry to barge in on you like this."

"No you're not," he called over his shoulder on the way down the hall.

I looked—not snooped—around his living room while he was gone, taking in the details I'd missed in my initial cursory glance. A pile of shoes sat just inside the door, sitting in a jumble like they'd just been toed off and kicked in that general direction. It was easy to see why—the pale beige carpet would easily attract dirt, but it looked spotless everywhere I could see. A coat rack beside the door sported three or four different coats of varying weight. A set of keys hung on a simple brass hook screwed into the wall above the shoe pile. A second one hung empty beside it. I filed that away for future reference.

Mike came wandering back down the hall in a pair of sweats and a T-shirt, running a comb through his wet hair. "Okay, why do you need to get into my desk?"

"Anderson's fucking up our case."

"How so?"

"He arrested Noah Chavez because that spelled bowl from the crime scene had his maker's mark and fingerprints on it." I perched on the arm at the opposite end of the couch. "But anyone could've bought a bowl from him. All it proves is it wasn't washed first."

He shrugged. "Motive, means, and opportunity. Check."

"Oh come on. You too? Even I know this is circumstantial, and as you're so keen to remind me, I'm not an actual cop."

"What makes you think he's innocent?"

"I'm not entirely convinced either way. But Officer Tsosie is. He all but begged me to keep digging, even gave me his cell number. This is sloppy investigating, Mike. Anderson just wants the case off his desk. We can't just send this to the DA and hope she can convince a jury to convict a possibly innocent man. It's not right. We need proof beyond a reasonable doubt. And I've got a lot of reasonable doubts."

His lips twitched in a smile. "I think I'm rubbing off on you. So, you want to keep digging. What's in my desk that you need?"

"The backup copy of our case notes. I can't print off another copy without the assigned officer getting an email notification, and I don't want Anderson to know I'm digging around."

He nodded and stood, heading for the foyer. I expected him to grab the keys off the hook, but instead, he shoved his feet into one of the pairs of shoes and grabbed a heavy coat first.

"Where are you going?"

"Where do you think? I'm not going to miss out on this little extracurricular adventure. I'm bored as hell. We'll collect the file and then grab some coffee and go back over everything again. If we missed something, we'll find it."

I couldn't help but smile. Emily and Mike, on the case. Suddenly, the world seemed right again. I walked over to him and flung my arms around him in a spontaneous hug. He put one arm around me and patted my back awkwardly.

Yup. Definitely not gay.

We took my car, thinking it'd be less conspicuous. I parked in the visitor parking rather than the employee lot, and Mike hunkered down under my winter hat and sunglasses to wait in the car. It was comical, and I was tempted to snap a picture for posterity, but he was already grumpy about my "Sunday Grandma" driving—his words, not mine. My grandma had a worse lead foot than anyone I'd ever met.

I waved to the officer at the reception desk on my way in, not even having to flash my badge since he knew me well enough to buzz me in. I strolled casually through the squad room, stopping at the water cooler on the way to Mike's desk because I thought holding a water cup might make me less suspicious. Why anyone would be suspicious of my presence somewhere that I legitimately worked, I have no idea. In the moment, it seemed like the thing to do.

When I reached Mike's desk, I slid into his chair and set the paper cup down, then pulled the keyboard over and woke up the monitor to log into the system, pretending I had something I needed to do. After a quick glance around to determine that no one seemed to be watching me, I unlocked the center desk drawer and opened it. Inside lay the haphazard mess of papers and photos pertaining to the Reed case that he'd shoved in there the previous day. I pulled them all out and straightened them into a tidy pile, then peered into the drawer. No file folder.

I opened the file drawer, which contained several hanging folders, most of them empty. Behind those were a few empty folders, and as I grabbed one I noticed a thick file in the very back. The tag read: Gentry.

Gentry. Where had I heard that name before? Curious, I pulled it out and flipped it open.

"Hey Emily, how's it going?"

I snapped the folder shut like the guilty snoop I was and lifted my eyes to find Officer Abrams smiling at me. "Oh, hey Rashida. It's going okay. You?"

"Fine. I heard you got reassigned to Anderson. How's that working out?" Her dark eyes strayed curiously to the file in my hands but didn't linger long before returning to mine.

"Um, alright I guess." I shifted the folder in my lap, letting my fingers cover the label as I tried to figure out how to end this conversation as quickly as possible. "I'm just trying to get ahead on some paperwork."

"Ugh. It never ends, does it? I swear this job is like thirty percent law enforcement, seventy percent paperwork. Anyway, say no more. I'll get out of your hair." She smiled and began to withdraw but snapped her fingers and turned back to me a moment later. "Oh, I almost forgot! A few of us girls do happy hour on Tuesdays at the Crow's Foot. You should come by sometime."

"Uh, sure, that sounds fun." It was also the first time in my two months of working for the SFPD that anyone but Mike had invited me to do something outside of work. I couldn't help but be a little suspicious, but Rashida's warm smile smoothed out most of the wrinkle like a flat iron for the psyche.

"Awesome! Looking forward to it." She threw a little wave and turned, wandering down the row of desks.

I released a breath I hadn't realized I'd been holding and looked back down at the folder in my lap. Flipping it open, I scanned the first page, which was a police report. Marissa Gentry. Death by suicide. It came to me in a flash. Gentry.

Mike's previous consultant. Mike had said very little to me about her, but it was clear her death had had an effect on him. We'd thought she might've been connected to the first case we worked on but hadn't been able to prove it. Why did he have a hard copy of her file in his desk drawer?

The file was an inch thick, which surprised me for a death by suicide. That ought to be fairly straightforward, shouldn't it? I thumbed through the first few pages. Police report. Autopsy report. Photographs. Interview transcripts. The rest were handwritten notes. Page after page of hand-written notes, all in Mike's familiar scrawl. I wanted to read more, curious about the woman who'd come before me, but Mike was waiting in the car.

I quickly stuffed the Reed case notes into the empty folder and tucked the Gentry file underneath it, then locked up Mike's desk and signed out of the computer. I should've put the Gentry file back where I found it, but I was too curious to leave it behind. With both files tucked under my coat, I headed back out of the station without incident.

Mike was behind the wheel when I reached the car. Rolling my eyes, I slid into the passenger's seat.

"Got it?" he asked.

I pulled the Reed file out of my coat, keeping it closed so he couldn't see the other tucked against my chest. "Got it."

He nodded and backed aggressively out of the visitor's spot while I buckled my seatbelt and willed my heartbeat to slow. I should just show him the file, I told myself. Ask him about it. But something stopped me. Call it intuition, maybe, but I didn't think he'd appreciate me snooping in his desk, even if I had stumbled across it innocently enough in pursuit of an empty file folder.

"Hey, I came across Marissa Gentry's file in your desk while I was looking for an empty file folder," I said, watching him out of the corner of my eye as I tested the waters. "Wasn't she your last consultant?"

"Yeah."

I gave him a beat to say more, but he didn't. "So . . . why do you have a copy of her file in your desk?"

Silence. His head was turned away as he watched for a spot to pull out into traffic, so I couldn't see his face. The quiet click of the turn signal was the only noise in the car. Tick tick tick.

"Mike?"

"It's just—it's complicated. Her death never sat right with me."

"Sure, I get it. She was your partner."

"Yeah." The car lurched forward as he punched the gas and pulled out of the driveway, accelerating swiftly down the road but settling right on top of the posted limit.

"So, you think maybe it wasn't suicide?"

His fingers tightened on the wheel. "I really don't want to talk about it. Let's just focus on the case, okay?"

"Okay." I let it go. But I still wanted answers. I wrapped an arm around my midsection, feeling the stiff paper folder beneath my coat. Maybe, just maybe, I'd find some in there.

CHAPTER 27

I pulled my coat closed tighter as I trudged across the frozen ground, following Mike and the beam of his bobbing flashlight. Our review of the details of the case hadn't led to any sudden revelations, so here we were, trespassing on a dead man's property after dark to revisit the crime scene, hoping there was something we—and the crime scene techs—had missed the first time around.

Yeah, we were grasping at straws a bit. But sometimes the truth really is staring you in the face the whole time. It's just not particularly often that it works out that way.

It had snowed earlier in the day, but the clouds had cleared out by sunset, and now the sky overhead was starry, with the waning crescent moon hanging low on the horizon. All was quiet and still. We weren't sure if the housekeeper or groundskeeper were still coming around. I imagined they weren't getting paid, so my bet was no. But to be sure we didn't encounter them, we'd decided to wait until after we knew they'd be gone for the day for our little trek into the wilderness, even though we had no plans to go anywhere near the house itself. Neither of us wanted to be caught on camera, even if we weren't really doing anything wrong.

Okay, trespassing is technically wrong, and we didn't even have Mike's badge to lean on if we were caught. Getting caught was pretty much the furthest thing from my mind as I trudged through the crisp night air, though. I was mostly thinking about coyotes and snakes, convinced that every hint of movement at the edge of the flashlight's beam was a predator lurking in the darkness. Hadn't the groundskeeper said something about checking coyote traps? I didn't want to become the next meal for a hungry pack.

It was enough to almost make me wish I had a gun.

It was more than enough to make me wish Mike had one.

I quickened my steps, following so close behind Mike that he could probably feel my breath on the back of his neck. "Maybe we should come back in the morning. It'd be better to check the sweat lodge out in the daylight anyway, wouldn't it?"

"You afraid of the dark, Davenport?" He chuckled.

"No, of course not. Just things that see better in the dark than I do. Which is—" I stumbled over a rock and bumped into Mike's broad back. "—pretty much everything that's out in the wilderness after dark."

"Trust me, anything out here is more afraid of us than we are of them. Besides, we're almost there. See?" He lifted the flashlight, and its beam illuminated the side of the sweat lodge some twenty feet away.

We crossed the remaining distance without incident, and Mike lifted the hide flap that served as a door, holding it for me as I ducked inside. I hadn't realized how much ambient light the stars and moon had provided until it was gone. Inside the dome was utter darkness until Mike followed me in with his flashlight. I pulled my phone out of my pocket and turned on its flashlight function, figuring it'd be more useful in an enclosed space than it would've been outside. It was. I panned the light over the ground, which was bare around the edges of the dome and fire pit but covered in woven rugs and animal skins in a wide ring around the fire.

I started around the edges, looking for footprints in the dirt we might've missed. Mike shined his flashlight around the walls and up to the top of the dome, then down onto the fire pit.

"The stay-lit charms kept the embers going long after they should've burned out," he murmured aloud.

"And the victim had enough peyote in his stomach to smell sounds and hear colors," I added. "And it may have increased his body temperature and sweating on top of the effects of the heat and steam."

We lapsed into a companionable silence, walking the grid carefully. I squatted to examine what looked like an impression in the dirt, turning my phone so the light hit at an angle rather than directly on it.

"Hey, come over here. Does this look like a footprint to you?"

Mike joined me and dropped to one knee, bending over to study the ground. "I see what you mean. That looks like toes, there. A partial bare footprint. Good job, Emily."

His words warmed me, and I held the light steady while he took a picture with his phone. "I wasn't paying a lot of attention to Noah Chavez's feet, but if that's an adult male footprint, I'll eat my shirt." I held up my hand to it, careful not to touch the ground. "It has to be a small woman's foot, or a child's."

"Could've been the girlfriend or one of his clients.

According to the housekeeper, the sweat lodge was a regular feature of his wellness retreats. Let's keep looking."

We spent the next forty minutes going over the lodge from top to bottom but found nothing else. The footprint could have been significant, or it could have been nothing at all. We had no way of knowing, really, not without combing through the victim's client roster and inspecting their feet. Which wouldn't have been easily accomplished even before the case had been marked closed, given that they were spread all over the country—and, in some cases, the world.

"This was a waste of time," I grumbled as I flung open the door flap and ducked to step out in to the night air—and locked eyes with a rather large coyote standing outside. The creature's eyes glinted in the darkness, reflecting the light of my phone until I slapped it against my body with a squeak and backtracked, letting the flap fall back down again.

"What is it?" Mike asked, stepping around me to reach for the flap.

I grabbed his wrist. "Coyote."

"Remember what I said about them being more afraid of us?"

"It didn't look afraid. I think we should just stay in here until it leaves."

"Don't be ridiculous." He pushed the flap back and stepped outside. Against my better judgment, I followed, crowding against Mike's back and peeking around him. The coyote stood right where it had a moment ago, watching us.

"Shoo." Mike waved both arms. The coyote held its ground and cocked its head to one side.

I cleared my throat. "We, uh, mean you no harm little guy. Or, uh, girl. We were just leaving." I tugged on Mike's arm, trying to draw him in the direction of the car. Mike walked with me, but we both kept our eyes on the coyote, which after a few steps began trotting along with us. Its jaw hung open, displaying a row of viciously sharp teeth but also a lolling tongue.

"I don't know much about coyotes," Mike said. "But I don't think they're supposed to do that."

"It's probably just distracting us while the rest of its pack surrounds us," I murmured. No idea why I felt the need to whisper, but I did. "We need to make like a roadrunner and zoom."

"Unless you can run like a roadrunner, I don't think that's a good idea. Coyotes like a good chase."

"Not. Helpful."

The coyote trotted closer, no longer keeping pace but closing the gap rather quickly. My feet froze to the ground, and this time it was Mike who bumped into me. I clung to his arm and managed to remain on my feet. The coyote yipped and skittered away, then flopped on its side and rolled on its back, mouth yawning, chuffing in what could only be described as canine laughter. I swear by all that's holy, the damn thing was mocking me.

Emboldened, I stepped out from behind Mike and shook a finger at it. "Get out of here, you mangy mutt, before I make mittens out of you!"

It stopped abruptly and rolled back onto its feet, posture suddenly tense. Its reflective eyes were intense, focused, and glinted red in the darkness. I fought the urge to hide behind Mike again. There was a curious sort of intelligence behind those eyes, and if I'd had any lingering misgivings about this being a normal everyday coyote, they were swiftly forgotten. In fact . . .

My mouth went dry, but I managed to croak, "It's a witch."

"What?" Mike looked between the coyote and me and back again.

The coyote appeared as startled as my partner. It took a step back, its eyes locked on me. Its lips twitched, showing a glint of teeth.

"You are, aren't you?" I pressed. "You have magic in you. I can sense it."

The coyote skittered back a few more steps, weaving to the left, then turned and ran off into the darkness.

I stared into the darkness after it, utter confusion assailing me.

"That was a witch?"

"Yes? No? I don't know. It had magic. That, I know for sure. I didn't notice it at first. I think because it was so out of place that my mind didn't really process it."

"You seem surprised."

"Yeah, because shapeshifting magic isn't real."

"We need to talk about this some more, but I think we should do it in the safety of the car." He nudged me in that direction with a hand at the small of my back.

I went with him, my thoughts spinning like a tilt-a-whirl. My phone was in my hand, calling Dan before I was even consciously aware of it. I jumped a little when he answered.

"Hey sis, what's up?"

"Are you home?"

"Yeah."

"Are you alone?"

"Uh, no."

"You've got forty-five minutes to get rid of her. Mike and I are on our way, and we need to talk."

CHAPTER 28

I t turned out Dan wasn't aware of any shapeshifting magic either. There was only one person I could think of who might be, and that's how I ended up making the freezing trek through the bitter cold at dawn the next morning with John Warren hiking quietly alongside me.

He hadn't asked for details when I'd called to set up a meeting with Kassidy, the mysterious recluse who lived on the Pojoaque Pueblo, nor did he ask when I met him at his house to strike out for Kassidy's cabin. In fact, he'd barely said a word to me, but it felt more like a companionable silence than a snub. He was a quiet, thoughtful man, the sort who liked to think things through before he spoke or acted. I appreciated that about him, but I still felt like I had some air to clear.

"So, about the other day . . . I think my brother may have given you the false impression that the fire in the oven was my fault. Don't get me wrong, I'm no Martha Stewart in the kitchen, but I'm not *that* bad."

He smiled, his eyes lifting up the slope of the nearby mountains. "Noted."

"I didn't even know you worked in Santa Fe. I guess I assumed you worked on the Pueblo."

"I do, but our fire department is staffed by volunteers, and the calls aren't frequent. Thank God."

My eyes slid over to him, curiosity stirring in my gut. "Ahh. So, you work full-time in Santa Fe?"

"Not full-time, no. Mostly in the winter, when I'm close to home."

"Oh, so what do you do during the rest of the year?"

He flashed me a small smile. "You're very curious."

"Sorry. Fault of mine, I guess."

"No need to apologize. I travel a lot in the warmer months, fighting wildfires."

"Oh, wow. I remember the big Las Conchas fire. Were you at that one?" Hey, he basically gave me a green light to ask questions.

"Yeah." He was quiet a moment, eyes downcast. "That was a rough one. Over a hundred and fifty thousand acres burned."

"I was in Albuquerque at the time, and I remember we could see the smoke from there. It was a big deal. We were something like fifty miles away as the crow flies."

He nodded. "I go out of state, too. Primarily New Mexico, Arizona, and California. I've had some specialized training. My skillset is often in demand, so I go where I'm needed."

"Oh? What kind of skillset is that?"

He chuckled. "I think it's my turn to ask a few questions."

Gotta admit, I walked right into that one. "Oh. Okay, sure. What do you want to know?"

"You bought my painting."

Noticed that, did he? The painting in question was literally the only one I owned, so I couldn't even claim not to know which one he was talking about. "That's not a question."

"True." A quiet laugh rumbled from his chest. "Why did you buy my painting?"

"It spoke to me. I saw it at the cafe and I just . . . It drew me in. Shortly after I saw it, I realized how little effort I'd put into making my apartment a home, so I decided to buy it. I didn't even know it was yours until I bought it—well, or until now. I mean, I figured it wasn't impossible there could be more than one John Warren in the area."

He nodded, expression thoughtful. Seconds passed, enough that I wondered if I was clear to ask another question—or if I really wanted to, knowing tit for tat was involved. Then he said, "Would you like to see my studio sometime?"

"That's probably not a good idea."

"Why not?"

"So many reasons . . ."

He nudged me with his elbow. "It's just art, Emily."

But it wasn't, was it? He knew things about me, things I hadn't told more than a handful of people about. He'd helped me experiment with my powers, and the connection we'd shared when his magic flowed through me had felt . . . intimate. He was an attractive man, I couldn't deny that. But he was a witch. I didn't date witches as a rule. And then there was Barry. I still didn't know what to do about Barry. "I can't afford to make any big purchases right now."

"I wasn't expecting you to. But if you don't want to come, that's okay." He fell silent once more, and I was content to keep walking in silence as long as he was. That turned out to be twenty feet or so. "Kassidy has been asking after you. Wondering if I've heard from you, if you'll be coming to see her again. Why haven't you come around?"

At least this one was a little easier to answer. "I already owe Kassidy one favor, and she's just enigmatic enough that I'm kind of worried about what might happen when that favor comes due."

"Ahh." He nodded slowly. "Yes, Kassidy's information is rarely free. And yet, here you are."

"A man's life is at stake."

"Every day is a gift, and each breath a risk."

"Whether you take that breath on the inside or outside of a cell matters to most people."

The log cabin had been growing steadily closer as we walked, and now I could smell the woodsmoke lifting from the chimney and see the wind chimes hanging from the porch. There was no wind to speak of this morning, but every now and then a faint chime sounded, a whisper of sound on an otherwise quiet morning. John's fingers curled gently around my upper arm, drawing me to a stop. I looked up at him curiously. His brown eyes were serious as he regarded me.

"You're right to be cautious, Emily. Trust your instincts."

"Who—or what—is she?"

"I don't know. She's been here longer than I've been alive, and to look at her . . . She hasn't aged a day. Some call her Asdzą́ą́ Nádleehé, the Changing Woman, and bring her offerings of food, clothing, and household goods. I doubt she truly is the spirit herself, but I don't have a better explanation for her timeless presence either."

I was familiar with the Asdzą́ą́ Nádleehé myth from my research on the Navajo. The Changing Woman was believed to be the creator of the Navajo and said to age with the seasons, becoming young again each spring. But she was also supposed to bring fortune and long life to those who honored her, so I understood why the locals might hedge their bets when confronted with some sort of inherited custodianship of a woman who didn't seem to age the way normal people did. I hadn't sensed magic in Kassidy when I visited before, but that didn't mean she couldn't be using charms to appear younger than she was.

"So there's no record of when she first came to the Pueblo?"

He shook his head. "My people don't keep records the way yours do. But tales of her presence span generations. I remember my great-grandfather telling stories about meeting her when he was young. She's a bit of an enigma, rarely sighted or spoken to, but all know she is there. It's a comfort to many."

"You seem to interact with her regularly enough," I said as we walked up the concrete steps outside. "How did that happen?"

"I believe that is a question for another time. We're here." He smiled at me even as he raised his hand to knock.

"Kassidy isn't cornering the market on enigmas," I mumbled.

"Come in, John!" Kassidy called from inside.

He opened the door and motioned for me to go inside. I stomped as much of the muck from my boots as I could on the front stoop before stepping inside. Warmth enveloped me immediately, and my hands lifted automatically to unbutton my coat and slip it from my shoulders. I glanced around the room, unsettled as I was before by how much bigger the inside of the cabin was than the outside suggested. I'd expected to find Kassidy at her massive computer desk, but the monitors were black and the chair empty.

"Good morning," Kassidy said in her Irish lilt, and my eyes homed in on her in the kitchen. She'd pulled her red hair back from her face with a wide shell-patterned head-band, displaying both her healthy pink cheek and the reddened mass of scar tissue on the other side. I briefly wondered why, if she were using a charm to make herself look younger, she hadn't covered her scars. The smell of breakfast finally hit home, tickling my nostrils and making my empty stomach rumble. I'd run out of the house that morning without more than a cup of coffee in my belly.

"Sorry to interrupt your breakfast."

"Oh, you're not interrupting at all, dearie. In fact, I made more than enough for all three of us, if yer hungry."

John took my coat and hung both of our coats up on the hooks beside the door, then headed into the kitchen, unbuttoning the cuffs of his flannel shirt and rolling the sleeves up as he went. I hesitated until he glanced my way and gave a subtle nod of his head as if to reassure me the offer of breakfast had no strings attached.

"Sure, that sounds great. Is there anything I can help with?"

"Plates and silver are on the table. Be a dear and set it for us."

I headed over to the table to do just that, idly watching John and Kassidy move around in the kitchen. They worked with the ease of people who had done such things many times before, and I wondered what exactly John's relationship to Kassidy was. They didn't behave like lovers, but definitely had the comfortable familiarity of long-time friends. A few short minutes later, we gathered around the table for the repast, which consisted of some sort of potato, meat, and vegetable hash, fresh from the oven biscuits, and scrambled eggs.

"I've never seen a potato hash quite like this," I said as I spooned a healthy portion on my plate. I have almost never met a potato I didn't like.

"Oh, it's quite simple to make but so good on a cold morning," Kassidy said. "All you need are boiled potatoes, meat, and thinly sliced cabbage. Crisp it all up with some salt and pepper, a dash of paprika, and you've got a proper bubble 'n squeak."

I tasted a bite, and the simple but homely dish danced on my tastebuds. "Mmmm. Wait, did you say bubble and squeak?"

"Aye. At least, that's what they called it in my house growing up."

"Bubble for the boiled potatoes, and squeak for the ham —in this case. But she usually makes it with some sort of pork, be it ham, sausage, or bacon." John plucked the ketchup from the center of the table and set it in my reach. "It's even better with ketchup."

Kassidy huffed. "John thinks just about everything is better with ketchup."

"A lot of things are, especially when there's no chile available."

Chuckling, I squirted a little ketchup on half my pile of potatoes. "I'll try it both ways."

"Ever the peacekeeper." Kassidy's blue eyes sparkled as she plucked a biscuit from the basket in the center of the table. "But you know we won't be satisfied until you tell us which you like best."

Laughing, John and I both reached for a biscuit and our fingers brushed in the basket. I flicked a glance in his direction, but he merely smiled and moved his hand to tilt the basket toward me in invitation, waiting until after I'd snagged one to take another for himself.

We all dug in, and I was content to eat quietly while John and Kassidy bantered back and forth about the weather, the price of gas, and any number of other mundane topics. But about halfway through the meal, Kassidy's blue eyes settled on me, and I couldn't help but feel the weight of her gaze.

"So, what brings you to my door this morning, Emily? I don't think it was my cooking, though you're always welcome at my table."

"Mmm. Now that I know you can cook like this, you might see more of me," I joked. Because, really, I wasn't any less wary of the woman. But I could make light of it with the best of them. "But you're right, that wasn't what drew me here this morning. I'm working on a case—I'm a consultant with the Santa Fe PD. Did I mention that?"

"No, you did not." She rested her elbows on the table, holding her dainty teacup with both hands as she studied me over the rim. Her eyes bored into me, and I fought the urge to shift uncomfortably in my seat.

"I've kept up my end of the bargain and will continue to do so." I mentioned how Kassidy's information came at a price. Part of that price was telling no one where the information she gave me came from.

"Mmm. Now, what is it about this case you think I can help with?"

"Well, it's less about the case and more about something weird I encountered the other night near the crime scene."

"Weird things are my specialty. You have my attention." There was still food on her plate, but she seemed content with her tea for the moment, her full focus on me.

"Well, there was this coyote. Only I don't think it was a coyote. It had magic."

John coughed, interrupting the conversation. He took a

quick sip of coffee and coughed a few more times, thumping his chest with his fist. "Sorry. Wrong pipe."

"What do you mean it had magic? You saw it performing spells?" Kassidy picked up right where we left off.

My eyes lingered on John for a moment before I answered. "No, it wasn't actively using magic, but it had magic. I sensed it the way I can sense witches."

"You can sense witches? Interesting," Kassidy mused over another sip of tea, then set her teacup aside.

"Isn't that a normal conduit power? You're the one who told me what I am."

"What I have on Conduits could barely fill a hand-written page. It was enough to identify your gift, not an instruction manual." She picked up her fork, gesturing with it. "Shapeshifters went extinct decades ago, but that was more of a genetic mutation than anything else. I'm not sure if they would have, oh, how would you say it . . . appeared on your sonar?"

"Radar," John supplied helpfully.

Kassidy pointed her fork at him. "Yes. Thank you, John. Those poor afflicted creatures couldn't sling a spell to save their lives. Their magic was wilder, more primal than that."

My mind stretched, grappling with what Kassidy had already revealed. I wasn't sure what was more fantastical, that werecreatures had existed or that they'd somehow gone extinct before I was born. "But they did have magic," I said, seeking clarification once I wrapped my mind around the subject. Could I have encountered a supposedly extinct werecoyote? A mind wondered.

"Yes. They were an unfortunate side effect of witch inbreeding back when bloodlines mattered more than they do now."

I thought about my own family and their vaunted ancestry. "They still do, in some circles."

"True, but society is a bit more enlightened now than they once were about the effects of inbreeding." She waved a hand. "Anyway, I doubt it was a shapeshifter you encountered."

"Okay, what about a witch? Is shapeshifting magic a thing? I asked my brother, who had a much more thorough magic education than I did, and he'd never heard of it."

"I'm not sure. I'd need to consult the Archive. The human mind is so . . . limited." She grimaced, then shook her head and refocused. "Did the coyote seem normal, other than the magic you sensed?"

"No. I mean, I haven't encountered many coyotes, but this one seemed intelligent."

"Intelligent how?"

"I, uh, may have threatened it, and that seemed to make it angry."

"Perhaps it was responding to your tone of voice?" John suggested quietly.

"And then when I realized it had magic, I asked it if it was a witch and it seemed . . . startled. Scared, even. And it ran away."

"Fascinating," Kassidy said. "What was its behavior like before that?"

"Um. It seemed . . . I don't know. I was afraid of it, but it maybe seemed more curious than aggressive. Playful, even. I think—I think it was making fun of me at one point. That's when I lost my temper."

"Hmm." Kassidy's eyes drifted to John. "Are you thinking what I'm thinking?"

"Probably not." He leaned back in his chair. He'd been sitting there holding his empty fork since the choking incident. I was the only one who'd managed to finish breakfast around the conversation—there isn't much that'll stop me when you put a plate of good food in front of me. You'd think I was starved as a child or something.

"What are you thinking?" I asked.

"Well, it sounds kind of like Coyote."

"Ahh," John said.

My eyes darted back and forth between them. "It was a coyote. I told you that."

"She means *the* Coyote," John said. "A trickster spirit who appears in the stories of countless Native cultures."

"Ohhh. Yeah, I'm familiar with some of those. But I don't think Coyote was ever in the business of murdering people. Was he?"

"No," John replied, his expression somber. "But when he appears it is often as a warning. My people have a saying. 'If Coyote crosses your path, turn back and do not continue your journey.'"

"I can't just abandon a murder investigation because a trickster spirit put in an appearance. If that's even what it was. A Pueblo man has been charged with the murder, and I'm not convinced he really did it. If I don't figure out who did, he could end up in prison for the rest of his life."

"Which Pueblo?" John asked.

I pushed back my chair and stood, frustration getting the better of me. "Does it matter? Are you more likely to help me if he's Pojoaque than not?"

John's brows pinched together, thin lines appearing in his forehead. "Relax, Emily. I was just curious."

Kassidy shifted her eyes between us, then stood. "I think I'll do a bit of that research now." She took her tea with her as she headed across the room to her desk.

"Thank you, Kassidy. Truly. I really appreciate it," I

called after her, feeling like an ass. I'd come here with my figurative hat in my hand, needing their help, and then I'd basically called John a racist for no reason. Frustrated with myself as much as the situation, I picked up my empty plate and piled my used silverware on top of it. The least I could do was help clear the table.

I avoided John's eyes as I passed him, but I heard the scrape of his chair legs on the floor as he pushed back from the table and his quiet footfalls following me into the kitchen. While I rinsed my plate in the sink, he scraped the remains of his breakfast into the trash and reached around me to put his dish and fork in the sink. His chest brushed my shoulder as he did, the warmth of him at my back for a few seconds before he withdrew to return to the table. I rinsed his dish too, then turned off the water and leaned against the sink.

"I'm sorry," I said when he returned with the leftovers in their glazed pottery serving bowls. "I shouldn't have jumped to conclusions."

He set the bowls on the counter and opened one of the cupboards to fetch containers for leftovers. "It's okay. It wasn't an outrageous conclusion to jump to. But, for the record, it really doesn't matter to me which Pueblo he's from. I'm not even sure why I asked. If someone from my Pueblo had been arrested for murder, I would've heard about it. News travels quickly here."

I walked over to stand beside him, plucking the smaller bowl from the counter and scraping leftover eggs into the smaller plastic container. "I'm really in a bind, here. My normal partner is on admin leave, and the guy who took over the case—he just wants to close it as quickly as possi-ble. Maybe this coyote thing has nothing to do with the case at all, but I can't just write it off as a coincidence. We found a bare footprint at the scene that doesn't match the victim or the supposed murderer, and I can't write that off either. I can't shake the thought that the two are connected. That the coyote is a witch using some kind of shapeshifting magic."

His hands stilled briefly, then continued the act of scraping the leftover bubble and squeak into a larger plastic bowl. "There's something to be said for following your instincts. Just . . . be careful, Emily."

"Follow my instincts. Okay. On that note, is there something you're not telling me?"

He hesitated a moment, then nudged the plastic bowl toward me. "Can you put the lids on these?" Then he headed back to the table for another load.

Yeah. There was definitely something he wasn't telling me. But he was right about one thing. I needed to be careful.

CHAPTER 29

By the time Kassidy surfaced from her research, John and I had cleared the table, tucked the leftovers in the fridge, done the dishes, and spent an uncomfortable twenty minutes sitting on the couch in silence. I wanted to press him about whatever it was he was holding back, but something made me hesitate. Maybe it was that I didn't really know him all that well, or that neither of us owed the other any particular favors. Okay, well, I probably owed him for introducing me to Kassidy, letting me use him as a guinea pig when testing out my powers, and bringing me to see her again this morning. I'd have to find some way of making things square—maybe even nudge the karmic balance in my favor a bit—before I could start making demands.

Kassidy's printer hummed to life a moment before she spun her chair to face us, smiling.

"I hope that smile is good news," I said.

"It could be. But before we dive into that, let's discuss the matter of payment."

"I'm listening."

"You've learned more about your conduit powers since

we last spoke, yes? I'd like to hear what you've found." I opened my mouth to reply, but she quickly held up a finger and continued. "And whatever you learn in the future."

I waited to make sure she was finished this time. "An exchange of information, eh? Okay, that seems reasonable. But my name stays out of your archive, and in the interest of transparency, there's not much you don't already know so far."

"I swear it." She held up her hand solemnly.

"Okay, let's see what you've got."

Kassidy passed me a handful of printed pages, still warm from the printer. I flipped through them. The first few pages were about Coyote legends, myths, and supposed sightings. Next came a few pages containing an uncomfortable amount of detail about shapeshifters, the mutated witch kind. Included was what closer reading would reveal to be a rather stomach-turning account of a mid-17th century autopsy on a still-living one. Finally, there were a few pages on a topic we hadn't discussed at all.

"Skinwalkers?" I said. "I thought they were just boogey-men. Isn't there a ranch in Utah or something famous for supposed sightings?"

"There are almost as many stories about skinwalkers as there are about Coyote," Kassidy said. "I don't know why I didn't think of them sooner, but you had me thinking about shape-changing spells. This is much more likely—at least around here at this nexus of Pueblos."

John stood abruptly, his features pinched. "I just remembered, I have to, uh, make a call. I'll be outside if you need me."

He was across the room and out the door before I'd fully processed what'd just happened. "Do I even want to know what that was about?"

Kassidy's lips curved in a knowing smile. "Poor John. His people are a bit touchy about this subject. They believe to speak of a skinwalker is to invite its attention."

"Ahh, I see. Well, I've got no problem with it. Carry on."

"Skinwalkers are vengeful witches who use their gifts for dark purposes, and they often take the form of animals, in particular coyotes. While Coyote is known for being a trick-ster, he is playful—not malevolent. A skinwalker delights in scaring people and harvesting their fear to fuel their dark magics."

"That's . . . not really how magic works. How do we know this is real and not just folklore? I can't go chasing some fairy tale." I was momentarily grateful John had excused himself. Had he been present, I wouldn't have let myself be nearly so blunt.

Kassidy shrugged her slender shoulders. "I'd say it's part truth and part blarney. These things usually are. I mean, there's a story behind every fairy tale. They just get more fantastical with every retelling."

"So, a Native witch with shape-changing magic that even your archive knows nothing about."

"Indeed. If you do manage to capture the pitiful thing, I'd be most interested in studying it."

"How in the hell would I go about capturing it?"

"Well, you do have that on your side." She pointed toward the door.

I squinted. "John?"

"No, dearie. Your coat. It's warded for protection against magic, isn't it?"

I couldn't figure out for the life of me how she knew that. I studied her for a long moment in silence.

She chuckled and waved a hand. "Don't bother asking, dearie. We're not *that* close."

It was on the tip of my tongue to argue that she knew what *I* was, but considering I'd learned that from her, it wasn't a particularly valuable bargaining chip. "Yes, I do have that. And I have my abilities. I can stop the witch from casting spells if I can touch them. But how am I supposed to draw them out?"

"That, I don't know. The last time you saw the coyote was near the crime scene. Perhaps another visit is in order."

"Perhaps. But that's not much of a plan."

Kassidy smiled. "Plans aren't my business. Information is. If you need more, you know where to find me. Don't worry about going through John. I'm always here. Well, unless you'd like the excuse to call him." She winked.

"So, you two aren't an item?"

Soft laughter filled the room as Kassidy tipped back in her chair. "Oh my goodness, no. I mean, he's a dear friend, and he's certainly attractive. But there's nothing between us but mutual respect. Have at him, but"—her cheerful expression sobered—"have a care. He *is* dear to me, understand? And I protect those I hold dear."

I had no idea what that protection might entail, but I had more than enough reason to be wary of Kassidy. "Noted. Well, if that's all, I'll get out of your hair."

Her expression brightened again, and she nodded. "Yes, yes, crime to be fought and all. You take care of yourself, and don't be a stranger." She turned back around to face her desk and went back to tapping on the keyboard and clicking the mouse.

Knowing a dismissal when I saw one, I retreated with my fistful of lore and collected my coat, donning it before I stepped outside. When the door opened, John turned from where he stood some ten paces or so from the porch to regard me.

I trotted down the steps to join him. "All done."

He nodded mutely, and we started walking back the way we'd come, following our footsteps in the snow. "Kassidy told me your people don't like to talk about, uh, you know."

He nodded again.

"I respect that, but I could really use some help sorting the truth from the myth. If this really is a—you know—I'm going to have to find them, somehow."

He sighed. "I'm sorry, Emily. Some things simply aren't spoken of." His footsteps slowed, and he reached for my arm, drawing me to a halt. "But if it is what you think it is, you won't have to worry about finding them. They will find you. Once you get their attention, they just can't help themselves. They'll be drawn like a moth to a flame, and you—" He lifted a hand like he was about to touch my face but laid it gently on my shoulder at the last moment. "You shine brightly."

There was such earnestness in his eyes that I wasn't sure if he was flirting or being sincere. I wasn't sure how to respond either way, so I just said, "Thanks. I think. But you're really going to let me go into this without knowing what I'm really up against?"

His dark eyes turned sad, and his hand dropped from my shoulder. "Honestly, I'd recommend you stay as far away from it as possible. We should get moving. I have to report for duty in an hour."

We walked the rest of the way in silence. I was disappointed, maybe even a little angry with him for holding out, but at the same time, I mostly understood his internal conflict. He'd been supportive enough in the past that I believed he truly wanted to help, but his beliefs and the connection to his culture ran deep, which was getting more and more unusual in the modern era. Children on the

Pueblos grew up steeped in tradition, but then they started going to school and mixing with non-Native children. They walked the cultural divide and learned about traditions and cultures beyond their own. By their teenage years, they identified as American teens as much as Pueblo teens. After high school, some went on to college—an act which further distanced them from their heritage—but for the rest, well, there were few options for work on the Pueblo, forcing most to look elsewhere. And, unless they found work close enough to commute, that meant moving off the Pueblo and into the general population.

But John still lived on the Pueblo. He clearly maintained a strong connection to the beliefs and traditions of his people, and no amount of my asking was liable to change his mind.

Fortunately, he wasn't my only port in this storm.

CHAPTER 30

"Ms. Davenport. I'm surprised to see you again so soon." Officer Tsosie met me once more in the lobby of the Tesuque Pueblo Police Station. I'd called ahead to make sure he'd be there. It was too long a trip to make without knowing for sure.

"I'm a little surprised to be back so soon, but is there somewhere we can speak privately?"

He nodded and led me into the back, down a short hallway, and into a small conference room. As I settled into a mesh swivel chair, he asked, "Do you want some coffee or a bottle of water?"

"No thanks, I'm okay."

"Alright." He pulled out a chair adjacent to mine and sat, swiveling to face me. "Is this about Noah?"

"Yes. I've been looking into the case some more and I have a lead, but . . . well, I'm just going to say it. I think Mr. Reed may have been killed by a skinwalker."

The older man flinched. He didn't laugh, didn't brush it off, didn't so much as shake his head. "What makes you think that?"

"I found a partial footprint at the crime scene that doesn't match anyone we know had been there, and I had a very strange encounter with a coyote while I was there." I went on to explain the incident in detail, along with what little I knew about skinwalkers, while he listened attentively. The more I talked about it, the more fidgety he got, but he didn't bolt from the room or try to stop me. "So, that brings me to why I'm here. I know that my information isn't complete, and I know your people consider discussing the subject to be taboo, and I'm an outsider on top of that, but I'm hoping you're interested enough in keeping Noah out of prison to make an exception."

He sighed and pushed back his chair. "I think I'm going to need a cup of coffee for this. You change your mind?"

"Does that mean you'll help?"

"Yeah, it does."

I smiled, relief coursing through me. "Then I'll take you up on that water."

Once Tsosie returned with beverages, he wasted no time in getting back to business. "There are a lot of things my people won't speak openly about with outsiders, but skinwalkers . . . It's not about keeping our traditions private. We don't even speak of them amongst ourselves. It's about not drawing the attention of the skinwalker. Anyone asking about them might be one, on the hunt for his next victim. I'm curious, though, where you got your information. It's too accurate to have come off the internet."

"I'm not at liberty to discuss my source. But I'm glad to know the information I have is accurate."

He nodded thoughtfully. "It's not inaccurate, but it's also incomplete. Skinwalkers are almost always men, and they don't just take the appearance of any animal. They prefer predators. Coyotes, wolves, mountain lions, anything that hunts, and especially ones that hunt at night. They stalk their prey in darkness and harvest their fear to fuel their profane magics. It is said they can possess the bodies of their victims if one locks eyes with them, making them say things—do things—they wouldn't normally. But skin-walkers are not irrational creatures and do not kill as a matter of course. There is always a motive behind their violent actions, just like normal people. Revenge, anger, something."

"Do you think Mr. Reed's co-opting of Native American culture might piss one off enough to want to kill? I was told that skinwalkers hate impostors, and he certainly seemed to be that. On multiple levels."

"Perhaps. Skinwalkers . . . they have a dark wind blowing through them, and just like any other wind, it can blow from any direction." His chair creaked as he shifted in it, leaning back some. "It's funny you should come here asking about skinwalkers Ms. Davenport—"

"Please, at this point I think you should call me Emily."

"Okay, but only if you call me Billy." He waited for me to nod, then continued. "Anyway, like I was saying, it's funny you should ask about skinwalkers because I'm pretty sure there's one active in the area."

"Oh?"

"It wasn't my first thought when the white man turned up dead, but there's been an uptick in mischief around the Pueblo. People complaining about coyote sightings and tres-passers at night scaring them or their animals, knocking or scratching on their windows or walking on their roofs."

"That seems to fit the bill. How long has it been going on?" I picked at the label around my water bottle while I listened.

"A few months, at least. It's hard to pinpoint exactly when, because it's not like people are filing in to make reports. We've had a few official complaints, but it's mostly just word of mouth. Anyway, there aren't many of us left on the Pueblo, and even fewer witches. Most of them have been around the Pueblo their whole lives, and I know them well. I like to think I'd notice if one of them went evil. Then there's Howard Johnson."

I blinked. "Like—"

"The hotel chain, yes." He chuckled. "People name their kids the strangest things sometimes."

"Okay. What about Howard Johnson?"

"Howard was always a smart kid with a bright future. He left the Pueblo for college and never came back—until about three months ago. According to the rumor mill, he was fired from some big law firm in Albuquerque for mucking up a big case."

Something about that tickled the back of my mind, but I couldn't quite figure out what. "Any connection to the vic?"

"Not that I know of. But when it comes to skinwalker suspects, he's at the top of my list. There's something off about him. He's not the same kid he used to be."

"Time changes people, and he's probably not happy about being back home with his tail between his legs."

"I hope you're right. But our troubles here started not long after he came back. It's stuck in my mind."

"I don't suppose he's a member of the NAC?"

Tsosie tilted his head. "What makes you ask?"

"Access to peyote. Potentially."

"Ahh. I believe he is. Or, at least his family is."

I nodded. The pieces fit, but there was still something missing. Oh yeah, actual evidence linking him to the crime.

"It sounds like we—or maybe just you—need to go ask this guy some questions, find out where he was the night Nate Alan Reed died."

He dropped his eyes and turned an alarming shade of white for his complexion, staring into his coffee mug for a long moment. "If he is what we suspect he is, it's going to take more than just me to bring him in."

"Oh, right. Powerful spellcaster possessing dark magic. Any strong witches on the Pueblo you think might help?"

"One comes to mind, but Noah's not gonna like it." He took a sip of his coffee and grimaced, and I doubted it was from the dark roast.

"Why's that?"

"Because the only man I know who's confronted a skin-walker and lived to tell the tale is Ray Chavez, our medicine man."

"Ahh. Noah's grandfather, right? But he's not in a position to complain right now. Either way, I think this is one of those ask forgiveness rather than permission scenarios."

"Agreed."

He unholstered his phone from the clip on his belt and tapped the screen a few times before putting it to his ear. I looked away to give him some semblance of privacy, though if he'd wanted it he would've stepped out of the room for it.

"This is Billy. Is Ray around? . . . Uh-huh . . . No, no message. I thought I'd come by, actually. There's something I'd like to speak with him about." He shifted in his seat, and I glanced at him to find him looking up at the ceiling as if beseeching the heavens. "It's official business, I'm not at liberty to discuss it." His eyes dropped, and I looked quickly away once more. There was a longer pause this time before he said, "That'll work, thanks." He hung up and shifted his attention back to me. "He's unavailable, but his grand-daughter—Maria, you sort of met her before at Noah's house—said I could come by in a few hours."

I nodded, remembering the young woman. "Can I come along, or . . . ?"

He thought about it for a moment, then nodded. "Sure. But I've got some stuff to take care of in the meantime. Why don't you come back around noon, and we can ride over together."

"Sounds good." I stood, taking my water bottle with me, and extended my right hand. "Thanks, Billy. I really appreciate your help."

He shook my hand. "I think you've got that backwards, but you're welcome. Be careful out there. Once you get a skinwalker's attention—"

"Yeah, I know. You become a target. I'll watch my back."

True to my word, I glanced around warily as I stepped out of the police station, but nothing struck me as out of place or sinister. My car sat in the lot where I'd left it, and while it was difficult to say if it was untouched at least nothing was visibly broken. Still, there was an itch between my shoulder blades, and I couldn't quite shake the thought that I was being watched. A caw drew my attention to a leaf-less tree on the other side of the parking lot and the silhou-ette of an inky black bird perched on a limb. A shiver ran down my spine as I stared at the bird. It couldn't be. Could it? I was too far away from the thing to discern a magical signature.

I shook myself. "It's just a bird."

Reminding myself what Billy had said about skinwalkers being largely nocturnal, I walked—briskly—to my car and climbed inside. I started the car and sat behind the wheel for a moment, rubbing my hands together. I adjusted the rearview mirror to angle it toward the tree. The bird was nowhere to be seen. Chiding myself for a fool, I returned the mirror to its normal position. But one thing was for sure: I didn't feel safe. I wished Mike were there with me. Since I wasn't capable of conjuring him, I did the next best thing. I put my phone in its dashboard cradle and called him to give him an update on what I'd learned.

"Wait, did you say Howard Johnson?" Mike asked, interrupting me mid-sentence.

"Yeah, I know. Kind of cruel of his parents, wasn't it? I knew a girl in college whose initials were KKK. I felt for her. I was one maternal grandmother away from being—"

"No, no. Hang on a sec." The sound of papers shuffling crackled from my phone's speaker. "Is he a lawyer?"

"Yeah. Er, maybe. Tsosie said something about him being fired from a law firm in Albuquerque."

"Remember the sweat lodge lawsuit? The attorney on record for the plaintiff was Howard Johnson."

My heartbeat kicked up a notch. "When was the case dismissed?"

"November third, last year."

"Tsosie said Johnson moved back to the Pueblo about three months ago. That fits the timeline."

"Sounds like we have a new suspect."

I filled him in on my upcoming meeting with Ray Chavez and arranged to meet him at my apartment in a few hours. I can't say that his deep voice coming out of the car's speakers made me feel safe, but it did soothe my ruffled feathers a bit, and I was able to get the car moving while we chatted. But Tsosie's words of warning—echoing John's— were an ever-present buzz in the back of my mind that I couldn't shake, and while I hadn't had a particular destination in mind when I left the police station, a sign caught my eye a few miles down the highway, offering just the sort of comfort I craved.

CHAPTER 31

The cowbell tied to the inner handle gave a hollow clang as the door swung shut behind me, and I hoped I didn't look as out of my element as I felt. I'd never really felt like I'd needed to own a gun before, not even when I'd first moved to Santa Fe, a single woman living alone in an unfamiliar place where she knew no one. It had all felt like an adventure, and as someone who had never lived alone, transitioning from a large household at home to dorm life at UNM, I was too excited—or foolish, some might say—to feel anything else.

A heavily tattooed man behind the counter, wearing a leather vest over a tight white T-shirt, looked up from a magazine—or maybe it was a catalog—and nodded at me. "Afternoon."

I nodded back and crossed the small storefront, breathing in the smell of gun oil and furnace coils as I approached the counter, which doubled as a display case. Beneath the thick glass sat a variety of handguns and knives, while rifles and shotguns hung on the wall behind the clerk.

Resting my hands on the edge of the counter, I leaned over to look inside.

"Looking for anything in particular?" the clerk asked, putting aside his reading material. It was indeed an outdoorsman's catalog, I confirmed with a glance before lifting my eyes to meet his. He was an older Hispanic man, his skin not so much lined as sagging. He had a faint mustache above his mouth, but was otherwise clean-shaven. I briefly wondered how he accomplished that without cutting himself, but quickly pushed the thought aside to focus on the matter at hand.

"No. I mean, I don't have a particular model in mind." My eyes were drawn to a piece similar to the one Mike carried. "Maybe that one?"

He lifted a dark brow but unlocked the case with a key hanging from a coiled stretchy bracelet around his wrist and removed the gun from the case. He fiddled with it, ejecting the magazine and showing me it was empty and the chamber clear, then pulled over a felt pad and set it down in front of me. I picked the weapon up, blinking at the heavy weight of it in my hand, the unexpected coldness of the metal against my fingers.

After watching me for a few seconds, he took the gun from my loose grip and put it back. At my questioning look, he shook his head. "That one's a little too much for you, missy."

I bristled. "Excuse me?"

Wordlessly, he moved down the counter and pulled something else from the case, going through the same magazine and chamber check as before, then setting it in front of me. It looked like a smaller version of the first one, but it was bright magenta. I gave the man behind the counter a narrow-eyed glare but picked it up anyway. It was lighter as well as smaller, though still heavier than I'd expected from looking at it. The clerk rattled off the details about it, most of which were lost on me, but I did catch the words Glock, safe action, and six-round magazine. He encouraged me to point it at a target on the wall and cautioned me not to point it anywhere else.

"Do you have something less . . . pink?"

He leaned over the counter, hands planted in a wide stance on the edge of the counter. "You ever own a gun before, missy?"

I was in over my head, and no matter how much of a chauvinist this guy was, I was smart enough to know when I needed help. "No, but I don't want some girly pink gun."

He chuckled and took the piece back and put it back in the case. "You looking for something recreational or more for self-defense?"

"Self-defense."

"Concealed or open carry?"

"Um . . ."

"You need a license for concealed carry, but you can buy a concealable firearm without a license. They tend to be smaller."

Smaller sounded better. "Okay, concealable would be good. I'd like to have the option, at least. I can worry about the license later."

Over the next ten minutes, he paraded a variety of pistols before me. To his credit, none of them were in fashion colors. I ended up selecting a Glock 26. Of all of the ones he showed me, it felt the best in my hand, wasn't too heavy, and had a larger ammo capacity.

Look, I hoped I'd never have to fire a single bullet, but if I did, I sure as hell didn't want to run out.

"How much for this one?"

"Seven hundred, plus tax and fees."

I blinked slowly and my mouth went dry.

"Pink one's cheaper," he offered.

I narrowed my eyes at him, but he just smirked.

Seven hundred dollars. That was way more than I'd expected, and given my recent underemployment, it gave me pause. I picked up the gun again and held it in my hand, thinking about the sense of vulnerability that'd driven me in here in the first place. Then I thought about what it'd been like to stare down the barrel of that shotgun two days ago and what might've happened if Mike hadn't been there to tackle me to the floor and return fire. And while it was great to have a partner to watch my back, I needed to be able to protect myself too. And with him on admin leave, well, one of us ought to have a gun, I reasoned. It was my turn to protect him.

"I'll take it."

The clerk put a form in front of me and slapped a pen down on top of it. "I've got a range out back," he mentioned while I filled out the paperwork. "For fifty bucks, I'll go over the basics with you before you leave."

"Sure." In for a penny, in for a pound. I pushed the finished form across the counter toward him and checked the clock on the wall. It'd barely been fifteen minutes since I arrived, so I still had plenty of time to kill. Oof. That was one idiom I was going to have to rethink, as a gun owner.

The clerk took the gun and my paperwork from the counter, his eyes skimming the information I'd filled out. "It should only take a minute for the background check. Ammo's over there," he said, pointing at a shelf. "You're going to want ball for the range and hollow point for carrying." He shuffled away and started entering my info into the computer.

Turning, I scanned the displays of gun accessories while he was busy. They seemed to have a little bit of everything on display. Safety goggles, special holsters, belts, earplugs, bumper stickers, T-shirts, flags . . . I'd never once considered just how many gun-related items a gun store might sell. Then again, I'd never considered going into a gun store before. Pushing away from the counter, I wandered aimlessly through the shelves, knowing I couldn't really afford to get much of anything but it wasn't like I had anything better to do. When I got to the ammo, I had another moment of sticker shock at the price of the hollow point rounds. It amounted to, essentially, a dollar a bullet. If it saved my life, it'd be worth it. But I was grateful he'd mentioned the cheaper ammo for practice. A few minutes later, he called my name, so I wandered back with a box of each in my hands.

"I guess you're probably going to need a credit card," I said, setting the ammo boxes on the counter and reaching for my wallet.

"Actually, there's a small problem. Well, not really a problem just more of a delay." He scratched the center of his chest, every bit the bearer of bad news.

"Oh, is the system down? That's kind of the way my luck is running lately."

"No, it's up. But when I ran your application through the database, it was flagged for manual review."

"That's weird. I mean, I can't think of any reason why there would be any red flags." I mean, seriously. Middle-class white woman, no criminal record, faithful taxpayer . . . I was about as unobjectionable as they come. Or so I thought.

"I don't suppose you'd happen to be in the state witch registry?"

My stomach fell. I could practically hear it hit the floor with a wet splat. "Yeah, actually. I am. Why does that matter? Witches are allowed to buy guns in New Mexico, aren't they?"

"Don't shoot the messenger." He spread his hands in a helpless gesture. "All I know is most of the holds I see are either witches or criminals, and you don't look like a criminal."

"Thanks, I think. Okay, so how long does this manual review take? I have an appointment this afternoon that I can't miss."

"It's usually cleared up within twenty-four hours."

"Twenty-four hours?" My voice lifted in volume and pitch, but I forced myself to remain calm. It wasn't this guy's fault, all he did was plug the info into the computer. Sighing, I pinched the bridge of my nose between my thumb and index finger.

"I'll give you a call when the hold clears," he offered, "and you can swing by to pick it up then."

"Okay. Great. Thanks," I said through gritted teeth and turned to stalk for the door.

Once on the sidewalk outside, it didn't take long for the chilly air to cool my temper, but annoyance wrapped around me like armor as I stomped to my car and climbed inside. Of all the ridiculous nonsense I'd had to deal with since registering as a practitioner, this was just the tip of the iceberg. But it seemed like every day I learned a bit more about just how much more lurked beneath the surface. I'd known when I registered that my life might change, that my name and address would be in a public database. That people I'd known for years would look at me differently, that I'd have to face a bit of prejudice and suspicion. Never in my wildest dreams had I imagined that I might lose my job over it. That someone might actually try to kill me. That my constitutional rights might be withheld. Where would it end? I wasn't sure how much more I could take.

By the time I pulled out of the strip mall parking lot, the tears had started to flow. It was all just too much. I pulled off onto the side of the road less than a mile later and let the frustration and hurt wash over me until the tsunami of emotion receded. I can't imagine what I must've looked like to passersby, sitting on the side of the road and crying my eyes out, then screaming and pounding on the steering wheel for lack of a better outlet. Then crying some more.

After a solid fifteen minutes, I wiped my face and blew my nose, then started the car again and got on with my life because it was the only thing I could do to stay sane.

Swim or die, little shark.

CHAPTER 32

Billy and I arrived at twelve o'clock on the dot for our appointment with Noah's grandfather. The Chavez house was located in the heart of the Pueblo where the small adobe homes were clustered around a plaza that also contained a church. The warm brown adobe church looked newer than most of the houses, and its architecture was more modern than most of the old missions in the area with boxy, graduated peaks. I'd asked Billy about it, and he'd told me it had been built in 2004, following the destruction of the old one in a fire. I got the feeling there was a story there, but he didn't seem to want to talk about it. I knew better than to press—at least about something relatively unimportant.

We parked behind a dusty Prius and followed a broken flagstone path from the packed dirt driveway to the front of the small house. The front door, like its window frames, was painted turquoise, giving the house a bit more character than its neighbors. Large wooden pots shaped like half-barrels flanked the door, containing blossoming flowers in defiance of the yet-cold weather. The moment I stepped under the front awning, most of the chill of the air faded away. I didn't have to look for the symbols carved into the lintels to know that the area had been warded, magically temperature-controlled to give the plants a warmer environment to blossom in. A long metal trough sat under a nearby window, from which three spiky aloe vera plants sprouted, their spindly arms reaching for the sky.

Billy rang the bell after removing his hat, and after a few moments, the door opened. I easily recognized the woman who answered from our brief visit to Noah's house a few days prior. She narrowed her dark eyes and her lips twisted in a sneer. "You've got a lot of nerve showing your face around here, Billy Tsosie."

"Now, now, is that any way to treat an invited guest, Maria? We're here to see Ray."

Maria's eyes slid to me, and if looks could kill I would've dropped dead. Instead, I mustered a weak smile. Maria's focus shifted back to Billy, and she said something sharply in a language I didn't understand.

"Her name is Emily Davenport, she's a consultant with the Santa Fe Police, and she's trying to *help* your brother," Billy replied, displaying admirable patience. "Would you please tell Ray we're here?"

The young witch snorted but nodded, stepping back and holding the door wide. "Please, won't you come in?"

The mockery in the invitation wasn't lost on me, but when Billy motioned for me to go ahead of him, I did. "Thank you," I said.

Maria remained tight-lipped until we were both inside, then shut the door firmly. The inside of the house was warm enough that I slipped off my coat and draped it over my arm. Maria left us standing by the door, but Billy wandered deeper into the room to settle at one end of the sofa. I followed his lead, looking around curiously but resisting the urge to scope out the bookshelf along the way. The living room was small enough to be cozy, with scuffed wood floors covered in colorful rugs and exposed beams overhead. The air smelled like mesquite, probably from the fire burning merrily in the corner fireplace. If not for Maria's chilly welcome, I might've even felt at ease. As it was, I sat ramrod straight on the opposite end of the sofa with my coat folded across my lap. Silence hung in the air between us. Most of what I could think of to say I hesitated to say with Maria potentially in earshot. She was a spunky one.

After a few minutes, the sound of a door opening and closing brought our attention to the mouth of the hall. The old floorboards creaked as slow footsteps approached down the hall, and eventually, Maria came back into view, escorting a stooped old man with a full head of white hair and wrinkled skin the color of a roasted walnut. Maria helped him over to the only other seat in the room, a wing-backed armchair with a threadbare quilt draped over the back. She leaned into him and whispered quietly before he sat, then gathered the quilt up and draped it across his lap. Her hand rested briefly on his knee, and he gave it a pat.

"Thank you, sweetheart."

Maria bent and pressed a kiss to the top of his head, then withdrew to stand behind his chair, looming over the proceedings with suspicious eyes.

"It's good to see you, Ray. How's the winter treating you?" Billy said.

It wasn't until he turned his face toward the sound of Billy's voice that I noticed the film over his pupils. Cataracts. The fellow had to be mostly blind, if not entirely so, and when he smiled in response to Billy's question I could see he was missing a few teeth. If this man was our only hope of catching the skinwalker, I had a really bad feeling about it.

"I can't complain. Or, I guess I could but it wouldn't do me any good!" He wheezed a laugh, smacking his knee with a weathered hand. "Did Maria offer you some refreshments?" He inclined his head, continuing before Maria could do more than open her mouth to reply. "Maria! Why didn't you offer my guests refreshments?"

Maria snapped her jaw shut and glared at me like this was all somehow my fault.

"We're fine, really," I said, not eager to get any deeper on her bad side. "I drank about a gallon of coffee no more than an hour ago. If anything, I'll need to beg the use of your bathroom before we leave."

Billy nodded his head in agreement, then cleared his throat as if remembering Ray wouldn't be able to see it. "Agreed, no reason to go through any trouble. Though I must say, the reason for our visit today is sensitive in nature. It would be best left between the three of us."

Ray may have been old, but his wits remained quick. His mouth formed a silent 'ah' of understanding, and he bobbed his head in a slow nod. "Maria, my dear, would you please give us some privacy?"

The younger witch looked for a moment like she might stand her ground but thought better of it. "Yes, grandfather." She stepped out from behind his chair and headed back down the hallway, though she paused on her way past my end of the couch to say, "I won't be far if you need me."

The comment was not directed at me, but she eyed me like if she was needed it would be my doing. She jabbed two V'd fingers at her eyes, pointed them at me, then stalked off down the hall. A few moments later, a door shut firmly. I cast a what-was-that-about look in Billy's direction, but he merely shrugged and got back to the matter at hand.

"Thanks, Ray. First, allow me to introduce you to Emily Davenport, a consultant with the SFPD."

The elderly man turned his head and looked right at me with his sightless eyes. For a moment, I forgot that I'd already spoken, so he would know approximately where I was in the room. My spine tingled for that moment, fleeting though it may have been. As it passed, I reminded myself that this man was a witch and no more, that his status as a Pueblo medicine man conferred no extra mysticism.

"It's an honor to meet you, sir."

He humphed quietly and worked his jaw left and right before replying. "This has something to do with my grandson, does it not?"

"It might, sir. Bi—Officer Tsosie and I both have reservations about his guilt, and I recently, well . . ." I wasn't sure how to proceed and glanced at Billy for help.

"We want to talk to you about skinwalkers," Billy said. Straight and to the point, something I could definitely get behind.

Ray wrinkled his nose. "You think a skinwalker killed the white man?"

"Maybe. I don't know. But my partner and I had a strange encounter with a coyote near the crime scene, and Officer Tsosie mentioned there have been some activities on the Pueblo recently that suggest there may be one active in the area. Even if this person didn't commit the crime, they might be able to help me find who did."

There was a pause, several long seconds wherein the elder blinked his sightless eyes a few times, and then he burst out in knee-smacking guffaws that filled the room. Billy joined him, though not quite as uproariously. The older man laughed until tears ran from his eyes and he wheezed with the effort to breathe through it.

"Skinwalker . . . help . . . ahahahahahahaha!"

My cheeks flamed, but I cleared my throat and waited for him to simmer down so I could get a word in edgewise. "I didn't mean they'd, like, join Team Scooby. More that if they were in the area the night it happened, maybe they might've seen something."

Ray ran his gnarled hands down his cheeks, wiping away moisture. "Yes. I suppose that's a thought. But I'm more apt to believe your first instinct. If there is a skinwalker in the area—and God help us if there is—it almost assuredly killed the white man."

"What makes you so sure?" I glanced at Billy, but he looked as curious as I was.

"Because, little one, there isn't anything a skinwalker hates more than a pretender. He pretended to have connections to the land, to the spirits, to have all the answers for the poor lost souls he drew into his orbit. He practically taunted the creature, calling himself a shaman. A medicine man. A healer. It would not be able to resist."

It was all true, and it wasn't even everything. He'd also pretended to be a witch, and I hoped that hadn't pissed off the skinwalker too because some might accuse me of the same thing, and if John and Billy were to be believed, I was already on the damn thing's radar.

"So, assuming the skinwalker did kill Nate Alan Reed, how do we bring it—them—in?"

"Hmm. That is the question, isn't it?" Ray said. "My grandson would probably say that justice had been served."

"He did, in fact, say that," Billy said. "But given that he's currently behind bars and facing charges, I think he'd like us to at least try."

"True." Ray clicked his tongue a few times, his expression turning thoughtful. "It's been many years since I faced a skinwalker. It takes a certain kind of man to turn toward instead of away from the darkness in his heart, to use magic to hurt rather than heal. I had the benefit of knowing who it was back then, or at least suspecting. It took me months to perfect the magic to trap him, to force him into his human form and bind him to the earth so he could not use his trickery on me."

A skinwalker trap. Now we were talking. I leaned forward, listening intently. "When you speak of his trickery, do you mean his magic? You forced him back to human form and bound him?"

"Indeed. He wasn't so scary after that. But it required much preparation, and if not for the bond we shared, I don't know that I would have been able to lure him into the trap."

"Oh right, because the spell would've been visible to him. What'd you do?"

"I placed the spell on the ground and covered it with skins. He sensed the magic, but he couldn't tell its source, and he trusted me enough to draw nearer regardless."

I felt myself smile and tried to tamp it down before it became wide enough to draw suspicion from Billy. Because if we needed an invisible spell, I knew just the witch that could cast one. The only problem, which deflated that blossoming smile quickly, was that I didn't have a clue what that spell was—and neither did Dan.

"I don't suppose you ever committed this spell of yours to writing." It was a long shot, given what I knew about Pueblo traditions, but I had to ask.

"No. But I remember it. Would you like to see it?"

I was too surprised by the revelation that the old man could still see enough to sling magic to think too hard about the fact that my spell notation skills were extremely rusty. But if I could get the gist of it down, maybe Dan could intuit the rest. "Yes. Absolutely."

I knew better than to ask for paper. I couldn't risk offending Ray or Billy when I was so close to getting a critical piece of information. No, I was going to have to do this the old-fashioned way, the way my tutor used to drill into me when I was a kid, recreating spells on a page from memory. I'd always hated those lessons, believing them completely useless for a witch with no magic. But maybe, just maybe, my tutor's unswerving devotion to mental and emotional sadism was about to pay off.

CHAPTER 33

When I pulled into the parking lot outside my apartment complex, I spotted Mike's car in a visitor space. Despite the fact that the visitor spaces were quite a hike from my building, he never failed to park there unless they were full. And, of course, they were rarely full because most visitors parked closer to wherever they wanted to be. Chuckling to myself over my partner's predictable patterns, I found a closer spot for myself and hurried for home, taking the stairs two at a time. Of course, that meant I was panting a bit by the time I reached the top, but it just made it all the more dramatic when I threw open the front door with the transcribed skinwalker trap clutched in one hand.

Sadly, my dramatics were mostly lost on Mike and Dan, who sat across the kitchen table from one another playing cards. They both glanced my way briefly before returning their attention to their game. A small "pot" of brightly colored candy lay on the table between them. Whatever they were playing, judging from the pile of candy in front of him, Mike was considerably ahead.

"Go fish," Mike said, and Dan drew a card. Leave it to my brother to turn Go Fish into a betting game.

"Ha! Got one!" Dan placed two eights down on the table and waggled his brows at Mike. "Got you on the run now, detective."

I nudged the door closed with my foot and locked it, then walked over to the table. "Did you talk to him yet?"

"Talk to who about what?" Dan asked.

Mike smirked. "No, I figured I'd give you that honor."

"Gee, thanks." I shrugged off my coat and threw it over the back of a chair before plopping down in it.

"Seriously, talk to who about what?" Dan said.

"Do you have any kings?" Mike asked.

I snatched the cards from Mike's hand and placed them face down on the table. "Focus, man." I shifted my attention to Dan, looking him in the eye. "I've got something to say to you, and I don't want it to be a thing."

My brother's brows knit together and he leaned back in his chair, eyeing me. "Okay . . ."

"I need your help." I slapped the spell down on the table and pushed it toward him.

Dan's expression brightened immediately, transformed from suspicion to eagerness in the span of a second. "What's this?" He pulled the paper closer and scanned my meticulous scribbles, brows once again knitting. "No, really, what *is* this?"

I caught Dan up on everything while Mike collected the cards, moved the candy to the side, and dealt himself a hand of solitaire. When I finally got back to the spell in his hand, Dan blinked and peered at it again. "So, you think a legendary boogeyman straight out of Navajo folklore offed this guy and might be after you, so you got this spell from a blind geriatric medicine man on a Pueblo?"

"Basically. Only he couldn't have been fully blind, because he was able to demonstrate the spell for me. I did my best to transcribe it, but it's been a while since I did that, and I wasn't really sure *how* to transcribe some of it. But I was hoping we might be able to reconstruct it and you could do that trick of yours to make it invisible so we can catch the skinwalker and ask a few pointed questions."

Dan frowned, studying the paper. "It'd be better if I could see the spell for myself. This is . . . no offense, sis, but it doesn't make much sense."

"Well, keep in mind that this is Navajo magic, too. The lines are going to be a little different from how you were taught."

"Well, I'm game to try, but how do we know when we get it right?"

I shrugged. "If it works, I guess. We don't know anyone who can turn into a coyote to test it on."

"Wait a minute," Mike said, looking up from his game. "This is your big plan? You try to recreate a spell given to you by this Pueblo shaman and just hope that it works against a powerful witch who may have already killed once?"

"I didn't say there wouldn't be a plan B."

"I'm listening." He went back to drawing cards three at a time from the dwindling deck.

I'd hoped he wouldn't ask that. "I'm still working on it. Feel free to chime in."

He set the cards aside and leaned forward in his chair, crossing his forearms across the tabletop. "You need to loop Anderson in."

I scoffed. "There's no way he'd get on board. He thinks he's already got his man."

"Em, your heart's in the right place, but you need to think like a cop."

I pointed at him. "That's what you're here for, isn't it?"

"The chief would have my ass if he knew I was still involved in this. I'm on admin leave. I could get fired for trying to do police work right now. Hell, I've already done too much. I can advise you on how to go about this, but I can't participate. And if this skinwalker—this witch—really is the killer, you need to be able to prove it in court. That means you need to gather evidence or a confession—properly—and that means you need a cop on Team Catch-A-Skinwalker."

"Who, then? Anderson found himself a witch to pin the murder on and considers the case closed. He shrugged me off every chance he got because he's a bigot that hates witches."

Mike barked a laugh. "Is that what you think?"

"Isn't it the truth? He gives you shit all the time about being in Magic Crimes and wants to be done with this case so badly that he's willing to put an innocent man behind bars just to wash his hands of it."

"Jerk," Dan remarked, though his eyes remained focused on the paper in his hands, studying the spell intently.

"Mmmhmm." Mike leaned back in his chair. "I've worked with Anderson a long time. He can be a bit of an asshole but a bigot is a stretch."

"Are you telling me he has nothing at all against witches?" I folded my arms and eyed him.

"Emily, Anderson's married to a witch. I promise you, he's not against witches. He's just against Magic Crimes as a department."

I blinked, struggling to process this revelation as my mental picture of the detective shattered into a million pieces. "Why on earth would he be against our department if he's totally fine with witches?"

"Because he thinks all cops should be trained and prepared to investigate crimes against or perpetrated by witches, not just one—or even more than one. He railed against the formation of the department from the start because he saw it as institutionalized racism, an under allocation of resources to serve the witch community, and he gives me a hard time because I volunteered."

My jaw nearly hit the table. When he put it that way, it was definitely food for thought. I'd never considered the implications of a Magic Crimes department from that angle. It'd always seemed like a good thing to me, to keep the witch community safe. But a lot of those thoughts were wrapped up in Mike—honest, loyal Mike who wanted to protect and serve all people equally. What if the officer who'd been assigned had been someone with a darker agenda? And, for that matter, why had they thought that only *one* officer would suffice for the whole city? Our case load was insane. Was the creation of Magic Crimes yet another example of the marginalization of witches I'd begun to experience since joining the registry?

"He's not entirely wrong," Dan said. "What Magic Crimes really needs is witch detectives. No offense, Mike."

"None taken. You okay, Em? You're awfully quiet over there."

"Sorry." I shook my head but couldn't entirely rid myself of the thoughts spinning around in there. "If you're right . . . I've been really wrong about Anderson this whole time. But that doesn't excuse his sloppy work."

"Agreed. But you need to talk to him anyway and tell him what you've learned." Mike picked the cards back up again. "I'm willing to bet the DA is pushing back a bit on the case against Noah. They don't like circumstantial evidence, so he's probably going to have to cough up something else to make the charges stick."

I tilted my head at that. "So, if we do nothing, chances are Noah walks anyway. You couldn't have mentioned that sooner?"

"That doesn't mean the real killer isn't still out there."

"Right." I rubbed my face with both hands and pushed back my chair. It'd been a long day, and it was still early afternoon. "I guess I'd better get moving."

"I'll work on this while you do that," Dan said. "I think I've got some idea of what it's doing." He straightened in his seat and looked around while I grabbed my coat and headed for the door.

"I'll text you and let you know how it goes," I said as I pulled open the door.

Dan waved me off absently. "I'm going to need some room. Mike, can you help me move the coffee table?"

"Drive safe," Mike said. "And Em? You've got this."

I stepped outside and pulled the door shut behind me, taking a moment to close my eyes and inhale the crisp air deep into my lungs. My thoughts still ran rampant in my head, chasing each other around like hyperactive lap dogs. The last few days had been beyond overwhelming, between the case and my personal struggles. Suddenly I didn't want to go to the station. I wanted to crawl into bed and pull the covers over my head.

As I struggled to clear my mind, Mike's parting words came back to me.

You've got this.

He believed in me. That was enough.

CHAPTER 34

It took surprisingly less effort than I'd expected to get Anderson to listen to what I had to say. He'd been on the phone with the DA when I arrived at the station, and as Mike had predicted, she was not pleased with the evidence against Noah.

I filled him in on everything I'd discovered since Noah's arrest—leaving out Mike's involvement—including the magic coyote sighting at the crime scene and my trip to the Pueblo to talk to Billy Tsosie. I left out the visit with Ray Chavez. I'm really not sure why. I think part of me was still having trouble trusting Anderson, and I felt like Ray had taken a big chance on me.

We ran Howard Johnson's name through the database but got no hits besides a driver's license and a few parking tickets. He'd never been arrested, at least not in the state of New Mexico.

"So, we don't have anything on this guy besides a suspicious tribal cop and the lawsuit?" Anderson was a pen chewer, and the poor black pen sticking out of his mouth bobbed as he spoke.

"Not unless he's got really small feet. I did find a partial bare footprint in the sweat lodge I'm pretty sure forensics overlooked."

"Hmm." Anderson reached for his mouse, and a few clicks later, the forensic report appeared on the screen. I leaned over to read over his shoulder as he scrolled through it. It wasn't until he got to the very end that we hit pay dirt.

"Wait! There. See that?" I pointed at the screen.

"See what?"

"Coyote fur. They found coyote fur at the scene. It's in the list at the very end of the report, in the irrelevant samples section."

He scratched his jaw, making a thoughtful noise. "Do you think there's enough of the witch's DNA in a fur sample to get a match?"

"I have no idea, but we don't have a sample to match it with."

"Yeah. I doubt we have enough probable cause for a warrant to get it, either. That puts us pretty firmly back at square one."

I moved around him to lean against the edge of his desk. "We'll find something."

"Let's say that this magic coyote of yours really is Howard Johnson. What do we do even if we find it? We can't question a coyote, much less make it turn back into a human."

"That's what you've got me for." I pointed at myself for good measure. "I've got a spell that might force him back into his human form."

"Might? You're not exactly filling me with confidence here."

"It's a work in progress. Needs some, uh, refinement. But

it'll be ready soon." I hoped I wasn't over-promising, but I was confident Dan and I would figure it out.

"Okay, then why don't you go work on that and leave me here to work things from this angle?"

I lay a hand on my chest. "That sounds suspiciously like teamwork, Detective Anderson."

"Yeah, yeah, don't let it go to your head."

Chuckling, I straightened but hesitated to leave. "Actually, there is one other thing we should discuss."

His focus had already shifted to his computer screen, though he emitted an absent, "Hmm?"

"I need to bring in another witch to consult."

That got his attention. His eyes jumped to me. "Why?"

"Because I can't cast the spell."

"Why not?"

He was going to make me say it, right there in the middle of the squad room. "Because I can't cast any spells. I'm a . . ." I couldn't call myself a null anymore. I did have some abilities, just not the quintessential one witches are known for. But I also didn't want to start throwing the whole Conduit thing around. Not when I didn't fully understand what it meant, what the implications might be. "An anomaly."

He scratched his shaved head and squinted at me. "But you're a Davenport."

"Yes." I suppressed a sigh. "I'm a Davenport, and I'm a witch, but I can't cast magic. I can sense it in others and assist with spellcasting, but I can't hold magic inside me, and that means I can't wield magic myself. I'm well-educated in the arcane arts, but it's more theoretical and observational than practical." I really needed to find a more succinct way of explaining things, because this was going to come up again. And again.

"Huh," he said after a moment's consideration. "I dunno if the cap will sign off on another consultant, but I can ask."

"He'll work for free." I hadn't discussed that with Dan, but I was sure I could convince him.

"Why would he do that?"

"Because he wants to be a cop, and it'll look good on his resume when he applies to the academy."

Anderson made an agreeable noise. "It would, yeah. I'll tell you what. I'll get the cap to sign off on it, and if he pulls this off, I'll write him a letter of recommendation myself."

That would definitely sweeten the pot for my brother. I stuck out a hand. "You've got yourself a deal."

We shook on it, then parted ways. I dialed Dan on the way to the car and smiled when he picked up.

"I've got an early birthday gift for you, Danny boy . . ."

CHAPTER 35

D an and I spent the rest of that day and most of the next trying to reproduce Ray Chavez's spell. I'm not going to lie . . . Dan did most of the work. All I could do was tell him when things looked right or wrong based on my memory and dictation.

"Wait, that line is supposed to be more curved. It's kind of like a noose, with the lines wrapping around that center piece." I walked across the glowing lines on the floor and pointed at the spot in question. We had every piece of furniture in the living room pushed out of the way to make room for the large circle of runes now glowing on the area rug.

The entire spell misted away with an irritated sweep of Dan's hand. "This is hopeless. How long before the pizza gets here? I'm starving and I need a break." He sank onto the end of the coffee table since it blocked access to the couch and pushed his fingers into his hair.

"It should be here any minute now. We just have to keep trying. We can make this work."

"We've tried a hundred times, and the spell matrix hasn't

held once. Something is wrong, and I don't know what because this isn't my kind of magic. I'm classically trained, and this—this is Pueblo magic. It's Greek to me. Maybe if I saw him do it . . ."

"Not an option."

"What do you suggest we do, then? We don't exactly have a Pueblo witch on speed dial."

"Even if we did, they're so touchy about this subject it'd be hard to find one who would be willing to touch it with a ten-foot wand." My mind jumped to John and his aversion to even speak about skinwalkers as a theoretical. The guy ran into burning buildings for a living, so I couldn't exactly call him a coward, but apparently the subject of skinwalkers made his testicles shrivel. Maybe that should've had me running the other way too.

Dan lifted his head, his hair sticking up every which way. "What about that witch from the sherriff's department? Didn't you say he was Native?"

"Deputy Payne? He is, but I don't have his number. I could ask Mike to call him, but Payne isn't known for timely responses. Or being cooperative, for that matter." Nonetheless, I grabbed my phone and fired off a quick text to Mike. It wasn't a bad idea. Deputy Payne was already considered a sell-out by his people for going into law enforcement outside the tribal police. He might not agree to help us, but he at least had a lower barrier than others. In theory.

"You know, there is someone you're overlooking." Dan lifted his brows. "A certain tall, dark, and handsome firefighter."

"John?" I shook my head. "He wants no part in this."

"You asked him already?"

"Not specifically, but when—" I remembered at the last

moment that I couldn't say anything about Kassidy without violating the terms of our agreement. "—I asked him about skinwalkers, he completely shut down. Wouldn't even talk about them. It's super taboo to talk about, which is why we can't just wander through the Pueblos asking for volunteers."

Dan eyed me, no doubt noting my sudden course correction. My brother is a lot of things, but he's not completely oblivious. When he doesn't want to be, anyway. The doorbell rang, and I seized upon the opportunity to end the conversation at least temporarily. Turning, I headed for the door to collect our late lunch. Or early dinner. Whatever.

"This is a little different, don't you think? We're out of the theoretical, now. Maybe he'd be more willing to help knowing that there's one running around killing people and we plan to capture him."

I shook my head, reaching for the door handle. "No means no." Frustration tightened my shoulders, but I was more annoyed with my brother—as usual for days ending in Y—than John. No, the emotion that stirred in my gut when thinking about his refusal to help was more disappointment than anything. I mean, sure, I barely knew the guy. But he'd gotten under my skin somehow. It was why I'd been avoiding him in the first place. Maybe it was the damn painting. If I didn't love it so much, I would've smashed it to pieces. Part of me wished I'd just kept avoiding him. At least then I wouldn't have had the opportunity to be disappointed. I yanked the door open.

And because sometimes life is just as ridiculous as the movies, John Warren stood on my doorstep, holding a pizza.

"Are you moonlighting as a delivery driver now?" I squinted at him.

He cracked a small smile and held the box out. "No, but I encountered yours on the way upstairs. Peace offering?"

I looked at the box, then up again. "It's hardly a peace offering when it was already paid for." I took the offered box, managing a small smile. "But thanks."

"I gave him a substantial tip to leave the box with me."

I stood there awkwardly, staring at him through the open doorway, clutching the pizza like a lifeline.

Dan swiped the box from me, stealing even that small comfort. "Hey Johnny Boy, we were just talking about you."

And there went my idiot brother, opening his big mouth. Figuratively and literally, as he fished a slice of pizza out on his way to the table and aimed it at his face hole. I sighed.

"Can I come in?" John tucked his now-empty hands in his coat pockets. "I won't take up too much of your time."

After a moment's hesitation, I stepped aside and motioned him into the apartment, then closed the door behind him to shut out the cold. He looked around the rearranged living room, then back to me with one brow lifted.

"Dance rehearsal." My tone fell intentionally flat, and I started to fold my arms but the spell in my hand got in the way. I tucked it under my arm. "What brings you by?"

"I wanted to apologize for my behavior the other day. I was caught off-guard when the subject of—when the subject came up. I handled it poorly and I, well, I want to help."

"Awesome," Dan said around a mouthful of pepperoni and cheese. "We need it."

I shot my brother a look, but he just grinned and wandered into the kitchen, temporarily out of sight. When I returned my attention to John, he remained rooted in place,

not making any sort of move to make himself at home. He
hadn't even taken off his coat. I respected that. He was
waiting for me to make the call despite Dan's cavalier
invitation.

"Dan's not wrong. We really could use some help. But . .
." I glanced over my shoulder at the kitchen, then grabbed
John's wrist and tugged him deeper into the apartment,
down the hallway and into the bathroom. He went along
without comment, but curiosity glinted in his dark eyes as I
closed the door and turned toward him again, keeping my
voice low. "I have conditions."

"I'm listening," he murmured.

"First, you can't ask where the spell came from."

His eyes flicked down to the spell tucked under my arm.
In the closer quarters of the bathroom, I couldn't help but
notice his slightly spicy cologne, and it was going to my
head. He smelled really good.

"That spell?" He reached for it, but I backed away.

"Yes, that spell. But you're not seeing it until you promise. The only thing I'll tell you is that it's Pueblo magic, and
it's not stolen, illegal, or harmful."

He considered the request a moment more, then
nodded. "Alright. I agree. What else?"

"You can't tell Kassidy about it. Or anyone, really. But
especially not Kassidy. I wouldn't feel right about giving it to
her. Think of me what you will, but don't ever think that I
don't respect traditions that aren't my own."

A smile tugged at his lips. "I'm mighty curious what's on
that paper now."

"Agree to my conditions, and I'll show you."

"Are there more?"

"No."

"Then I agree." He reached for the paper again, fingertips brushing my sleeve as I let him pluck it free. He turned it face up and studied it in silence, brows inching closer together and forehead wrinkling. The silence stretched for a dozen or so seconds, and then he tilted his head and rotated the page, studied it some more, then shook his head and handed it back to me. "What is it?"

"It's a skinwalker trap."

His eyes widened, and he emitted a low whistle. "Does it work?"

"I hope so. But I'm the only one who's seen it, and I tried to transcribe it, but Pueblo magic is beyond my expertise. So we've been trying to recreate it from my memory and my notes."

He leaned forward slightly, balancing on the balls of his feet. "Show me."

We went back out into the living room, where Dan hovered over the open pizza box with a quarter of a slice in one hand and an open can of soda in the other. Two more cans sat on the table beside the box.

"You two kiss and make up?" He grinned. "Weren't in there long enough for much else."

I smacked the back of his head lightly in passing, then leaned over the table to grab a slice of pizza. "He's on board. Go show him what we've got."

Six hours later, all three of us were sprawled on the floor with our backs to the wall, staring at the glowing circle in the center of the room, the first stable version of the spell we'd managed to produce. Or, rather, the first stable version Dan and John had been able to produce between the two of them. They both looked exhausted but satisfied with the fruits of their labors.

"Think it'll work?" I asked, studying the now-familiar sweeping and curling lines of the spell.

Dan yawned widely. "Got any spare skinwalkers to test it on?"

"Not funny." John rubbed his face and sighed.

"Well, we might not be able to test that part of the spell, but we can definitely test the binding part. Who wants to go first?" I asked.

"Not it," Dan said, flopping over on his side and curling up with a couch pillow.

"Work, work, work," John mumbled as he hauled himself to his feet, tossing over his shoulder to me, "You're lucky I like you."

"Aw, that's sweet. I like you too," Dan replied, sounding half-asleep already.

I rolled my eyes, then shifted my attention to John as he approached the circle. But as soon as one of his feet crossed the edge of the circle, the spell flickered like a failing bulb and then vanished.

Stepping back, he scratched his head and then cast the spell again. Or tried. The glow around him, normally so strong while he casted, had grown so weak that I could barely see it. He was tapped, his mystical magic muscle unable to absorb any more. I stood and walked over to him, putting a hand on his arm and drawing power from the earth to feed to him. The glow around him brightened, and he blinked a few times before trying the spell again. This time it came together more easily, but when it stabilized and he stepped into its circumference again, the spell once again collapsed.

John rubbed the back of his neck and stared at the floor. "What are we doing wrong?"

"Maybe it only works on skinwalkers," Dan said.

I could've sworn I'd heard him snoring a moment prior.

"Or maybe it doesn't work because you're the one that cast the spell," I said, thinking out loud. "I mean, you can't bind your own magic, right? Maybe that's causing the matrix to collapse. Anyway, we can try it again tomorrow. You two are dead on your feet."

"I'm not on my feet," Dan protested, then proceeded to climb to said feet as if to prove that he wasn't actually dead on them. He zombie-shuffled over to stand next to me and took my hand. "Gimme some juice."

I obliged, and Dan cast the spell this time. It took him longer than it had John, no doubt because the style of magic was still so foreign to him. But he managed to reproduce the spell easier now that he'd seen John do it. When he finished, he released my hand and motioned to John, who stepped forward into the circle, paused, and turned to face us. The glowing whorls lingered in place. The spell remained stable.

"Did it work? Are you bound?" I asked.

John looked uncertain. "I can't tell. I'm tapped, so I couldn't sense much of anything to start with."

I crossed into the circle myself and approached him. He held out a hand, and I placed mine in his, then attempted to feed him mystical energy. But it was like there was a kink in the straw. It wouldn't pass from me to him. Elation washed over me.

"It's working. You guys, it's working!" I twisted to look behind me, finding Dan once more on his ass.

He flopped onto his back and raised a finger in the air, giving it a slow twirl. "Yay."

Chuckling, I backed out of the circle, bringing John with me. As soon as he cleared the glowing ring, whatever impeded the flow of energy between us vanished, and I was once again able to feed him magic.

A small smile curved his lips. "That feels nice."

It did. I stared into his eyes for a long moment before I caught myself swaying toward him and made myself cut him off and step back. "Great. Well, at least we know the binding works. Even if the spell doesn't reverse the shapeshifting, at least the witch will be bound."

"What's next?" John asked.

Dan moaned from the floor. "Sleep."

"Yeah, that's probably a good idea."

"I'll get my coat," John said.

"Oh no, you don't. I'm not letting you drive in this state." I caught his arm and led him toward the sofa, pausing to push the coffee table out of the way. "You can sleep here."

"Are you sure? Where's Dan going to sleep?"

I looked down at Dan, who was either already asleep or doing a fair impression of it. "He looks fine there, but he can sleep with me if he wakes up and wants to drag his ass down the hall."

John sank down on the sofa without further argument, and I fetched Dan's pillow and bedding from the hall closet. John ignored the sheet and just grabbed the blanket and pillow, stretching his long frame out on the sofa and covering up. Looking down at him, gratitude swelled inside me. Sure, he may have disappointed me at first, but then he'd come through in a major way. I'd become accustomed to disappointment over the years. But someone who showed up, well, that didn't come along every day.

"Thanks, John."

His eyes fluttered open. "Hmm?"

"For your help. We couldn't have done it without you. I mean it."

"You're welcome." A smile lingered on his face as his eyes drifted closed once more.

I grabbed a spare afghan from the closet and draped it over Dan before retreating to my own bed. I was so tired I expected sleep to come easily, but I lay awake for another hour or so, thinking about our next move. We had the trap. We had a suspect—sort of. Now I just had to figure out where to set the trap . . . and how to get the skinwalker inside it.

CHAPTER 36

Before he left the next morning, John and I had a chat about finding the skinwalker. He told me that Reed's property would be a good place to start because skinwalkers are territorial and I'd already encountered it there once. We speculated that after killing Reed, the skinwalker may have laid claim to his territory and would keep coming back. Of course, there was no telling what sort of timetable its patrols might take, but it was the best idea we could come up with, so I was willing to give it a try.

To his credit, John did offer to go with us to confront the skinwalker. I didn't even get the sense that there was any lingering reluctance, but since Dan seemed comfortable enough with the spell by then—and I doubted Anderson would sign off on yet another consultant—I assured him we'd be fine. He didn't press the issue, but I could tell he wasn't happy about it, and he wouldn't leave until I promised to text him before and after the event so he'd know we were okay. Like we were friends or something. But I couldn't really call him merely an acquaintance either. I mean, he'd worn himself out trying to help, and it wasn't the first time he'd come to my aid either. It was like he just couldn't stop himself, and I got that. I was a sucker when it came to helping people too, and while I didn't put my life on the line running into burning buildings to do it, neither of my occupations were without peril.

Tonight, for example, I was trotting off into the wilderness with my brother and my fill-in partner to confront a powerful spellcaster who'd already killed one fake witch. I had no plans to be the next.

We'd waited until well after dark to head out to Reed's house, parking beside the narrow dirt road that ran alongside his property. Anderson handed out flex cuffs, one pair to me and one to Dan to slip in our coat pockets, and I passed out the charms that Mike had driven out to Taos to pick up for us while we were busy deciphering Ray Chavez's spell. I had no idea what he'd paid for them but no doubt they'd been sold at a premium.

The walk-softly charms would keep our footfalls as quiet as possible, while the no-stink charms would dampen our scents. Shield charms would've been nice, maybe even a few air blasts, but those weren't the kind of thing Charming stocked, and we didn't have time to make any special orders. Even Dan, who'd grumbled about using "retail charms," had to admit he couldn't produce them quickly enough to suit our timetable. After draining his magic reserves the day before, he'd needed downtime to recuperate, and he'd need every ounce of magic muscle he had at his disposal tonight. My spelled coat would have to do for me. As for Anderson— well, he had his badge and gun. Hopefully, Dan and I could keep the skinwalker focused on us.

No. Hopefully the trap would go off without a hitch, and the skinwalker wouldn't be able to sling any spells.

When we were ready, we crowded together and Dan

used his invisibility trick to conceal us and his spell invisibility trick to hide the spell's magical signature.

"Remember," he said, glancing between us. "Stick as close to me as you can. Seriously. Get up in my personal space."

Biting down a retort, I nodded and took the lead since I was the only one who'd been out here before and had a general idea where I was going. Dan crowded against my back while Anderson stuck close to his. I have to confess, I would have much preferred to have Mike with us. Given the revelations about Anderson, I didn't distrust him as much, but I didn't fully trust him either. The weight of my new pistol at my hip wasn't much comfort. I'd gotten the call that the background check had cleared and picked it up that afternoon, just in time for our little adventure. I knew how to use it, thanks to the clerk at the gun shop, but I hadn't practiced enough with it to be comfortable and confident with it. It still felt foreign. Uncomfortable. Then there were the second thoughts I was having about actually shooting someone. Maybe I should've left the damn thing at home.

The temperature had risen steadily over the last few days, the sky was clear, and the moon hung in the sky, making our visibility not too terrible, but I wished Mike had picked up some night vision charms for us too.

My thoughts swirled around in my head while we walked. There wasn't much else to do as we crowded together and trudged across the darkened landscape but watch, listen, and think. I thought about the coming confrontation, but that occupied only a small part of my overactive brain. I thought about how much I missed my work at the hospital and the friends I'd made there. Then again, none of them had reached out to me since I was fired, so how good of friends were they, really? Work friends, occupying that gray area between personal and professional. But I supposed we'd never really hung out socially outside of holiday parties. Then again, I hadn't reached out to any of them either. Friendship was a two-way street, after all. Maybe they'd been trying to give me some space to process? Surely all of them couldn't be biased against witches. They'd never displayed any anti-witch sentiments where patients were concerned, though our recent issues with the overdoses had made them warier of random magical outbursts. Understandably so.

Speaking of anti-witch sentiment, I also thought about the unfair treatment I'd received since registering. I'd known that this sort of thing happened from time to time, but I'd had no idea how pervasive it had become. And I'll say something you'll almost never hear me say . . . Dan was right. Specifically, he was right about Magic Crimes needing witch detectives. But in order for there to be witch detectives, there needed to be witch cops. And in order for there to be witch cops, they had to be recruited. I wondered if the SFPD had ever had a recruitment drive targeting witches. I wondered if the top brass would even want to have one. When all this was over, Mike and I were going to have to have a long talk.

But first, I had to deal with the matter at hand. By the time the shadowy outline of the sweat lodge emerged from the darkness, my adrenaline was high. I scoured the landscape for signs of activity. Once I thought I saw something move, but I wasn't sure. We eventually came to a stop about ten feet from the sweat lodge. Dan's fingers brushed mine, and I turned my hand to curl my fingers around his and drew power from the earth to feed to him, allowing him to cast the big, complicated spell without expending as much effort. His gain was my loss, of course, because using my ability wasn't entirely without cost. But I didn't expect to have to use it much, so preserving Dan's strength seemed more important.

The spell began to take shape before me, a glowing circle about fifteen feet in diameter, filled with whorls and sigils that were more familiar to us both now but which neither of us fully understood. However, I was positive now that the compulsion spell on the bowl from the crime scene was Pueblo magic. When Dan finished, he twisted the spell so it disappeared from sight and released my hand, breaking the connection between us.

As the magic drained out of me and back into the earth, I experimented with trying to hold onto some of it, but it was like trying to catch water with a colander, slipping through my metaphorical fingers no matter how hard I tried. I always felt strangely empty when it was gone, but shook off my self-pitying thoughts and turned to lead the way to the sweat lodge. I felt around for the door flap and threw it back, leaving it open as we filed inside.

Once inside, we separated. Dan took out a flashlight and clicked it on since we no longer required stealth. The trap was set. Now we had to bait it. I lingered in place until my eyes adjusted to the new light level, then moved farther into the lodge, away from the sloped walls and toward the pit in the center. We relocated the rocks to the edges and gathered firewood and kindling from the wood pile outside to start a fire.

A few minutes later, we sat around the pit, the merrily crackling fire sending sparks dancing up into the air. Vents in the hide-covered roof drew the curling smoke out into the night. Then we waited.

"Know any good ghost stories?" Dan asked after a few minutes of sitting in silence.

"Shh," Anderson said, sparing me from having to be the heavy.

Dan mumbled to himself but fell silent, and we returned to sitting quietly, ears straining for sounds of activity outside.

After the first hour, I made myself stop checking the time on my phone every few minutes. A few hours later, the popping sound of a fresh log being added to the fire jolted me from a half-dozing state. I blinked rapidly and rubbed my eyes.

"Most. Boring. Stakeout. Ever," Dan whispered.

"Shh," Anderson said.

"Why do we need to be quiet, anyway? Maybe some noise would h—"

I clamped a hand over his mouth, suddenly fully alert. I could've sworn I heard something. I tilted my ear toward the phantom sound, listening carefully. Until Dan's warm, wet tongue slithered against my fingers. I jerked my hand away with a grimace, wiping it on my jeans.

"Thought I heard something." I kept my voice to a bare whisper.

Then the noise sounded again—a distant coyote howl. The others straightened where they sat, so they must have heard it too. We sat in tense silence for a few more minutes before Dan took out his phone and tapped at it a bit. I gave him the side-eye because this was hardly the time for texting a buddy. Then again, other than Tracy, I wasn't sure Dan had any buddies.

A moment later, he stopped and gave me a meaningful look just as my phone vibrated in my pocket. I pulled it out and glanced at the notification lighting up the small rectangular screen.

Dan: We need to make some noise. Roll with it.

Before I could reply or pass the message on, he said, "This is really relaxing. We should do this more often."

I couldn't tell if he was speaking loudly or if my ears were overly sensitive from sitting there in silence for so long. Before Anderson could shush him, I jumped in.

"It's not the same without Nate. He just had such a chill vibe, you know?" I made a rolling motion with my hand and tried to catch Anderson's eye.

"It, uh, feels less authentic," Anderson said, managing to play along after a brief stumble. I didn't get the sense that he'd been involved in many undercover operations.

"I know, right? No one led a spirit journey like Nate," Dan said. "He just had a way of going deep, you know? I think it was his natural Navajo spiritualism."

I grimaced, fairly certain someone's ancestor was rolling in their grave. Another howl sounded outside. Closer this time.

I pushed to my feet, stretching with an exaggerated groan. "I think I need to get some air and cool off."

Dan looked at me like I was crazy. I quickly tapped and sent a message.

Me: It's more likely to approach if it can catch one of us alone.

His fingers flew and my phone vibrated again.

Dan: Be careful.

I tucked my phone away and left the light and warmth of the fire behind, stepping out into the crisp night air. My footsteps carried me some ways from the sweat lodge until I stood about where I estimated the center of the trap was. If playing bait meant we could catch this thing—this witch—I could do that.

Alone in the dark, I tipped my face up at the stars and did my best to attune the rest of my senses to the world around me. The lush, earthy smell of the arid wilderness filled my nostrils while the quiet of night wrapped around me like a blanket. It wasn't completely silent. The wilderness never is, not naturally anyway. I caught the faint sound of small creatures moving about, crickets chirping their nightly symphony. I turned my eyes from the starry sky and that's when I saw the moonlight reflecting off canine eyes in the darkness. Silly me, I'd expected to hear the damn thing first.

I stilled, not having to really try to look startled or intimidated. The coyote stood maybe thirty feet away, watching me. Even at a distance, I could sense its magic.

"Oh, hey there," I said loudly enough that I was reasonably certain the guys would be able to hear. "Do you, uh, want to come in? We were just about to start the drum circle."

I wasn't really sure what to expect, but I definitely didn't expect the creature to charge. My eyes widened, and instinct made me step back before conscious thought halted me. I had to stay in the circle, to give it a chance to work its magic. But the flight instinct was difficult to tamp down when faced with a toothsome, snarling predator bearing down on me. It rapidly closed on me and leaped into the air while I stood there rooted to the spot and prayed we'd gotten the spell right.

I knew something was horribly wrong a mere split second before impact, but it was too late to do a damn thing about it.

CHAPTER 37

The coyote slammed into me, and I flew backward, landing on my back in the dirt. The wind rushed out of my lungs, and I brought my arms up instinctively to defend myself, but the coyote didn't attack. Instead, it stood on me, pinning my shoulders down beneath its paws and glaring down at me with menace in its yellow eyes. Its lips were peeled back to show its pointed fangs, and its face was close enough to mine that I could see its nostrils flaring in the moonlight with each indrawn breath. I'd known the thing was bigger than the average coyote, but I hadn't quite gotten the full scope of it until that moment. It wasn't dire wolf-sized, but maybe the size of an extra-large regular wolf —easily three times the size of a regular coyote—and bulky. With all hundred-plus pounds weighing me down while it loomed over me.

My terrified mind scrambled for an explanation. Had the spell not worked at all? Was I even inside it? Had I misjudged where the invisible circle was on the ground? I didn't know what to do. I couldn't get to my gun, I had no magic, and the damn thing looked like it wanted to rip my face off. So, naturally, I ran my mouth off.

"Sorry, but you're not really my type. And, um, your breath is terrible."

The creature's eyes narrowed and a growl rumbled from its chest.

Dan exploded out of the sweat lodge, distracting the coyote from its prey—aka me. "Hey! Try punching closer to your weight class!" A magical glow surrounded him, and he conjured a ball of air faster than I could blink. He lobbed it at the coyote, which didn't even have time to scramble away. The burst of air knocked the creature off me and sent it rolling a few feet away. As it rolled, there was an explosion of magic around it. Fur and skin blurred together until it came to a stop and was a coyote no more.

I scrambled to my feet, staring at the slender nude human figure lying half-curled on one side, facing away from me. The narrow waist and rounded hips suggested female, which surprised me. If it wasn't Howard Johnson, who the hell was it?

Dan walked up behind me and smacked the back of my head. "Idiot. You missed the circle by like six inches."

That meant . . . "It worked." I was too awed to be annoyed with him. "You did it, Danny!"

He puffed up his chest. "Damn right I did."

Anderson walked up on my other side and shined his flashlight on the unmoving witch. The light settled on the back of her head after briefly panning over the rest of her. "That doesn't look like Howard Johnson, but I don't see any weapons. What'd you do to her?"

"Had to knock her into the circle," Dan said. "I might've knocked a little hard." He didn't sound sorry.

"Or it could've been the forced shapeshift." I took the flex cuffs out of my pocket and started forward.

Anderson grabbed my arm. "Or she could be playing possum."

I studied the unmoving witch for a long moment, then shrugged. "One way to find out." I shook off his arm and stepped forward. How much trouble could one naked, bound witch be?

Anderson went with me, but he unholstered his gun and stepped wide, moving around to the other side of the witch while keeping the light on her head. "Ma'am? Are you alright?"

There was no response, so I crouched behind the witch and took one wrist in hand, preparing to gently roll her on her stomach so I could cuff her wrists together. But as soon as I touched her, she tensed.

"She's awa—"

The witch rolled onto her back and flung dirt in my face. I recoiled, completely blinded by the surprise attack.

"Police! Stay where you are!" Anderson barked.

I fell on my ass and scrambled blindly away. "Don't let her out of the circle!"

My back fetched up against something solid, and I hoped it meant Dan had thrown up a ring of hardened air to keep the witch from escaping. I pushed my way up to my feet, blinking furiously to try and clear the sand from my stinging eyes.

Somewhere behind me, Dan cursed. "She's got something around her neck! Look out, Anderson!"

I pulled up my shirt and scrubbed at my eyes with it. It didn't help much. I managed to peel my eyes open, but my sight was blurry as fuck, and I wished I'd had an eyewash station handy. Or a river. Hell, even a bottle of water. My heart raced faster with every vulnerable second that passed.

"Whoa, whoa! Anderson, buddy, you don't want to do that!" Dan said.

"What's going on?" My heart pounded in a literal blind panic. "Dan! What the hell is going on?"

"She's gotten around the binding somehow, and I think she put the whammy on your partner. He's pointing his gun at us."

"What!?" Panic didn't take long to set in. Mind control magic. Tsosie had warned us, but we'd thought the binding would prevent it. "Can you do anything about my eyes? I can't see shit."

"Um . . . yeah, but it's going to be a little weird."

"Just do it!"

I felt a tingle behind my eyes, and then the scene came into sharper view. I saw Anderson pointing his gun, the witch behind him, her lips moving like she was whispering in his ear, and myself standing a few feet away, tears running in muddy tracks down my cheeks.

Wait. Why was I seeing myself? It took me a moment to realize what Dan had done. He'd linked my vision to his, lending me his eyes. He was right. It was definitely weird.

I took a step forward but watching myself do it was seriously disorienting, so I quickly thought better of it and stilled my feet. I lifted my hands in a universally peaceful gesture. "Okay, I can see we got off on the wrong foot. But if you give me a minute, I can explain."

The witch's lips stopped moving. I couldn't make out much of her features in the darkness. I wasn't sure if it was because Dan needed glasses or her face was painted, but all I could really see were the whites of her eyes and her teeth flashing between her lips as they moved.

"Spare me your lies, Emily Davenport," she hissed from afar.

"Oh great, so, we're halfway introduced. I'm sorry, I didn't catch your name." That voice, though. That voice was familiar.

"Release me from this prison, or suffer the consequences."

"All we want to do is talk to you."

She huffed. "Yes. Talk, talk, talk is all *you people* ever do. The time for talking is past. Now is the time for action."

Her fingers appeared on Anderson's shoulder, and he tipped his head toward her as her lips moved again, this time too quiet for me to hear. Anderson swung his gun arm, pointing it at me, and my heart leaped into my throat. The muzzle flashed as the crack of the gun firing echoed through the quiet landscape in a three-round burst. I hit the ground on instinct, not that it would've likely saved me from a speeding bullet. What did save me —or rather Dan, since I'd lost track of whose eyes I was seeing through—was the wall of air Dan had put up to keep the witch from escaping the circle. The bullets struck it and hung there in a tight cluster as if embedded in invisible drywall.

At least Dan was safe, but I found myself wishing Anderson had been less diligent about his range time. Taking advantage of the moment's confusion, I scrambled to my feet and rushed Anderson. I was uncertain of my trajectory since I was relying on Dan's point of view, but I knew I had to get to him before he decided to switch targets. I spread my arms to widen my wingspan, and it's a good thing I did because otherwise, I would've run right past them both. As it was, my left arm struck across his chest while he was still bringing the gun around to aim at me, and I wrapped both my arms around him and used my full weight to tackle him to the ground.

We landed in an ungraceful tangle of limbs that caused a flare of pain in my bruised shoulder. The gun went off again, but none of my flesh ended up perforated. While I felt around frantically for Anderson's gun arm, I noted with at least some satisfaction that I'd succeeded in separating Anderson from the witch. She'd retreated to the air wall behind her and had both hands lifted, palms facing the barrier and power gathering around her as she tried to force her way through.

The worst part? The damn thing flexed beneath her palms, splintering golden cracks spreading around her fingers.

"Dan! Stop her!"

"I'm trying!"

I held onto Anderson's arm with both hands, a knee planted firmly on his chest as he strained beneath me. I slammed his hand against the ground once, twice, three times before he finally lost his grip on his weapon. But the cracks spreading like gossamer threads from beneath the witch's hands were growing bigger by the moment. If I could get to her, I could stop her. But that wouldn't do me any good if Anderson picked up his gun and resumed shooting.

Who knew one damn witch could prove to be so much trouble?

CHAPTER 38

"Anderson! Snap out of it, buddy!"

He bucked beneath me, trying to throw me off, but fortunately, he was a marksman and not a wrestler. Dan's focus was entirely on keeping the barrier up. Magic streamed from him and into the spell until the whole thing lit up with glowing threads of swirling air.

In the eye of the storm, I forced my eyes open once more. They still stung, and my vision was blurry, but it was better than nothing. A breeze had picked up inside the circle, blowing my hair across my face. I shook my head and tried to toss it out of my eyes, unable to spare a hand to do so. But the bigger problem was that the human brain—evolved as it may be—wasn't capable of processing simultaneous visual input from two different angles. This brought a whole new meaning to "second sight," and I felt a headache stirring almost immediately.

"Dan, cut the sight spell!"

"A bit busy here," he said through gritted teeth, but a few seconds later the view from his end winked out, and I was left with my own impaired vision.

Of course, Anderson took that moment to successfully dislodge me. I fell into the dirt, but rather than come for me again he turned his back and went for the gun. I couldn't allow that. I scrambled onto his back and slid my good arm around his neck, establishing a quick and dirty chokehold. I'd never thought my experience grappling tweaked out meth heads in the ER would come in so handy. Anderson stopped going for the gun and tried to pry my arm off his neck instead, but I squeezed both sides of his neck with my arm, cutting off the supply of blood to his brain. He rolled onto his back, squishing me beneath him as he struggled against me, but I just wrapped my legs around him too and held on, counting in my head.

It takes as few as ten seconds to choke a guy out this way, even a guy Anderson's size. It's much faster—and safer—than cutting off their air supply. The downside? They usually wake up just as fast. I'd have a few seconds at best to get him off me and otherwise subdue him before he regained consciousness. I'd lost my flex cuffs earlier when I hit the deck, and I had no idea where they were at this point. However, Anderson did have regular cuffs on him. The question was whether I could find them and get them on him before he came to.

I spared a glance in the witch's direction. She hadn't broken through yet, but my vision was so blurry I couldn't see how close she might be. The wind inside the circle had picked up even more, whistling in my ears. It also stirred the dirt on the ground, though I didn't notice that until I inhaled some of it and had to cough.

After the longest twelve seconds of my life, Anderson finally went slack above me. I released the choke and pushed him away, then quickly patted him down for his cuffs and liberated them from the holster attached to his belt. Grateful I knew my way around a pair of handcuffs thanks to Mike's coaching, I quickly slapped them on his left wrist. As I reached for his right, he began to stir, but I was able to get both wrists cuffed thanks to his disorientation upon regaining consciousness.

"What the . . . Davenport?"

The fact that he was speaking was a good sign that knocking him out had interrupted the spell the witch had used on him, but I couldn't risk him being turned against us again. I took a gamble and slid my fingers into his right-hand coat pocket, grinning when I located his key ring. I pulled the keys out and tucked them in my own pocket.

"Davenport! What's going on? Are you crazy? Get me out of these things!"

"Sorry, bud. She's got mind control magic. This is safest for both of us, I promise." I patted his back. There really wasn't any time to explain. "Wait here."

I stood and brushed myself off, popped my neck, and strode purposefully toward the witch, who still had her back to me as she pushed against Dan's reinforced wall of air. My hair whipped around my head, the halves of my coat flapped at my sides, and both my lungs and my eyes burned, but determination drove me forward until I could lay a hand on the distracted witch's shoulder. I triggered my power, planning to suck her dry, but she jumped at the touch and spun, shoving a magic-wrapped hand at my chest. It connected like a jackhammer. I flew backward halfway across the circle, heels skidding through the dirt, and landed on my ass once again.

The whites of the witch's eyes glowed, telling me she was running at close to max capacity, and Dan had been right about something around her neck. It looked like an amulet of some sort, and it glowed brightly between her breasts. It must have had something to do with why the circle's binding hadn't taken hold. Somehow, I had to get it off her.

I pushed to my feet once more with a grumbled, "You couldn't be making this any more difficult, could you?"

I should've known sarcasm and angry witches didn't mix. *Challenge accepted*, her narrowed eyes said, and then she flung an unfamiliar spell at me. It spun through the air faster than I could blink, hitting me right in the face and wrapping around my head, clinging to my skin like I'd walked into an unseen spider web. My hands went up instinctively, like I could claw it off somehow.

"Stop," the witch said, and despite the racket the wind was making at the time, I heard her as clear as day. It was like she spoke directly into my head.

The certainty that she'd hit me with whatever she'd used on Anderson washed over me like a shock of cold water, but though I felt the weight of her compulsion wrapping around my mind, it didn't stop me from taking a step forward. Then another. I remembered with sudden clarity how the spelled bowl had failed to compel me to drink. How Ashley Iverson's ensorcellment charm had been fairly easy to shrug off. Was there something about my being a Conduit that made me resistant to mind magics?

"No!" she said. "Stop!"

The weight of her words was uncomfortable, but they failed to have the desired effect. I took another step forward. Then another. "Get. Out. Of. My. Head."

Features twisted in frustration, she lifted her hands and a bright ball of light appeared between them, starting out about golf ball-sized, but swiftly growing until it was closer to softball-sized. She pushed her hands straight out, sending the glowing sphere flying through the air toward me. I let it come, turning so it'd strike the side of my coat. When it did, the spell unraveled and dissipated harmlessly. Wishing I could see the look on her face, I pressed on, putting one foot in front of the other. I was tempted to draw my gun, but I wasn't sure I could see well enough to aim.

"Behind you!" Dan called.

I didn't have time to turn. Something crashed into the back of my head, bringing me to my knees. The world dimmed and spun, and if I'd been able to see better, I probably would've seen little chirping birds.

"Is that all you've got, Davenport witch?" I'd never *heard* a sneer before, but somehow she managed it. "Police consultant? Witch for hire? Hiding behind someone else's magic?" She punctuated her derisive questions with a mocking laugh. "You're no better than he was. You're just another *pretender*."

Another ball of light flew at me, this time right at my head. My addled brain didn't register it until it was right on top of me. I brought my hands up instinctively to shield my face. The spell struck my hands, which began to glow with mystical energy. I wasn't sure what the spell was supposed to do, but I was reasonably certain it wasn't that. I stared at my glowing hands in confusion, then blinked rapidly as the energy flowed up my arms and into my chest, tingling its way down my torso and legs before finally sliding into the earth beneath my knees and fanning out, just like magic I drew from a witch did.

That was new.

The implications were staggering. I could absorb magic from spells, not just from witches? Holy shit.

"H-how did you do that?" The witch's astonished voice drew me from my stunned stupor.

I struggled to my feet, head still ringing but full of newfound confidence. Okay, maybe cockiness. I stripped my coat off, flinging it on the ground before lifting one hand and gesturing with my fingers. "Come at me, bro."

My vision was finally starting to clear a little more, and I saw her take a step back. Was it hesitation? Fear? I couldn't be certain. I shook my head, feeling the last vestiges of her attempted mind control slide away.

"What's wrong? Coyote got your tongue?" Yup, definitely cockiness.

She threw an air burst at me, and I absorbed it easily.

"Duck!" Dan shouted, and this time I was able to avoid the magic mallet she tried to sneakily brain me with again.

I'm not sure how many spells she threw at me. All I know is that the more I absorbed, the more invincible I felt and the weaker she became. Air bursts, energy pulses, fire-balls . . . okay, okay, I ducked the fireballs. I wasn't feeling *that* cocky. Still, I closed the distance between us at a steady clip until only a few feet separated us. She was backed against Dan's wall by then, eyes wide as she stared at me.

I was finally close enough and could see well enough to make out her facial features beneath the dark paint. That was why her voice was familiar. It was Maria Chavez. Ray's granddaughter, and Noah's sister.

"Are you finished yet? Because he needs to read you your rights." I motioned at Anderson, still handcuffed on the ground nearby.

"I thought you said you just wanted to talk," she spat.

I snorted. "Yeah, I did. But then you mind raped a police officer and assaulted me with deadly magic."

"You started it!" She stomped her bare foot and gestured at the surroundings. "I know what entrapment is."

"If you think this is entrapment, then you absolutely don't know what entrapment is. But what I really want to know is why you were willing to send your brother to prison for your crime."

She opened her mouth briefly and then snapped it shut, glaring at me.

"What, you thought the dumb white cops wouldn't figure out how you lured Nate Alan Reed out here in the dead of night and tricked him into drinking enough peyote to ensure he'd cook in his own juices before he stopped tripping?"

Her lips remained sealed, like that whole right to remain silent thing had occurred to her without anyone reminding her.

"The one thing I don't get is why you used a charm when you could have just whammied Reed into drinking the peyote. Unless . . . wait. Did you want your brother to take the fall? Did you set him up?"

Maria let out a furious scream and threw another spell at me, but I was ready for it and channeled it harmlessly into the ground.

"You're gonna have to use your words. I'm not fluent in crazy bitch," I taunted. Sometimes I just can't help myself.

"I would have to be pretty stupid to use one of my brother's bowls to kill someone and leave it behind, don't you think?" Her upper lip curled in a haughty sneer.

I smiled back. "Who said anything about a bowl?"

"You did."

"Nope. I said charm. So, tell me, how stupid *do* you have to be to use one of your brother's bowls to kill someone and leave it behind?"

"I didn't know it was his! I thought it was just another piece of worthless tourist crap!"

I couldn't have wiped the smile from my face at that point if I'd tried. She seemed to realize what she'd done without my intervention, though, because she emitted another frustrated scream and beat her fist against Dan's wall.

"Whoever you are," Anderson said from the ground, having struggled into a sitting position to watch the show. "You are under arrest for the murder of Randolph Hirshman, aka Nathaniel Alan Reed . . ."

It takes balls for a guy to start reading someone their rights while they're the one in handcuffs. I had to give him props for that. Unfortunately, that put her attention on him, and it was harder to intercept a spell when it wasn't coming at me. Maria called on her magic once more, murderous intent in her eyes. I rushed her, hoping to distract her from finishing the spell, and almost made it. But the glowing ball of energy flew at Anderson seconds before I crashed into Maria and grabbed the glowing amulet hanging around her neck. The mystical glow around her winked out and she shrieked, threatening to burst my eardrums. I grabbed her shoulders, spun her around, and shoved her against the invisible wall, then grabbed her wrists and put one of her arms in a lock. She went up on the tips of her toes, shrieking.

"Anderson, are you okay?" I called.

"He took a direct hit," Dan said. He'd moved around so that he stood on the other side of the wall. "Give me a minute to bind her fully and you can check on him."

He had to drop the air wall to get to Maria for the binding, which also allowed him to pass me his own pair of zip cuffs. We secured her as quickly as we could, and I hurried over to check on Anderson, finding him unconscious but breathing. It could've been much worse.

Dan sidled up to me, one arm gripping Maria's slim

bicep. "So, do you need some time to process or can we talk about that cool spell absorption thing you did?"

It all came back to me in a rush. Discovering I could "catch" and negate spells, Maria's failed attempt at mind control . . . my head began to ache with the swirling possibilities, but it also could've been an eyestrain headache or a mild concussion from getting tossed around.

"Process. Definitely process."

CHAPTER 39

I wasn't the only one who needed to process. Once Anderson came to, we headed back to town—with a pit stop at a gas station so I could wash my face and flush my eyes—and booked Maria. Or rather, he booked Maria and we hung around to make sure there weren't any more problems. Fortunately, the fight seemed to have gone out of her. Dan put his coat around her when we got out of the car so at least some of her dignity was intact. I wasn't sure she deserved any, but it was decent of him.

Anderson seemed okay, but I was worried enough about the possible after-effects of the spell that I insisted on taking him to the ER to get checked out afterward. His wife met us there, and I got to meet her. Turns out, she's a hugger, and she was rather grateful to me and Dan for backing him up and making sure he got checked out.

It felt weird being at St. Vincent's. There wasn't really any way I could avoid running into former co-workers, especially since I'd often worked nights and we rolled up right smack in the middle of the overnight shift. I got everything from suspicious glances to friendly smiles, even a hug from Gracie at the front desk. Word had spread, the hospital rumor mill being what it was, so no one asked what had happened. I was grateful for that. I didn't want to rehash it. Not at three in the morning with everything else that was already rattling around in my head and my heart. I was beyond scattered. I was lucky I'd remembered to text John from the station.

While Dan flirted at the nurses' station, I sat in the waiting room, my hands cupped around a lukewarm paper cup of coffee, ignoring the comings and goings around me until a pair of silver and blue trainers stopped in my line of sight, toes pointed right at me. I counted to five, hoping they'd keep going, then looked up and found Dr. Russell Carson studying me with an unreadable expression. He motioned with his head, and I reluctantly stood and walked down the hall with him, away from the nurses' station. He ducked into an empty conference room and flipped the light on.

I joined him, shutting the door behind me and leaning back against it. "Okay, let me have it."

I don't know why I expected him to tear into me. Maybe because we'd worked together so closely for so long. Maybe because I was friends with his wife. But all he did was tilt his head and study me, a hint of curiosity in his eyes. "Is it true? You're a witch?"

"Yes, I am." And for the first time, I really felt like it was true. Like I'd finally accepted it myself, and even though nothing had changed about my spellcasting ability—or lack thereof—I couldn't call myself a null anymore, and too much had changed for me to masquerade as a mundic. I wasn't even sure I wanted to.

Disappointment flickered across his face, and the rejection stung. I liked Russell. Always had. And given that his own wife couldn't really call herself a mundie either, of all the people I worked with, he was the last I would've expected to harbor an anti-witch bias. My eyes began to sting, but the last thing I wanted was for him to see me cry. I pushed off the door and turned. "See you around, Doc."

But he caught my shoulder and turned me back, his hand lingering there as his solemn eyes met mine. "Why didn't you tell me? As long as we've worked together, we were—I mean, I thought we were friends."

I realized I'd read him all wrong, and then I wanted to cry again for totally different reasons. He wasn't disappointed that I was a witch. He was disappointed I hadn't told him. "It's a long story. A really long story." But, for once, it didn't feel like it was the end of the world if I told it.

"I'm off tomorrow night. Come have dinner with me and Suzi? There's something we'd like to share with you too."

With everything that'd happened, I'd forgotten all about the little witch Suzi was carrying, but I wasn't going to steal his thunder. If my smile was broad, hopefully he'd think it was just relief. "That sounds great, Russ. Text me tomorrow and tell me when and where to show up."

He hugged me. It probably should've seemed odd because he'd never done it before. But it felt as natural as anything to lean against him while he rubbed my back, like I'd finally found a safe harbor after a long time adrift at sea. I hadn't given him, or anyone at the hospital, enough credit. Sure, there were some who wouldn't have wanted to work with me if they'd known about my background, just like there were assholes out there that'd go out of their way to harass me now that I was registered. But I had to believe that they were the minority, that the good mundies outnumbered the bad.

Yes, I was a witch who couldn't sling a single spell, but I wasn't completely helpless, and I didn't have to go it alone. I had friends. I could join a coven. And I was going to fight like hell to get my job back because this was where I belonged.

CHAPTER 40

Noah Chavez was released the next morning, but when I didn't hear from him for a week afterward, I figured I wouldn't. That was a little disappointing. I mean, on the one hand, he had asked me to help him—which I had. But I'd also exposed his sister as the real murderer, so I could see where that might make a guy a little conflicted about saying thanks.

Mike was still on admin leave for most of that week, but the investigation into the shooting went smoothly and he was reinstated without issue, much to my relief. It wasn't that working with Anderson hadn't improved our working relationship, because it definitely had, but rather that every time a Magic Crimes case came down the pipe while he was out, it was assigned to someone else, and breaking in a new partner was exhausting.

While he was gone, I'd gotten in the habit of stopping by the station after my morning run to check in and see if I was needed to consult on something, and that continued after he got back. Sure, a text may have been faster, but it wasn't like I had anything better to do. To say I was climbing the walls at home would be an understatement. All Dan wanted to do was experiment with my conduit powers while he waited for a callback on his application to the academy, and there was only so much of that I could take. I'd been cold calling lawyers daily trying to find someone who would take my case, but either I couldn't afford them or they wouldn't touch it with a ten-foot pole. Which was a little weird, because they say lawyers will do just about anything for money.

I'd also finally gotten a call from Tracy, and we'd had a really nice talk one day over tacos. Though she was adamant that there'd been no abuse going on with Hector, she'd also confided that she was thinking about breaking things off. We bonded over guacamole and mutual wariness of controlling, macho men, and I thought we might even become friends. I didn't have many—okay, any—witch girl-friends, so that felt kind of good.

Mike wasn't at his desk when I got there, so I set our coffees down and plopped in his chair, grabbing the topmost file from the inbox to see what was on deck. My eyes caught on what had been underneath it—a plain white envelope sandwiched between the two file folders with my name on it. I picked it up and studied the front. There was a return address but no name, and the postmark said Tesuque, NM. There was more weight to it than I'd expect from a letter, but it wasn't particularly thick. Something metallic slid around when I tipped it, though.

I tore open one end of the envelope—it was addressed me, after all—and tipped it out over the desk. A small pewter medallion slid out and landed with a quiet thud on the desk, tugging along behind it a silver box chain that puddled around it. I squinted at it and detected no magical signature, but lately that didn't mean much, so I fished a pencil out of Mike's desk to turn it over since it'd landed facedown. The oval-shaped medallion was stamped in relief with the likeness of a saint and read, "Saint Jude" at the top and "Pray For Us" at the bottom. I couldn't for the life of me remember which saint Jude was, though I remembered hearing the name in celebrity-riddled commercials at movie theaters.

Curious, I pinched the paper inside the envelope and pulled it out. It was a simple sheet of lined notebook paper, the edges frayed from where it'd been ripped out. The message was short, written in a bold, blocky script.

Dear Ms. Davenport,

I'm sorry for not reaching out sooner, but after everything that happened, I didn't really know what to say. I'm still not sure, but I'm going to try.

I know now that what I did was wrong, and my own actions led to me being in that cell—wrongfully accused or not. I've made more than my share of bad decisions in my life, many of them fueled by alcohol. I've begun attending AA meetings, and while I can't make all my wrongs right, I hope by the grace of God I can find some peace with them and be a better man.

Billy Tsosie told me what you did for me, how you kept digging even after my arrest, and I'm beyond grateful. As for my sister, she's always been a passionate girl, but her outrage over Reed's liberties with our culture had become an obsession, and when she found out he was faking being a witch too . . . I should have seen the signs.

It's hard to reconcile what she's become with the sweet infant I once held in my arms and promised to look out for. I can't help but feel like I failed her somewhere along the way. I can only hope that God will help her come back to herself, because she's beyond my reach now. I pray every day for her soul.

Please accept this as a token of my gratitude. It feels appropri-

ate, yet insufficient. I really owe you one. You know how to find me if you need me.

God Bless You,

Noah Chavez

After marveling for a moment at the transformation of the angry Pueblo man into the humble one who'd penned the note, I refolded it and slid it back into the envelope for safekeeping. Some times accepting one's truth was harder than others. I knew that all too well. And sharing that truth with others . . . that was a whole other level of vulnerability I yet struggled with. Daring to pick up the necklace, I held it aloft and studied the aging saint's humble face as it dangled before me. I was about to look him up on my phone when Mike rounded the corner of the desk with a coffee mug in one hand and a newspaper in the other.

"You're in my seat."

"I brought you coffee . . ." I motioned at the to-go cups still in the carrier on the desk.

He waved his mug. "I have coffee."

"I brought you *better* coffee."

He paused a moment, then shrugged. "Point conceded. What do you have there?"

"A gift from Noah Chavez." I held it out to him, and he took it, glancing at the medal. A laugh burst from his chest.

"I guess that's appropriate."

"How so?"

He dropped the necklace back into my upturned palm. "Saint Jude. The patron saint of lost causes?"

"Oh." I rubbed my thumb against the medal briefly. Noah had no doubt meant it as a thank you for attending to his lost cause, maybe even encouragement to take up others. He had no idea about my own situation, and while I was neither Catholic nor religious, I'd take whatever help I could get. I unfastened the clasp and slipped the necklace around my neck.

After watching me fumble blindly with the clasp for a few seconds, Mike set his coffee down. "Here. Let me help."

I passed him the necklace and turned, gathering up my hair and shifting it out of the way so he could fasten the clasp. The silver chain settled in place, cool against my skin, and I tucked the medal under the neck of my T-shirt before rising to give Mike back his chair. Things felt more settled between us now. When he'd first returned from admin leave, we'd had a chat.

"Anderson says you handled yourself well in the field," he'd said.

"That was nice of him."

He'd studied me in silence for a moment. "It's possible I may have been coddling you a bit. I just wanted to keep you safe. After what happened with Marissa . . ."

He trailed off, but I bit my tongue and held my breath. I'd made sure his former partner's file was back in his desk before he got back—after scanning a copy for myself—but the guilt of prying where I wasn't welcome lingered.

"It's not that I don't think you're capable. I just wanted to keep you safe," he said eventually.

"It wasn't your fault, you know. She took her own life. You can't protect someone from themselves."

"I know. Just promise me something, Emily."

"Yeah?"

"If you're ever thinking about hurting yourself? Talk to someone. If not me . . . someone."

The vulnerability in his eyes had touched something deep inside me, and I'd fought the urge to wrap him in a hug. Instead, I'd lifted a hand with pinky extended. "Only if you promise the same. Pinky swear?"

He'd snorted but hooked his pinky with mine, and that was that.

A few hours of poring over Narcotics case files later, trying to figure out what was making local witches overdose in such spectacular and lethal ways, Mike and I were debating lunch options when the officer at the front desk called back to tell me I had a visitor waiting in reception. It was a day of firsts apparently, from my first piece of mail at the station to my first visitor. Hoping it wasn't my brother—I got enough of him at home—and grateful for the opportunity to stretch my legs, I headed for the front and found a plainclothes Billy Tsosie standing there with a box under one arm.

"Hey, Billy, what's up? Do you want to come back?" I jerked a thumb over my shoulder toward the squad room.

He smiled but shook his head. "No, thank you. I'm just a delivery boy today." He held the box out to me.

Curious, I stepped forward and took it from him. It wasn't taped shut, so I peeled back the flaps and found a small hand drum inside, nestled within a pile of wood shavings. Blinking, I took it out carefully and held it up for a closer inspection. It was about twelve inches tall and eight or so in diameter, crafted of unpainted wood and undyed hide stretched taut over both top and bottom. It looked old, unlike the drums I'd seen for sale in Cochiti Pueblo—basically the drum capital of New Mexico. Drums are important to Native Americans, so I had to believe this held some sort of significance, I just wasn't sure what that was.

There was no note attached, and none to be found inside the box either. I looked to Billy for an explanation, canting my head to one side.

"Ray Chavez sends his regards."

"Ah! Well, this is really nice of him. Please pass along my thanks." I carefully placed the drum back in the box.

"Tesuque drums are rare. It's been decades since we had a drum maker in the Pueblo," Billy mentioned, making sure I understood the significance of the gift.

"Really? Wow. I'm flattered, then. Truly. Thank you."

"To have a handmade pueblo drum in a home is considered a great blessing. Ray said he wishes you many, and thanks you for your service to the Pueblo."

I fidgeted with the box, flushed with a sense of unworthiness. "Even though I arrested his granddaughter?"

Billy put a hand on my shoulder. "Especially because you arrested his granddaughter. The bitterness in her heart led her down a dark path, and she had become like a cancer in our community. We just didn't know it, or at least didn't fully know what to do about it. It took great courage, not only to ask the kind of questions that needed to be asked, but also to stand up to someone with her dark power."

"I couldn't have done it without that sp—"

His hand tightened on my shoulder, and he gave me a warning look. I pressed my lips together and mimed locking them and tossing the key. Billy broke out in a broad smile and laughed, then dropped his hand away.

"Take care of yourself, Emily. No offense, but I hope we don't have to work together again."

I laughed, understanding what he meant. Jurisdictional conflicts were a bitch. "None taken. Have a safe drive home."

CHAPTER 41

W hat Noah Chavez had written stuck with me the rest of the day, maybe in part because of the lingering weight of the Saint Jude medal against my chest. He wasn't exactly cornering the market on bad decisions, and there were plenty of people I probably owed an apology to. One in particular haunted me, and that's why I ended up texting Barry after I left the station to see if he was available to get together for drinks later. Of course, that probably meant beer for him and ginger ale for me, but it was the spirit of the thing not the . . . thing for spirits. Not even if a little tequila might've loosened me up enough to make it easier. No, this deserved sobriety.

I could stop by Matt's and raid his liquor cabinet afterward if it felt necessary.

I picked a restaurant with a decent bar and an outdoor patio dotted with radiant heaters to keep the chill of the February night air at bay. Once we were settled at a table with our drinks—I'd splurged for a Shirley Temple rather than plain ginger ale—I listened while he recounted the events of the day. Barry was the kind of guy who never took

"How was your day?" as largely polite and requiring a simple answer. No, he would start with waking up, how he slept, what he had for breakfast, and then move on to everything he could remember that happened at work. Fortunately, his work stories were usually funny in some way, and I didn't mind listening to him talk most of the time.

Tonight, I was stalling more than anything. No matter what Billy Tsosie or Ray Chavez had to say about my courage, in this . . . I was a coward. I'd face a hundred skin-walkers if it meant not having to have this conversation. Barry kept talking, and I kept stalling, toying with the edge of my napkin poking out from under my glass. This was ridiculous. What I needed to do was rip off the bandage. Just get it over with.

"So then I got your text and of course I wouldn't pass up the opportunity to—"

"I'm a witch," I blurted.

Barry blinked at the interruption, tipped his head, then finished, "—spend time with you."

I stared at him in bewildered confusion, having expected a little more reaction than that. He gazed back at me with an easy smile, dimples on display. He had to have heard me. It seemed like he'd heard me. Did he hear me?

"Sorry, I didn't mean to interrupt. But I've been holding that back for a while now. I should have told you, and I'm sorry." I sucked a bit of syrupy sweetness through my straw.

He sat back in his chair, amusement shining in his blue eyes. "Well, I'm just a plain ol' human, if that's okay."

I furrowed my brow. "Why wouldn't it be?"

"You seem to think not telling me you were a witch was a big deal, but I hadn't shared my human status with you either."

"That's . . . not the same thing." His logic made my brain throb as my thought processes began to realign.

"Isn't it?" He shrugged.

Okay, maybe he had a point. Sort of. I was so used to push back from people who had a problem with witches that I forgot some humans legitimately didn't care, and I certainly hadn't given Barry the benefit of the doubt. But that only made me feel guilty in another way because he'd never said or done anything that should have made me think he'd have a problem with it. I was just afraid to tell him, for reasons that were all in my head, and had kept it from him like some shameful secret for two months.

Barry gave me a few moments to process while he nursed his beer, but eventually leaned forward and planted an elbow on the table, resting his chin on his palm. "Would it make you feel better if I pretended to be upset with you?"

I chuckled, but it sounded as awkward as it felt. "Maybe." I fiddled with my straw, tapping it against an ice cube to submerge it deeper and watching as it floated back up. Troubling thoughts clouded my mind. Was I actually disappointed that Barry hadn't been upset? Had I been looking for an out? And, if so, was it because I wanted out or because I was self-sabotaging?

"You're thinking really hard over there."

"Yeah." I lifted my eyes to his and searched them, longing to feel some sort of pull. Any sort of pull. Barry was a nice, normal guy. On paper, he was everything I'd ever wanted. But so much had changed in the last few weeks— hell, in the last few days—that I didn't know what I wanted anymore. And it wasn't fair to Barry to expect him to stick around while I figured it out. Not when he was ready to put down roots if I said the word, rather than moving back to Colorado at the end of the ski season. "The last time we were together, you said something about staying in Santa Fe long-term."

A smile curled the corners of his mouth up. "Yeah . . ."

"I think if I'm the only reason you'd stay, that you should go back to Denver."

His smile faded, confusion supplanting hopeful pleasure. "Really?"

"Yeah." Christ. I felt like I'd just kicked a puppy. And not one of those creepy pug-nosed little shits, but something seriously cute. Like a Golden Retriever. Dan may have enjoyed teasing me about the Barry vs. Barrington thing, but Barry—flesh and blood human Barry—was nothing like my cat. He was more like a Golden Retriever. Enthusiastic, loving, and at times endearingly oblivious. "Barry, the last few weeks . . . you have no idea what's been going on with me—"

"Because you didn't tell me."

There it was. A hint of anger tinged with hurt. I took it, because I deserved it. "I know. And I—I'm truly sorry."

"So, tell me now. This doesn't have to be the end of the road."

I shook my head. "I'm not saying it is, I'm just—just not ready for something serious right now, and you relocating, that's serious. I have a lot of work to do on me, to get my head on straight. So much has changed in such a short time, I just . . . I can't drag you down with me. You deserve better than that."

He sat back in his chair again, a pensive look on his face as he picked at the label on his bottle with a thumbnail. "I don't think you really understand why I offered to stick around. I mean, it wasn't a proposal. I just want to keep getting to know you. I think we could be good together."

"I barely know *myself* anymore."

His fingers tightened on the bottle. "Don't be flippant."

"I'm not. Believe me, I'm not. I'm not your garden variety witch, Barry. I spent most of my life thinking I had no powers at all, and now they're popping out of me left and right. I need to get a handle on that, and I need to figure out what my life looks like as a registered practitioner. So far, someone tried to run me down in a parking lot, I got fired from the hospital, hell, I couldn't even buy a gun without a twenty-four-hour hold."

His pale brows inched closer together, but he held his tongue. I held a hand out to him across the table, and he hesitated a moment before placing his hand over mine. "I don't know what you want, Em. Please, just tell it to me straight."

"I need to take a step back. And if that means you don't want to hang out, I understand. I do like you, Barry. You're probably one of the most genuinely nice guys I've ever met, and you deserve someone who can give you everything I can't."

He hung his head briefly, and his broad shoulders rose and fell in a heavy sigh. "Friends, then. And we'll see where the future takes us."

I squeezed his hand and bought another round. We spent the next half hour chatting about this and that, and it was only maybe half as awkward as I would have expected. Even dumped, semi-distant Barry was a better man than I deserved.

CHAPTER 42

On the way home, I decided what I really needed was some self-care. Specifically, a long hot soak in the tub. With a lavender bath bomb. And a glass of wine. Maybe a couple glasses of wine. I could almost taste the merlot by the time I got there, but when I opened the front door and found a stranger on my couch, I kissed all of that goodbye. There was a stranger in my house. In my sacred space.

Keys tightly in hand, I paused with the door half-open and swept my eyes around the room in search of my brother, but he was nowhere to be seen. The witch stood, buttoning the top button of the suit coat he wore over his black turtleneck as he assessed me frankly.

"Ms. Davenport, I presume?" he asked in lightly accented English. It sounded kind of Slavic. His brown hair was slicked back, and his jaw could've cut diamonds. There was an unmistakable formality to his bearing that threw me for a loop.

The sound of the toilet flushing down the hall suggested that Dan was home, and that's the only reason why I moved fully into the room and closed the door behind me. I nodded to the witch and dropped my keys in my purse, then set it on the table by the door.

"I'm home!" I called for Dan's benefit, hoping it would speed his return from the bathroom, then addressed the stranger again. "And you would be?"

"Pleased to meet you." His words didn't match his countenance. He didn't smile or approach to offer a handshake. "I'm Adrian Volkov."

I tilted my head. The name meant nothing to me, but he said it like it should. The bathroom door opened, and Dan ambled down the hallway. "Oh, there you are. How was the date?"

"It wasn't a date," I said absently, my eyes still on the elephant in the room.

"If you say so." Dan waved a hand and flopped onto the sofa. Within seconds, my cat materialized in his lap in that way that cats do. "So, shall we get down to business?"

"Business?" I repeated, still clueless and hating it.

"Yeah, tall dark and Russian here wouldn't tell me what he wanted. Just that he's here to see you and you were expecting him."

"I think there's been some mistake . . ."

Adrian inclined his head, brow furrowing in a faint frown. "I was told you would be expecting me, that your mother sent a letter."

Shit. Mom's letter. I forgot all about that. "I, uh, kind of didn't read it."

Dan laughed, rubbing Barrington's ears. "Classic."

I shot my brother a glare, not that it dissuaded him in the slightest. "I'm sure it's around here somewhere. Sorry, I've been a bit busy, I guess it slipped my mind. What brings you here?" If it involved my mother, it couldn't be good.

Adrian's features smoothed and he nodded curtly. "Then

I suppose it falls to me. Allow me to begin again. Emily Davenport, my name is Adrian Volkov, and I am a deputy to the Archon of the Southwestern Territory. It is my duty to inform you are under investigation by the Circle for fraudulently presenting yourself as a witch of an allied coven."

AUTHOR'S NOTE

Thanks for reading *Hollow Witch*! Sorry to leave you hanging there, but that seemed like the best spot to end this chapter of Emily's story.

No matter how much planning I do or how meticulously I outline, sometimes a book takes on a life of its own. That certainly happened this time! This book is a fair bit longer than I intended, but I guess that just means there's more of it to love.

I had a lot of anxiety when it came to following up on *Null Witch* since it's been quite a while since I wrote the first draft of that. Had I grown or changed too much as a writer to recapture Emily's voice? Thankfully, she came back to me like an old friend, and from here, we're going to grow together.

Emily's crime-solving adventures will continue in *Witch Hunt*, expected later this year (2021). In the meantime, I invite you to sign up for my newsletter for release dates, recipes, sneak peeks, bonus content, free reads and more.

ABOUT THE AUTHOR

 Disenchanted with her mundane human existence, Lori loves spinning tales of magic and creatures of myth & legend existing in the modern world. When not indulging in these flights of fancy, she enjoys cooking, crafting, gaming, and (of course) reading. She's also a bit of a weather geek and would like to go storm chasing one day.

Lori lives in Austin, Texas with her husband and three adorable kitties that don't understand why mommy doesn't like them climbing on her laptop and batting at the screen.

The kitties, that is. It'd be really strange if her husband did that.

www.loridrakeauthor.com
lori@loridrakeauthor.com

 facebook.com/loridrakeauthor
 bookbub.com/authors/lori-drake

Printed in Great Britain
by Amazon

70872202R00180